the Archie DIGEST LIBRARY

Archie®

– in –

Quiet Please

Spotlight

visit us at
www.abdopublishing.com

Exclusive Spotlight library bound edition published in 2007 by Spotlight, a division of ABDO Publishing Group, Edina, Minnesota. Spotlight produces high quality reinforced library bound editions for schools and libraries. Published by agreement with Archie Comic Publications, Inc.

Library of Congress Cataloging-in-Publication Data

Archie in Quiet please. -- Library bound ed.
   p. cm. -- (The Archie digest library)
  Revision of issue 184 (Dec. 2001) of Archie digest magazine.
  ISBN-13: 978-1-59961-260-7
  ISBN-10: 1-59961-260-7
   1. Graphic novels. I. Archie digest magazine. 184. II. Title: Quiet please.

PN6728.A72 A696 2007
741.5'973--dc22

2006051169

All Spotlight books are reinforced library binding
and manufactured in the United States of America.

Contents

Archie®

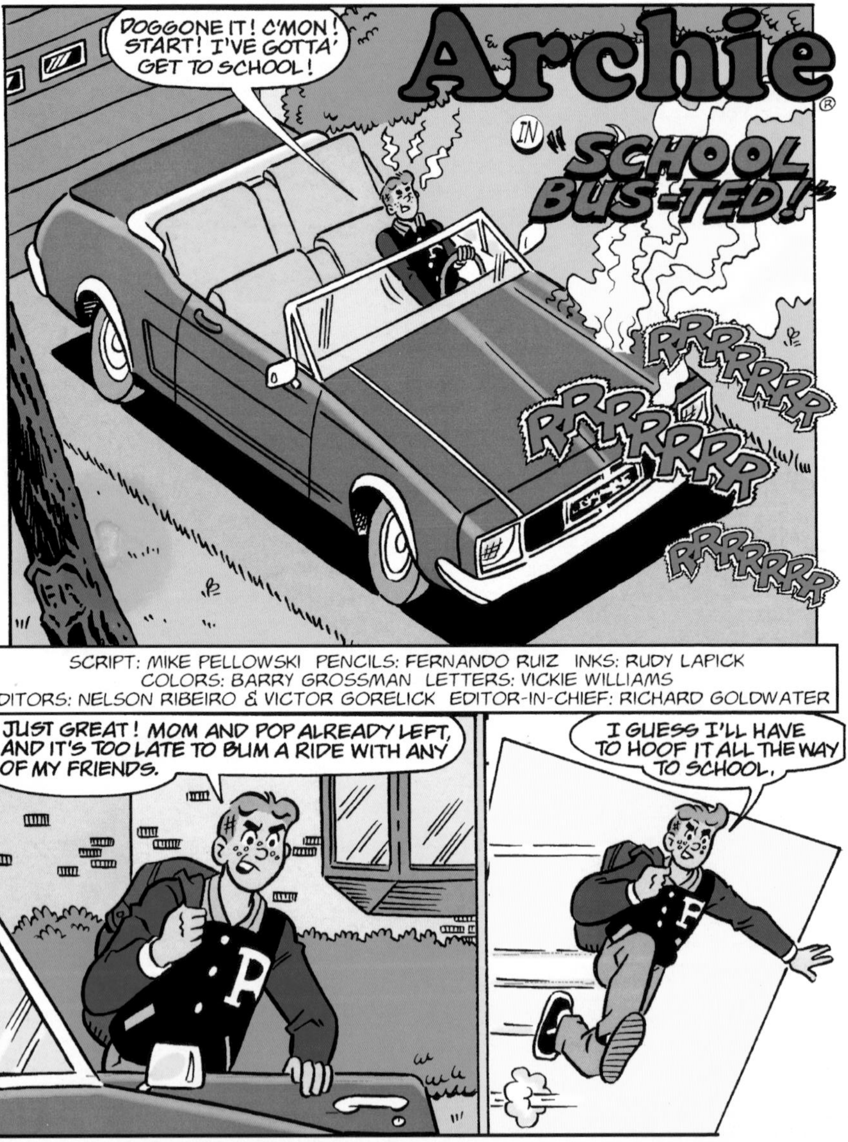
DOGGONE IT! C'MON! START! I'VE GOTTA' GET TO SCHOOL!
Archie® IN "SCHOOL BUS-TED!"
RRRRRRRRR
RRRRRRRRR
RRRRRRRR
SCRIPT: MIKE PELLOWSKI PENCILS: FERNANDO RUIZ INKS: RUDY LAPICK
COLORS: BARRY GROSSMAN LETTERS: VICKIE WILLIAMS
EDITORS: NELSON RIBEIRO & VICTOR GORELICK EDITOR-IN-CHIEF: RICHARD GOLDWATER
JUST GREAT! MOM AND POP ALREADY LEFT, AND IT'S TOO LATE TO BUM A RIDE WITH ANY OF MY FRIENDS.
I GUESS I'LL HAVE TO HOOF IT ALL THE WAY TO SCHOOL.

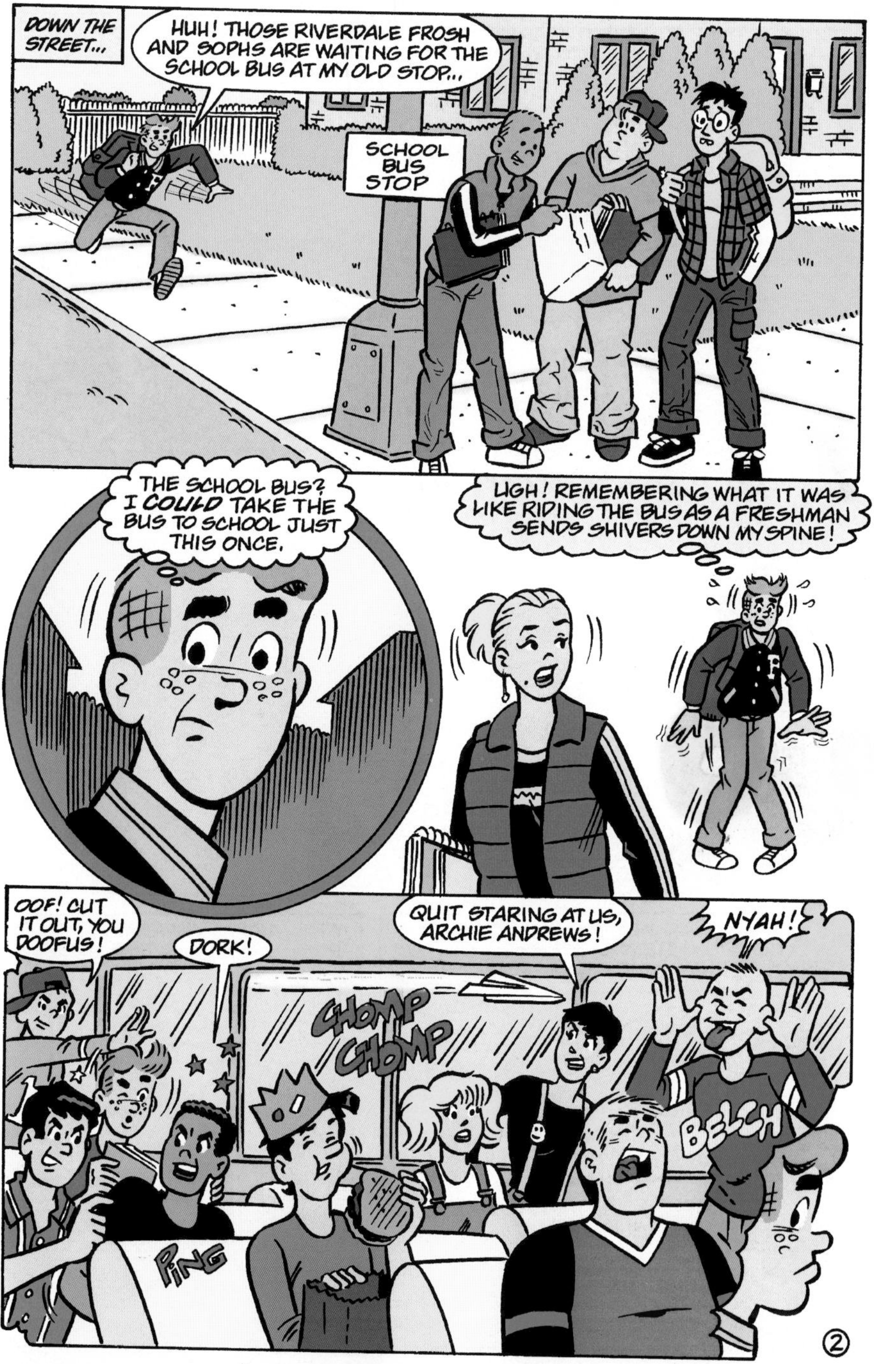
DOWN THE STREET...
HUH! THOSE RIVERDALE FROSH AND SOPHS ARE WAITING FOR THE SCHOOL BUS AT MY OLD STOP...
SCHOOL BUS STOP
THE SCHOOL BUS? I COULD TAKE THE BUS TO SCHOOL JUST THIS ONCE.
UGH! REMEMBERING WHAT IT WAS LIKE RIDING THE BUS AS A FRESHMAN SENDS SHIVERS DOWN MY SPINE!
OOF! CUT IT OUT, YOU DOOFUS!
DORK!
QUIT STARING AT US, ARCHIE ANDREWS!
NYAH!
CHOMP CHOMP
BELCH
PING
2

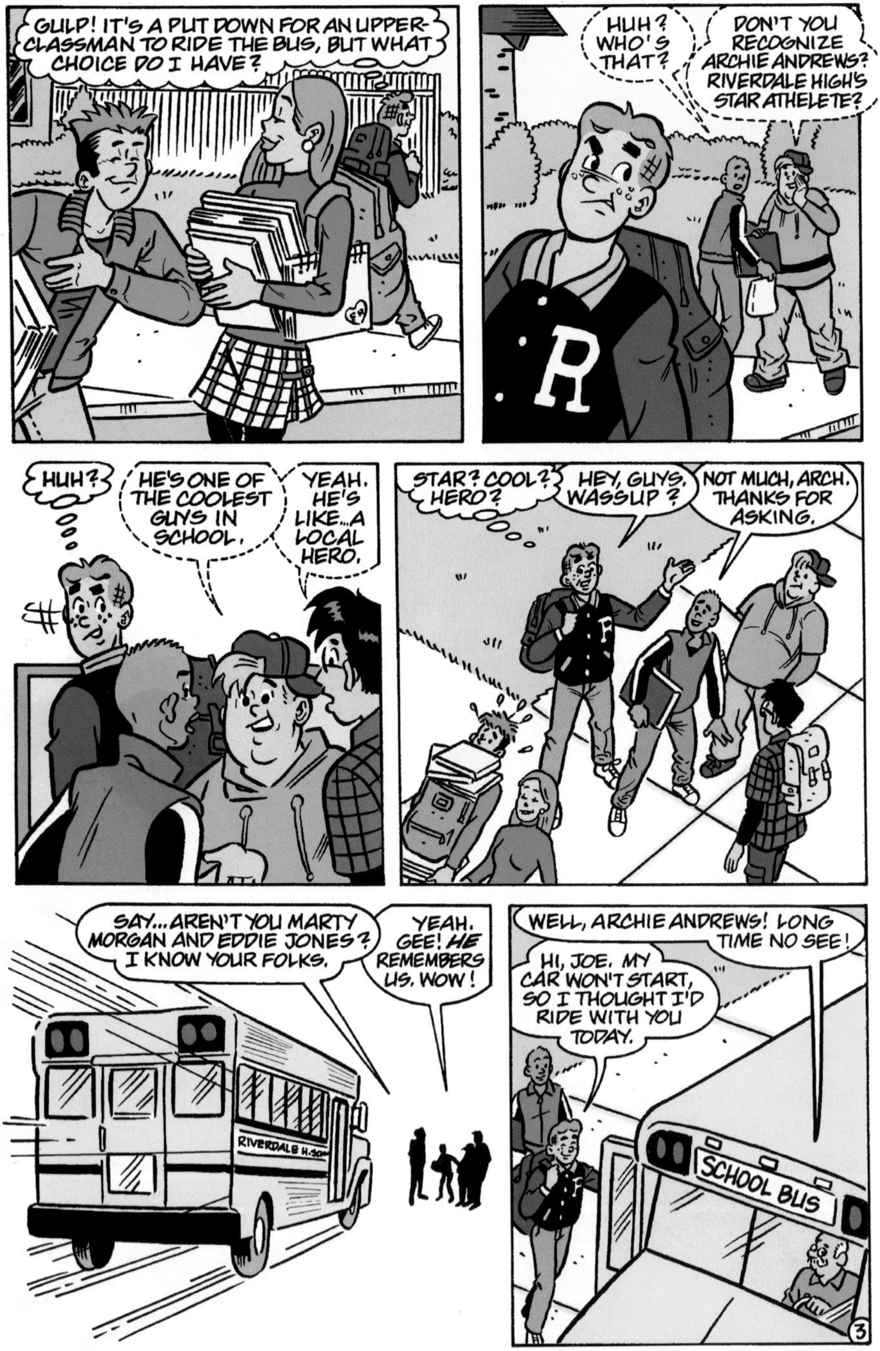
GULP! IT'S A PUT DOWN FOR AN UPPER-CLASSMAN TO RIDE THE BUS, BUT WHAT CHOICE DO I HAVE?
HUH? WHO'S THAT?
DON'T YOU RECOGNIZE ARCHIE ANDREWS? RIVERDALE HIGH'S STAR ATHELETE?
HUH?
HE'S ONE OF THE COOLEST GUYS IN SCHOOL.
YEAH. HE'S LIKE...A LOCAL HERO.
STAR? COOL? HERO?
HEY, GUYS, WASSUP?
NOT MUCH, ARCH. THANKS FOR ASKING.
SAY...AREN'T YOU MARTY MORGAN AND EDDIE JONES? I KNOW YOUR FOLKS.
YEAH. GEE! HE REMEMBERS US. WOW!
RIVERDALE H. SCH
WELL, ARCHIE ANDREWS! LONG TIME NO SEE!
HI, JOE. MY CAR WON'T START, SO I THOUGHT I'D RIDE WITH YOU TODAY.
SCHOOL BUS
3

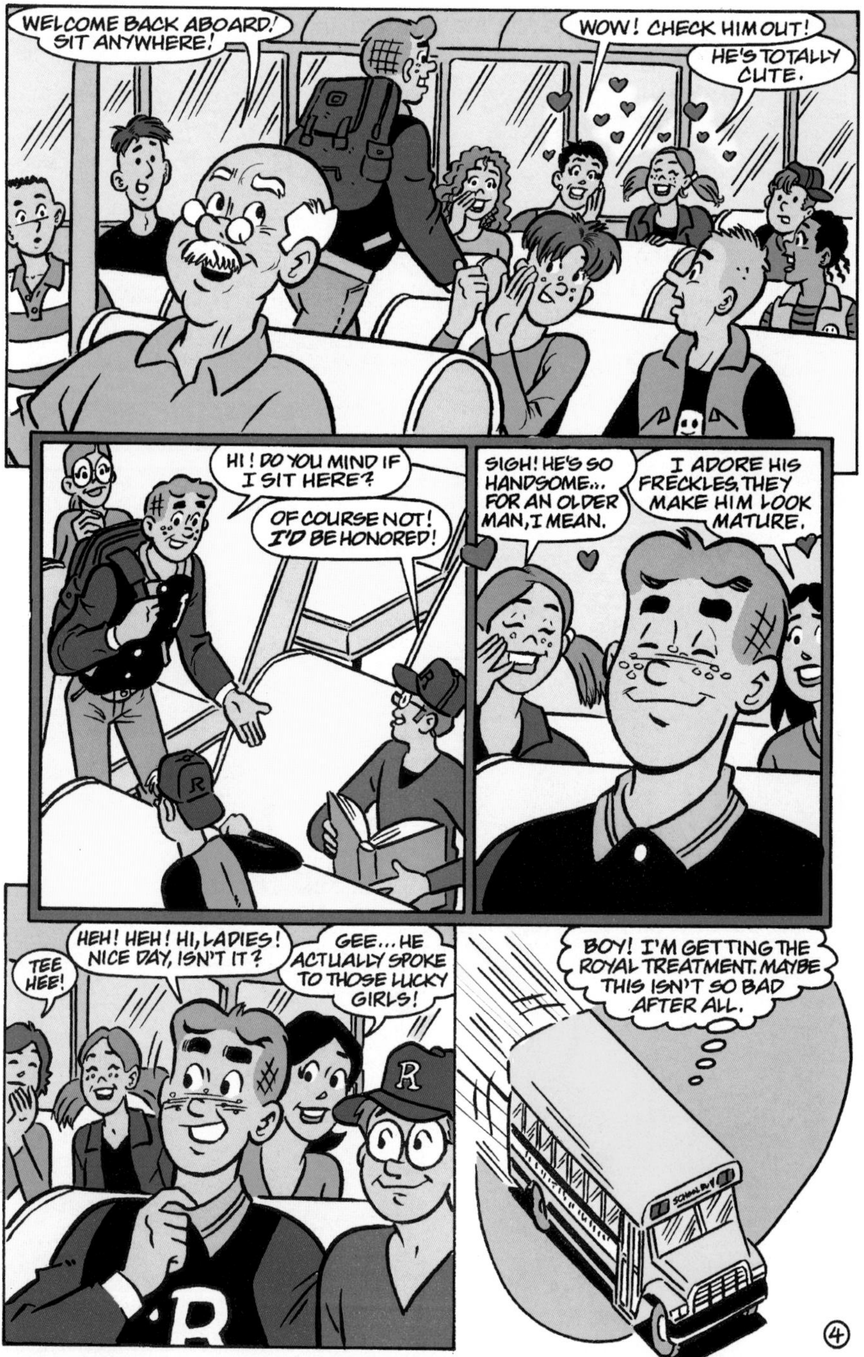
WELCOME BACK ABOARD! SIT ANYWHERE!
WOW! CHECK HIM OUT!
HE'S TOTALLY CUTE.
HI! DO YOU MIND IF I SIT HERE?
OF COURSE NOT! I'D BE HONORED!
SIGH! HE'S SO HANDSOME... FOR AN OLDER MAN, I MEAN.
I ADORE HIS FRECKLES. THEY MAKE HIM LOOK MATURE.
TEE HEE!
HEH! HEH! HI, LADIES! NICE DAY, ISN'T IT?
GEE... HE ACTUALLY SPOKE TO THOSE LUCKY GIRLS!
BOY! I'M GETTING THE ROYAL TREATMENT. MAYBE THIS ISN'T SO BAD AFTER ALL.
4

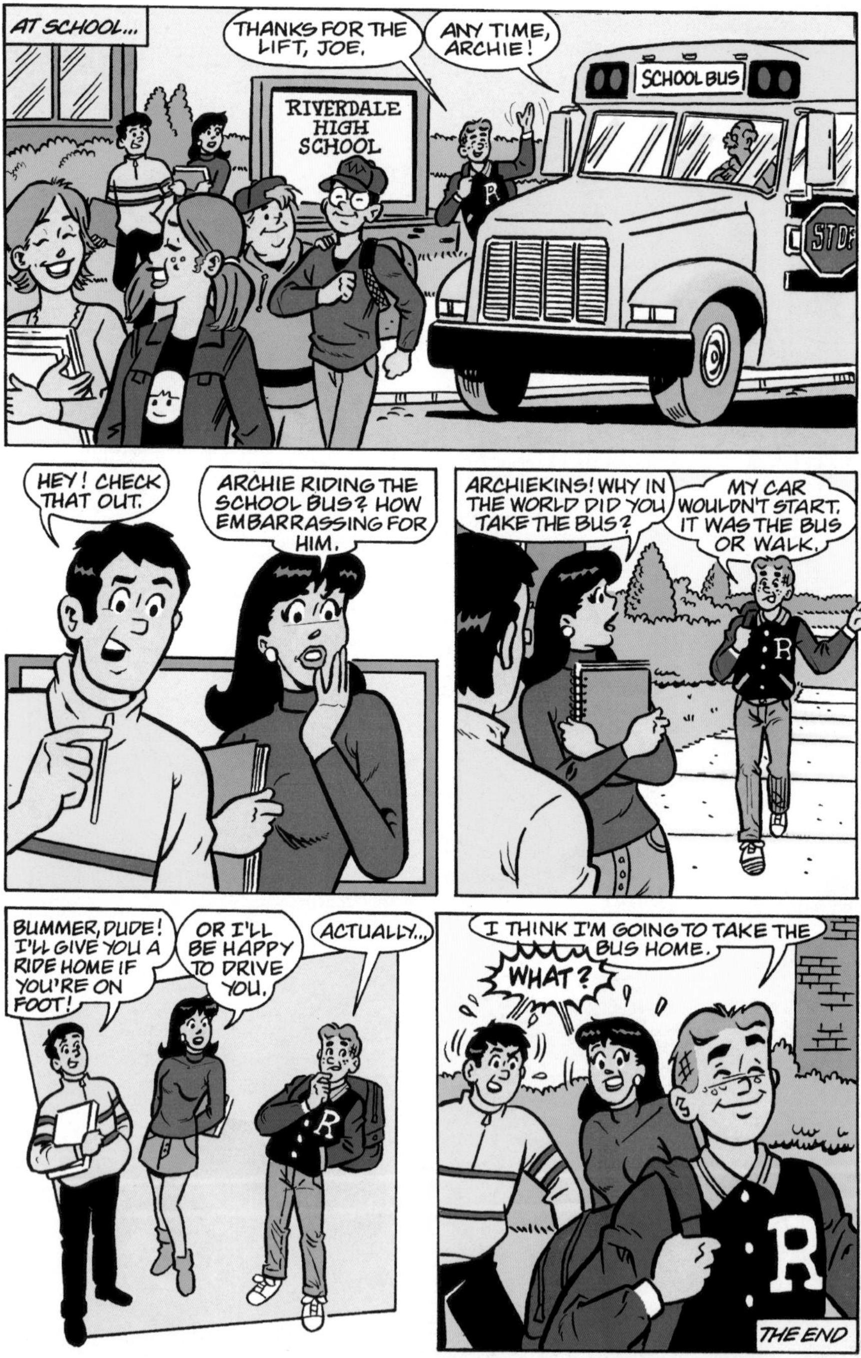
AT SCHOOL...
THANKS FOR THE LIFT, JOE.
ANY TIME, ARCHIE!
RIVERDALE HIGH SCHOOL
SCHOOL BUS
STOP
HEY! CHECK THAT OUT.
ARCHIE RIDING THE SCHOOL BUS? HOW EMBARRASSING FOR HIM.
ARCHIEKINS! WHY IN THE WORLD DID YOU TAKE THE BUS?
MY CAR WOULDN'T START. IT WAS THE BUS OR WALK.
BUMMER, DUDE! I'LL GIVE YOU A RIDE HOME IF YOU'RE ON FOOT!
OR I'LL BE HAPPY TO DRIVE YOU.
ACTUALLY...
I THINK I'M GOING TO TAKE THE BUS HOME.
WHAT?
THE END

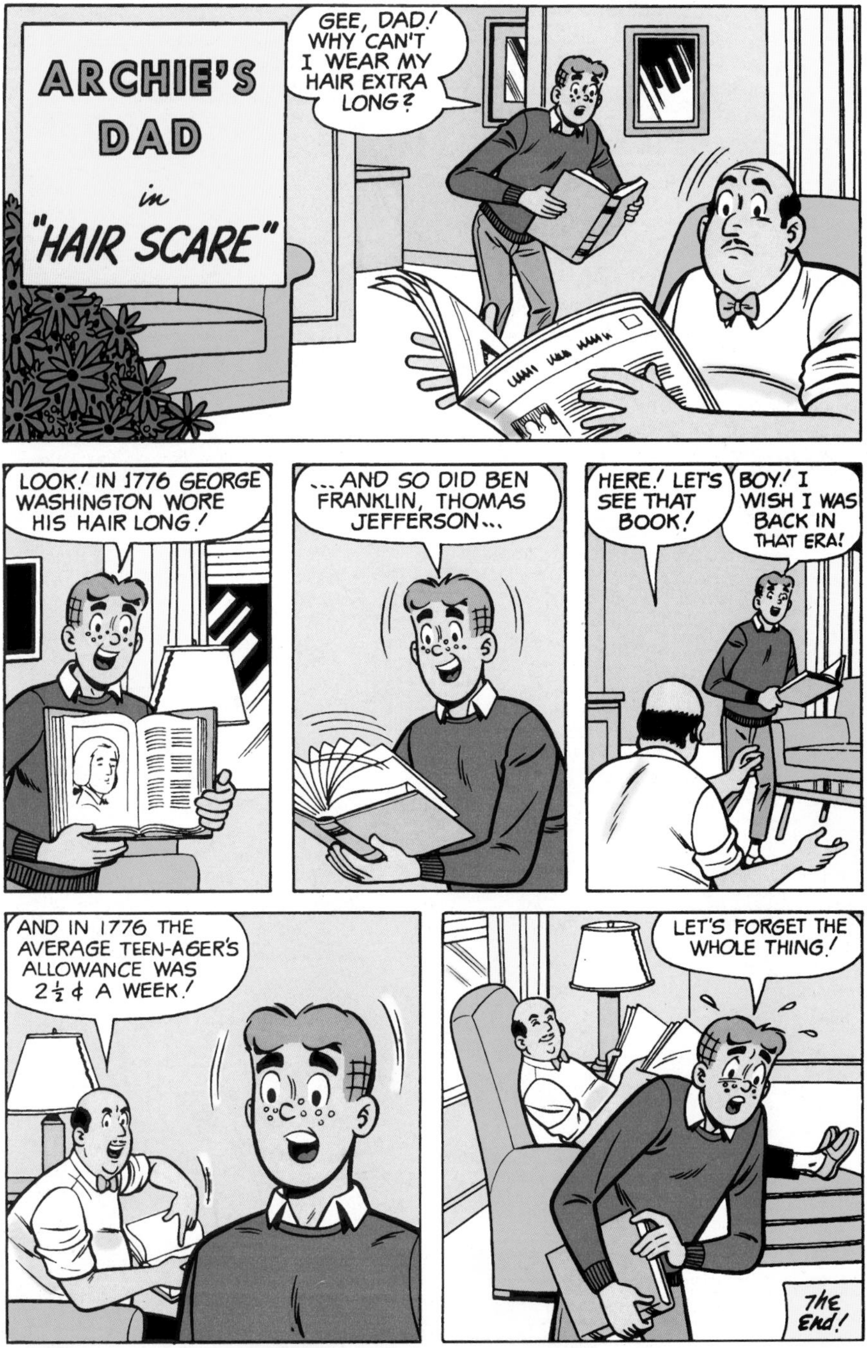
ARCHIE'S DAD in "HAIR SCARE"
GEE, DAD! WHY CAN'T I WEAR MY HAIR EXTRA LONG?
LOOK! IN 1776 GEORGE WASHINGTON WORE HIS HAIR LONG!
...AND SO DID BEN FRANKLIN, THOMAS JEFFERSON...
HERE! LET'S SEE THAT BOOK!
BOY! I WISH I WAS BACK IN THAT ERA!
AND IN 1776 THE AVERAGE TEEN-AGER'S ALLOWANCE WAS 2½ ¢ A WEEK!
LET'S FORGET THE WHOLE THING!
THE End!

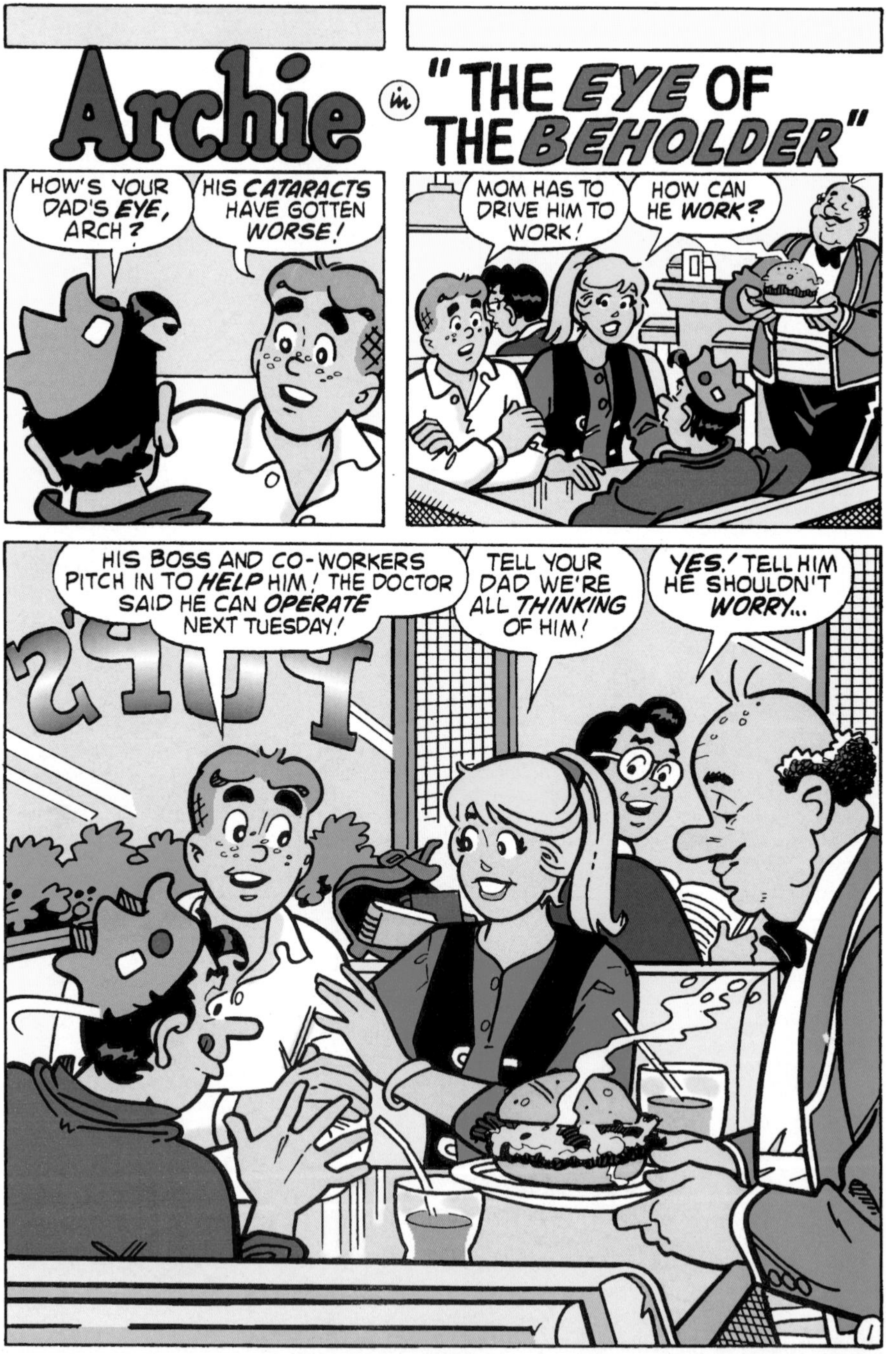

Archie in "THE EYE OF THE BEHOLDER"
HOW'S YOUR DAD'S EYE, ARCH?
HIS CATARACTS HAVE GOTTEN WORSE!
MOM HAS TO DRIVE HIM TO WORK!
HOW CAN HE WORK?
HIS BOSS AND CO-WORKERS PITCH IN TO HELP HIM! THE DOCTOR SAID HE CAN OPERATE NEXT TUESDAY!
TELL YOUR DAD WE'RE ALL THINKING OF HIM!
YES! TELL HIM HE SHOULDN'T WORRY...

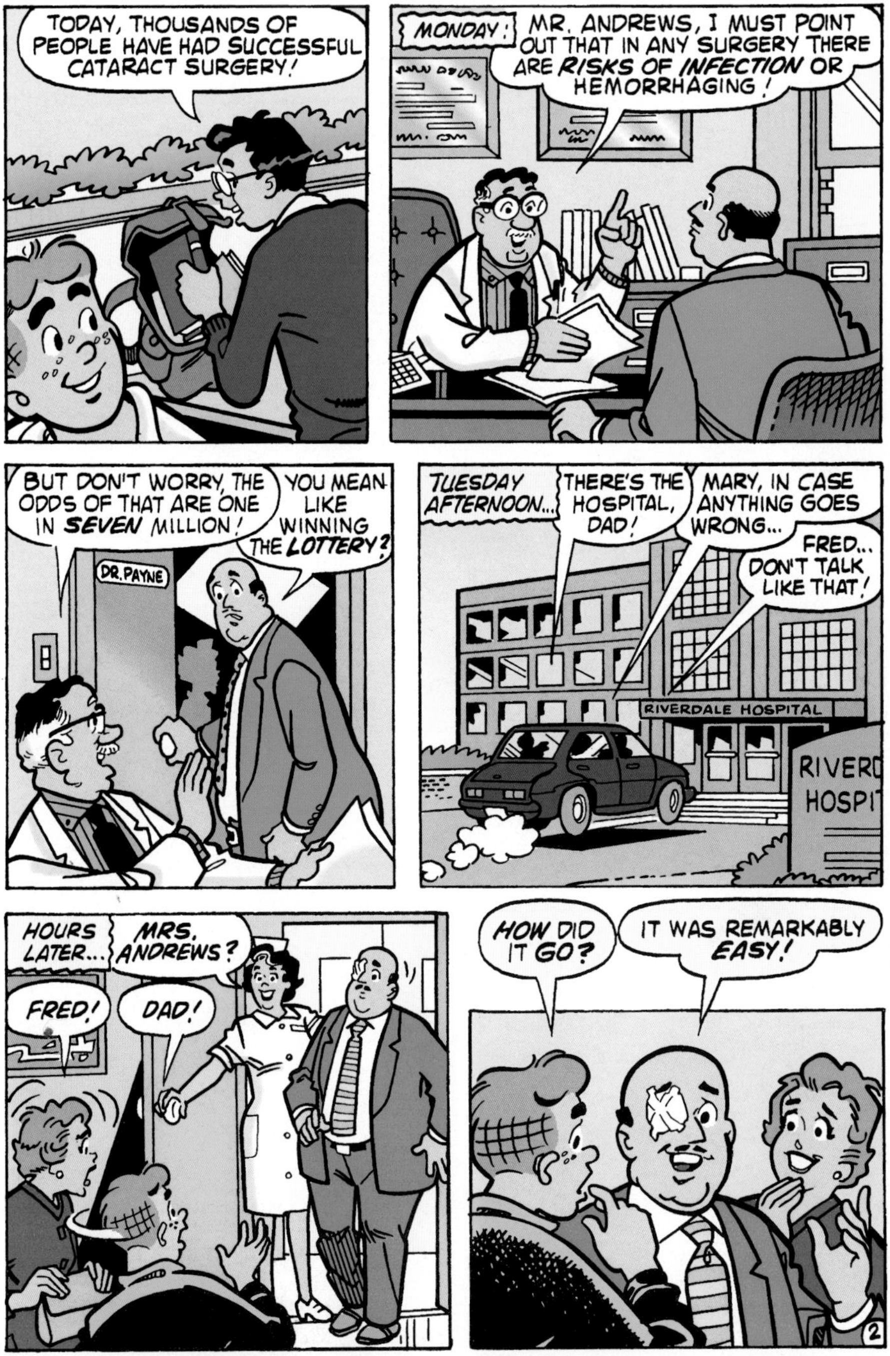
TODAY, THOUSANDS OF PEOPLE HAVE HAD SUCCESSFUL CATARACT SURGERY!
MONDAY:
MR. ANDREWS, I MUST POINT OUT THAT IN ANY SURGERY THERE ARE RISKS OF INFECTION OR HEMORRHAGING!
BUT DON'T WORRY, THE ODDS OF THAT ARE ONE IN SEVEN MILLION!
YOU MEAN LIKE WINNING THE LOTTERY?
DR. PAYNE
TUESDAY AFTERNOON...
THERE'S THE HOSPITAL, DAD!
MARY, IN CASE ANYTHING GOES WRONG...
FRED... DON'T TALK LIKE THAT!
RIVERDALE HOSPITAL
HOURS LATER...
MRS. ANDREWS?
FRED!
DAD!
HOW DID IT GO?
IT WAS REMARKABLY EASY!
2

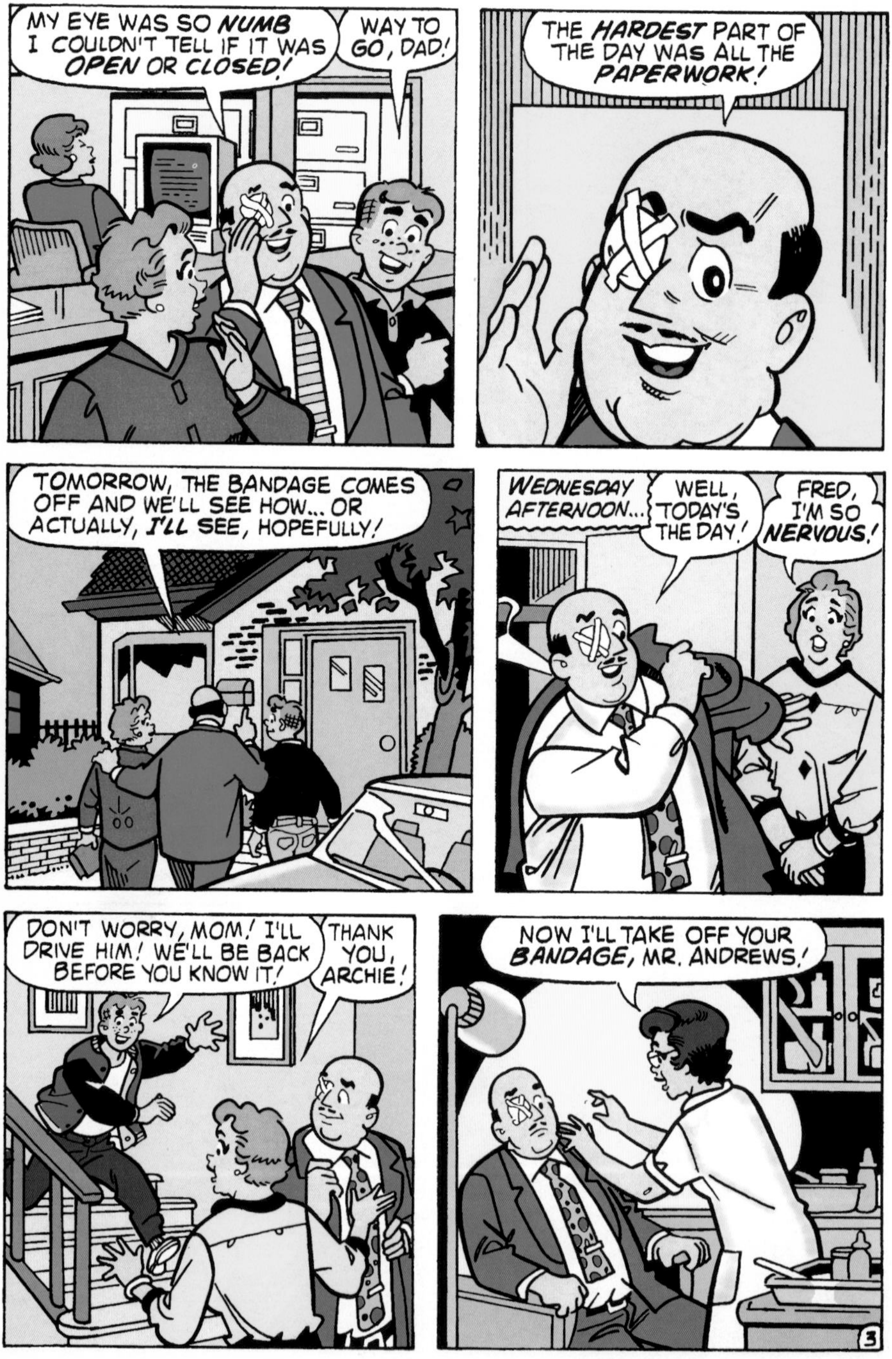
MY EYE WAS SO NUMB I COULDN'T TELL IF IT WAS OPEN OR CLOSED!
WAY TO GO, DAD!
THE HARDEST PART OF THE DAY WAS ALL THE PAPERWORK!
TOMORROW, THE BANDAGE COMES OFF AND WE'LL SEE HOW... OR ACTUALLY, I'LL SEE, HOPEFULLY!
WEDNESDAY AFTERNOON...
WELL, TODAY'S THE DAY!
FRED, I'M SO NERVOUS!
DON'T WORRY, MOM! I'LL DRIVE HIM! WE'LL BE BACK BEFORE YOU KNOW IT!
THANK YOU, ARCHIE!
NOW I'LL TAKE OFF YOUR BANDAGE, MR. ANDREWS!
3

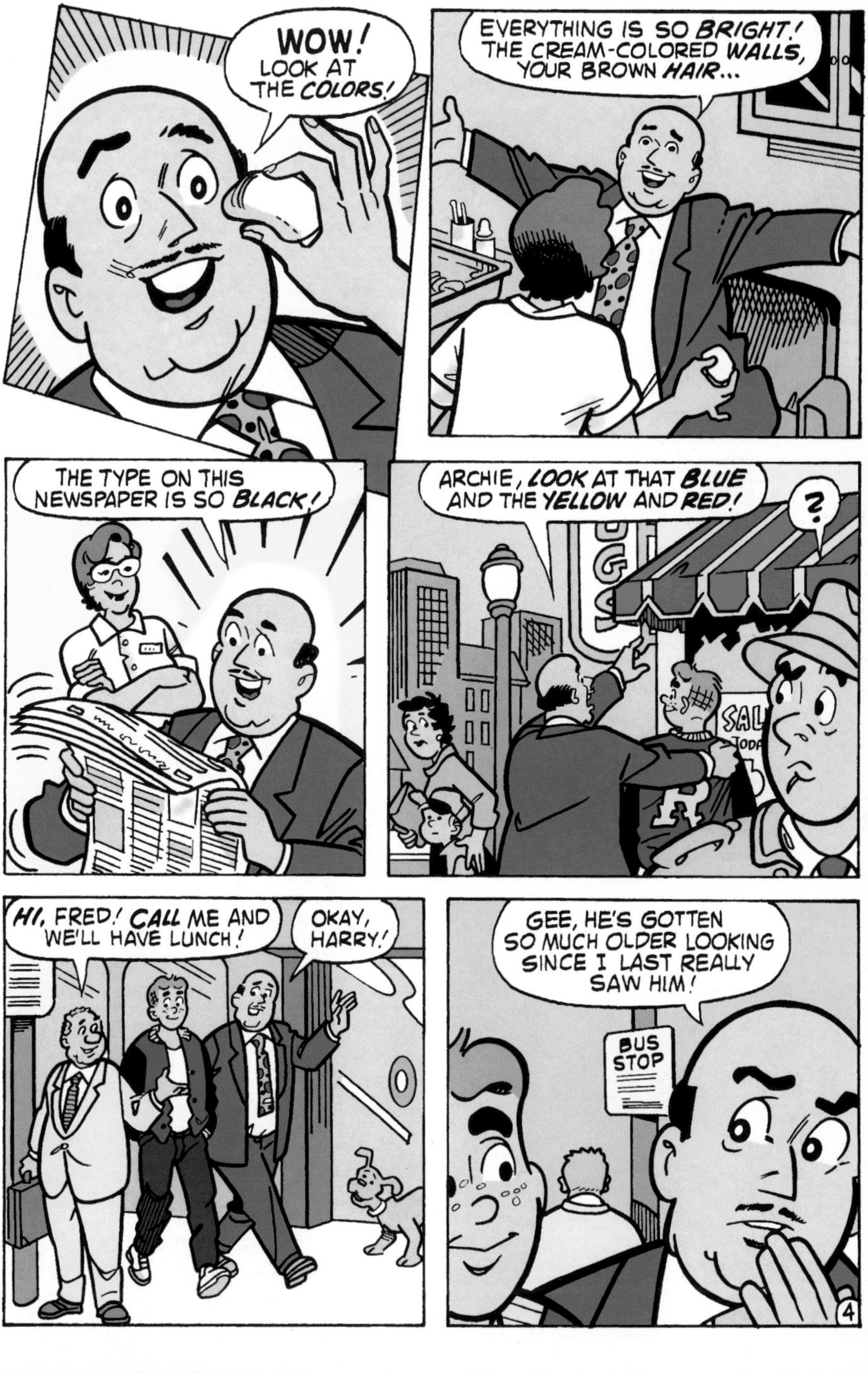
WOW! LOOK AT THE COLORS!
EVERYTHING IS SO BRIGHT! THE CREAM-COLORED WALLS, YOUR BROWN HAIR...
THE TYPE ON THIS NEWSPAPER IS SO BLACK!
ARCHIE, LOOK AT THAT BLUE AND THE YELLOW AND RED!
?
HI, FRED! CALL ME AND WE'LL HAVE LUNCH!
OKAY, HARRY!
GEE, HE'S GOTTEN SO MUCH OLDER LOOKING SINCE I LAST REALLY SAW HIM!
BUS STOP
4

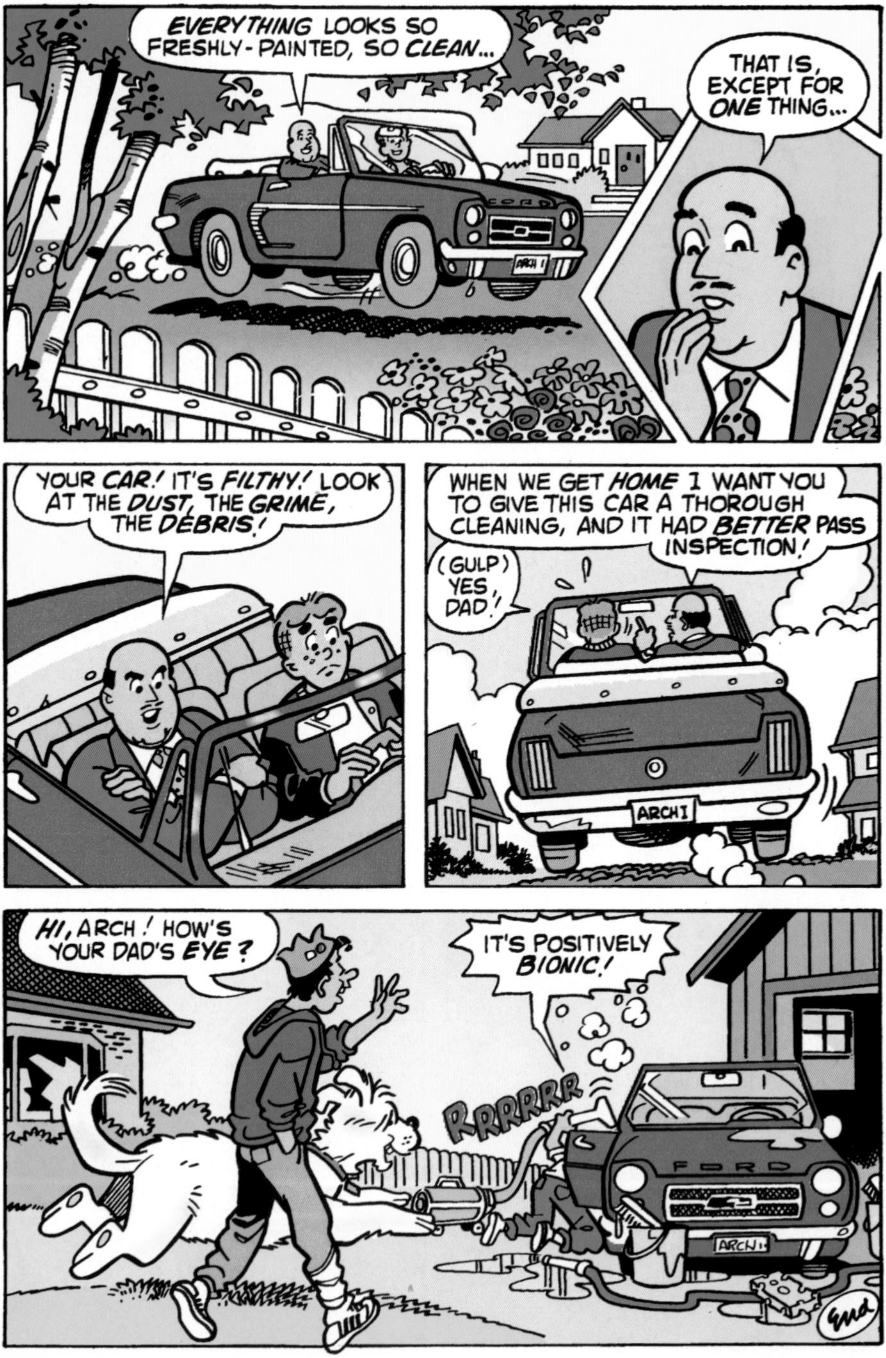
EVERYTHING LOOKS SO FRESHLY-PAINTED, SO CLEAN...
THAT IS, EXCEPT FOR ONE THING...
YOUR CAR! IT'S FILTHY! LOOK AT THE DUST, THE GRIME, THE DEBRIS!
WHEN WE GET HOME I WANT YOU TO GIVE THIS CAR A THOROUGH CLEANING, AND IT HAD BETTER PASS INSPECTION!
(GULP) YES, DAD!
ARCH I
HI, ARCH! HOW'S YOUR DAD'S EYE?
IT'S POSITIVELY BIONIC!
RRRRRR
FORD
ARCH I
End

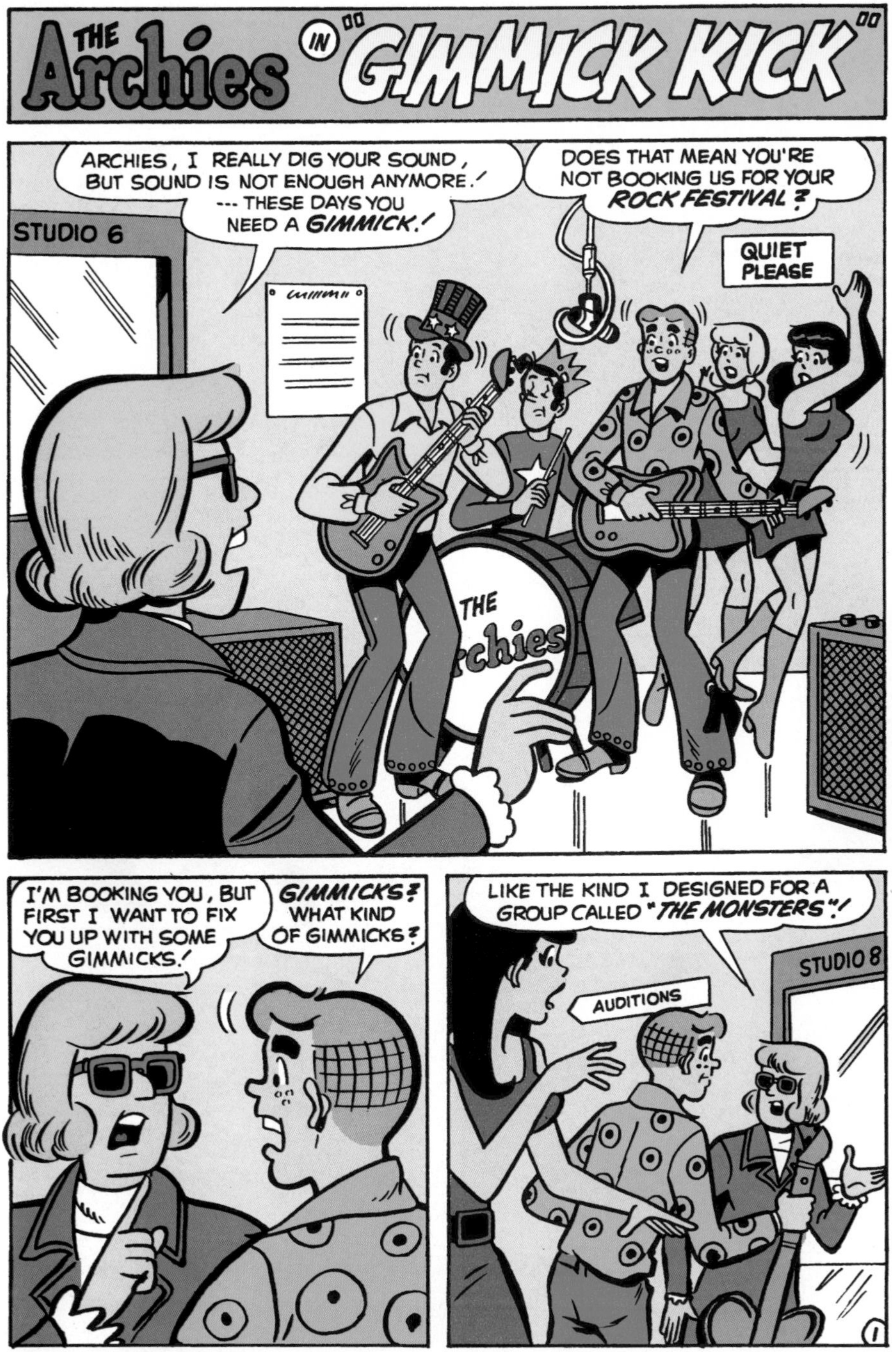
THE Archies IN "GIMMICK KICK"
ARCHIES, I REALLY DIG YOUR SOUND, BUT SOUND IS NOT ENOUGH ANYMORE.! --- THESE DAYS YOU NEED A GIMMICK.!
DOES THAT MEAN YOU'RE NOT BOOKING US FOR YOUR ROCK FESTIVAL?
STUDIO 6
QUIET PLEASE
THE Archies
I'M BOOKING YOU, BUT FIRST I WANT TO FIX YOU UP WITH SOME GIMMICKS.!
GIMMICKS? WHAT KIND OF GIMMICKS?
LIKE THE KIND I DESIGNED FOR A GROUP CALLED "THE MONSTERS".!
STUDIO 8
AUDITIONS
1

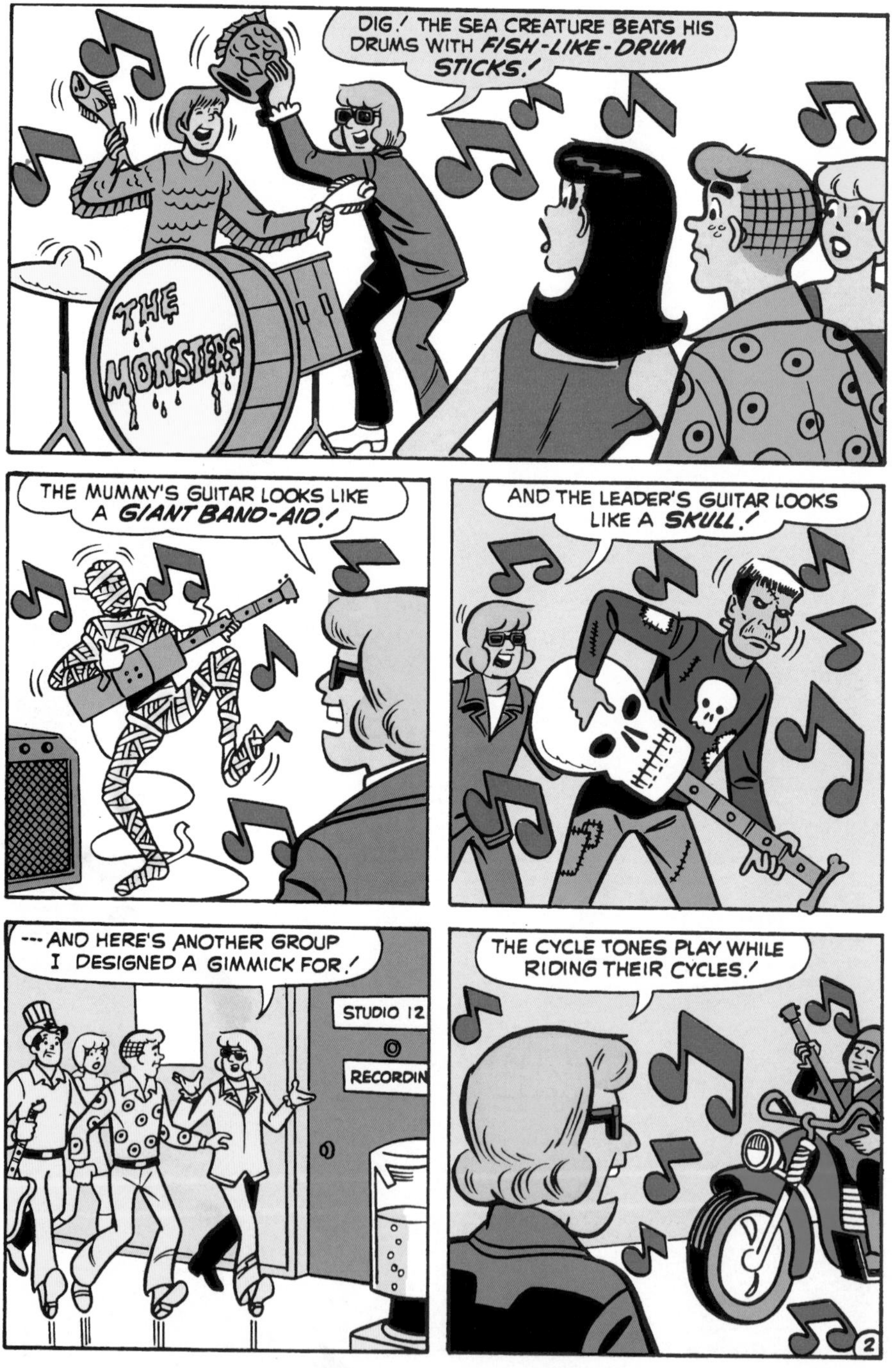
DIG.! THE SEA CREATURE BEATS HIS DRUMS WITH FISH-LIKE-DRUM STICKS.!
THE MONSTERS
THE MUMMY'S GUITAR LOOKS LIKE A GIANT BAND-AID.!
AND THE LEADER'S GUITAR LOOKS LIKE A SKULL.!
--- AND HERE'S ANOTHER GROUP I DESIGNED A GIMMICK FOR.!
STUDIO 12
RECORDIN
THE CYCLE TONES PLAY WHILE RIDING THEIR CYCLES.!
2

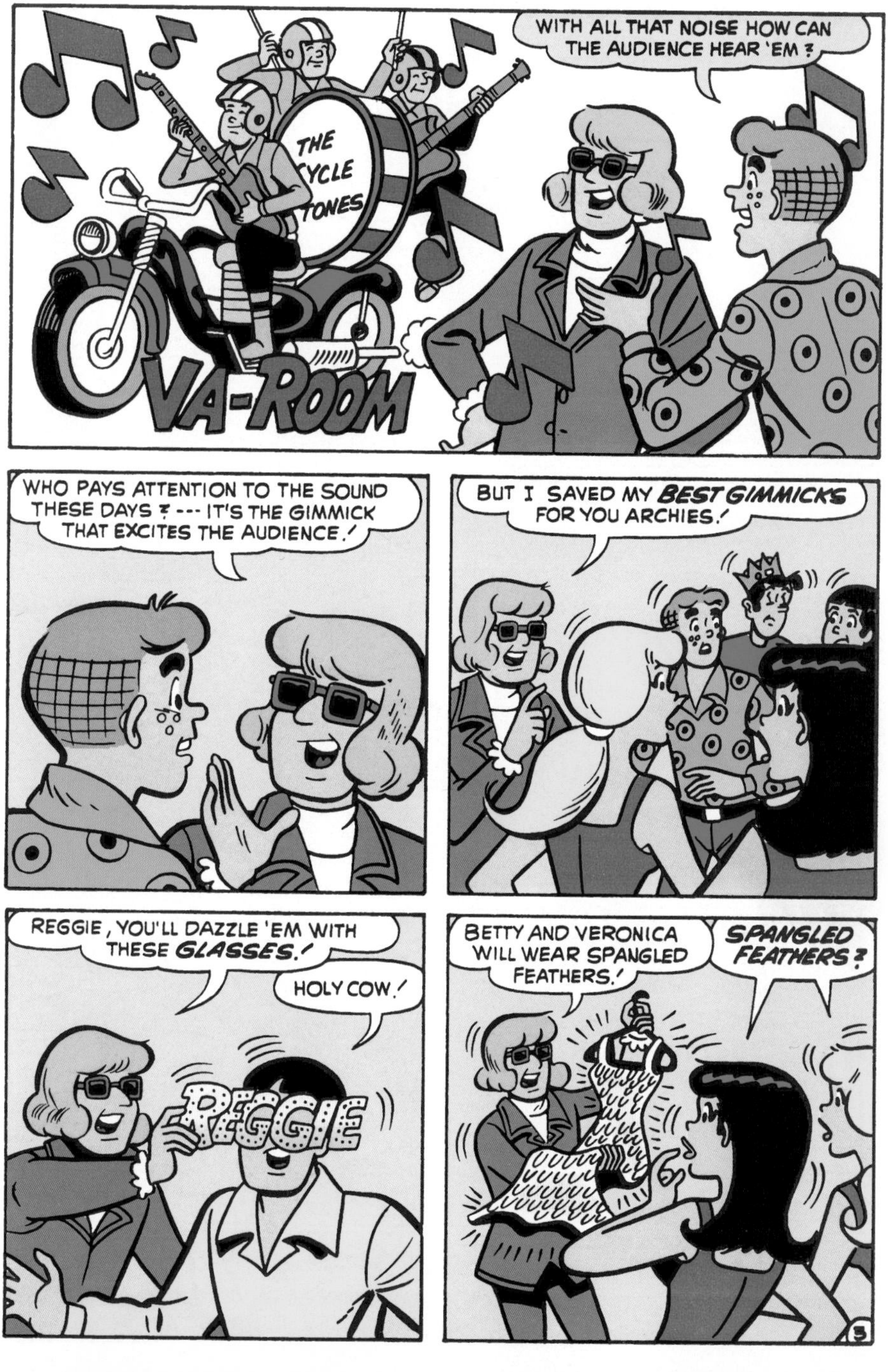
WITH ALL THAT NOISE HOW CAN THE AUDIENCE HEAR 'EM ?
THE CYCLE TONES
VA-ROOM
WHO PAYS ATTENTION TO THE SOUND THESE DAYS ? --- IT'S THE GIMMICK THAT EXCITES THE AUDIENCE !
BUT I SAVED MY BEST GIMMICKS FOR YOU ARCHIES !
REGGIE, YOU'LL DAZZLE 'EM WITH THESE GLASSES !
HOLY COW !
REGGIE
BETTY AND VERONICA WILL WEAR SPANGLED FEATHERS !
SPANGLED FEATHERS ?
5

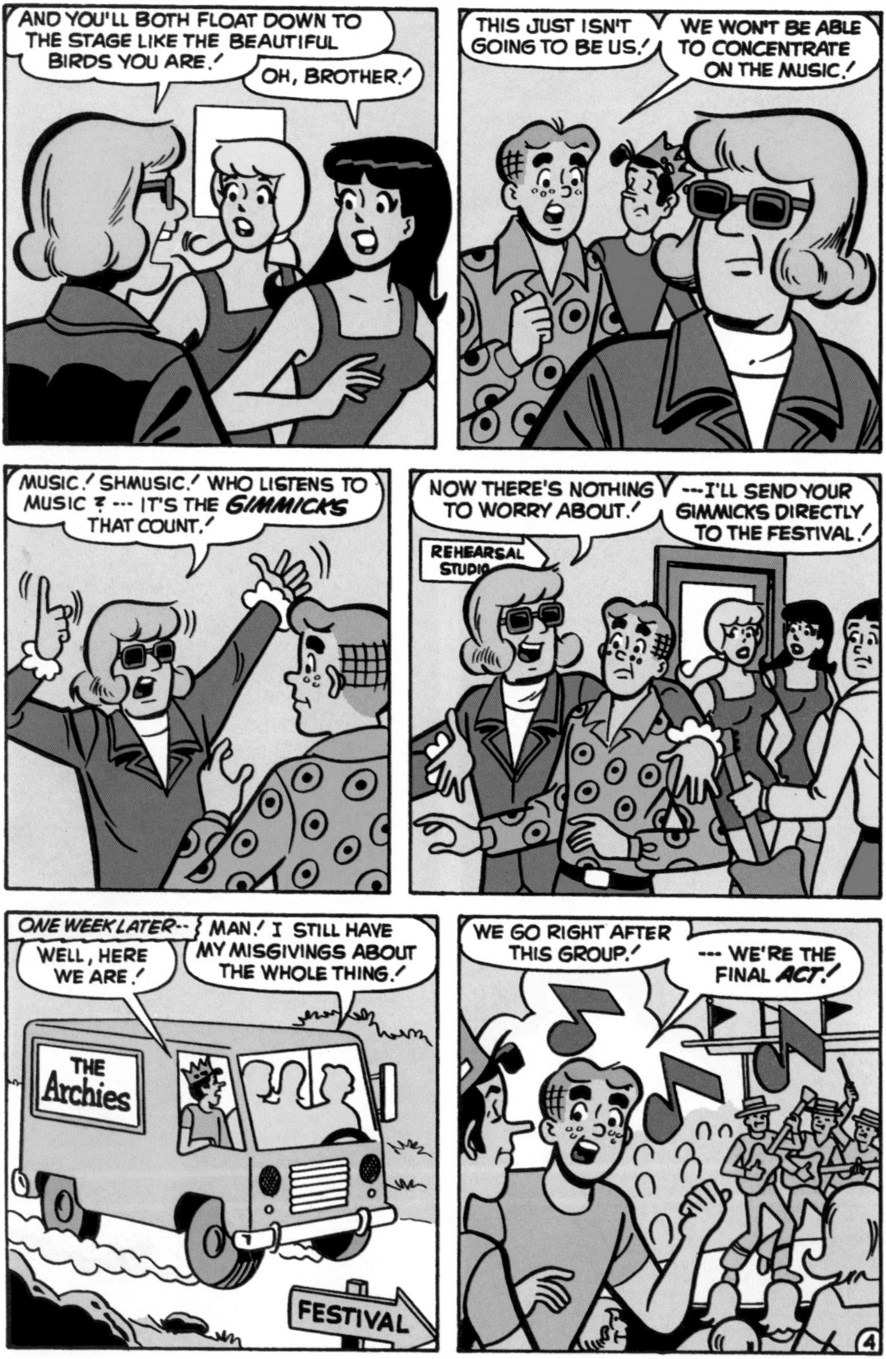
AND YOU'LL BOTH FLOAT DOWN TO THE STAGE LIKE THE BEAUTIFUL BIRDS YOU ARE.!
OH, BROTHER.!
THIS JUST ISN'T GOING TO BE US.!
WE WON'T BE ABLE TO CONCENTRATE ON THE MUSIC.!
MUSIC.! SHMUSIC.! WHO LISTENS TO MUSIC ? --- IT'S THE GIMMICKS THAT COUNT.!
NOW THERE'S NOTHING TO WORRY ABOUT.!
---I'LL SEND YOUR GIMMICKS DIRECTLY TO THE FESTIVAL.!
REHEARSAL STUDIO
ONE WEEK LATER--
WELL, HERE WE ARE.!
MAN.! I STILL HAVE MY MISGIVINGS ABOUT THE WHOLE THING.!
THE Archies
FESTIVAL
WE GO RIGHT AFTER THIS GROUP.!
--- WE'RE THE FINAL ACT.!
4

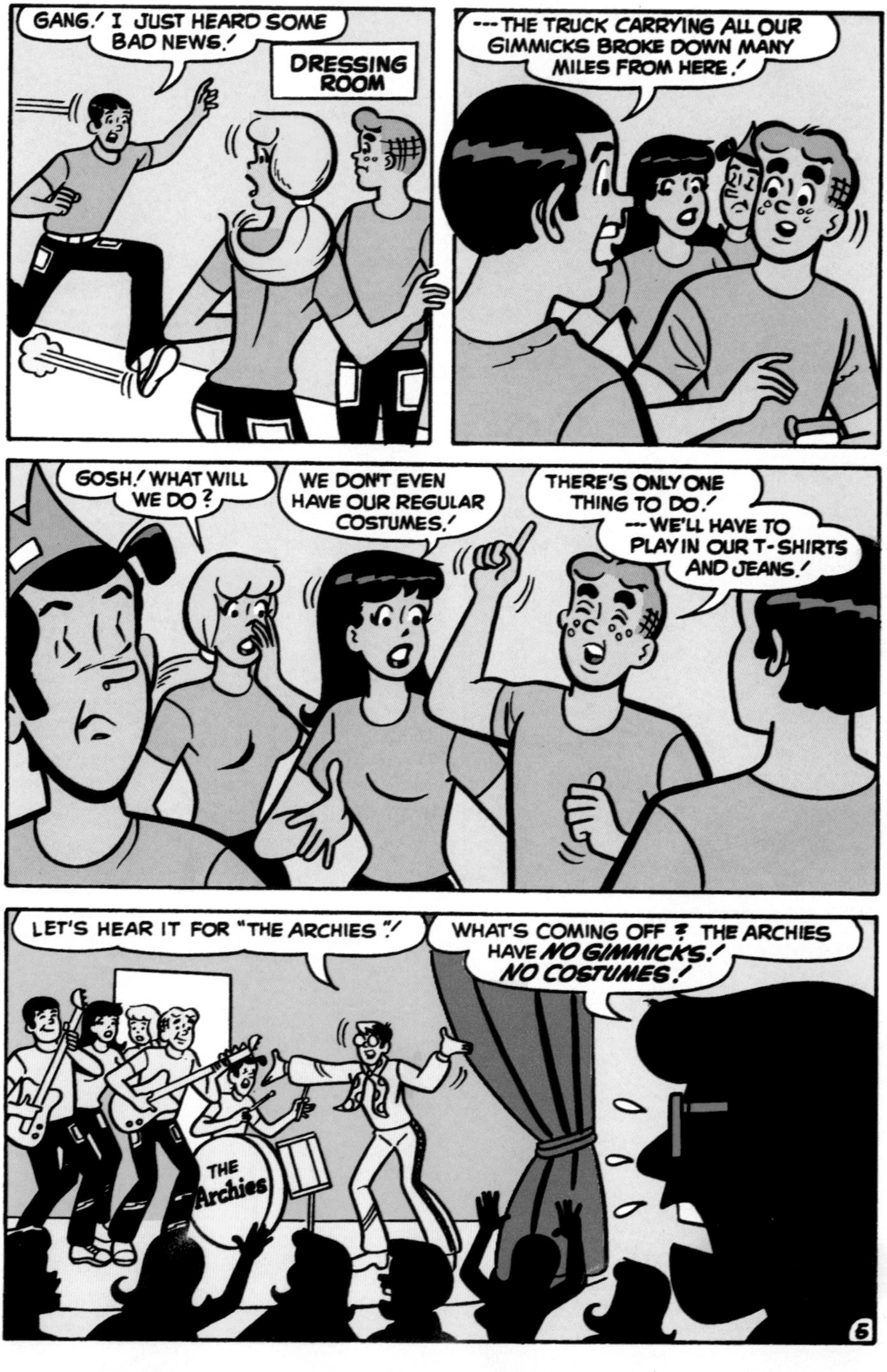
GANG! I JUST HEARD SOME BAD NEWS!
DRESSING ROOM
---THE TRUCK CARRYING ALL OUR GIMMICKS BROKE DOWN MANY MILES FROM HERE!
GOSH! WHAT WILL WE DO?
WE DON'T EVEN HAVE OUR REGULAR COSTUMES!
THERE'S ONLY ONE THING TO DO! ---WE'LL HAVE TO PLAY IN OUR T-SHIRTS AND JEANS!
LET'S HEAR IT FOR "THE ARCHIES"!
WHAT'S COMING OFF? THE ARCHIES HAVE NO GIMMICKS! NO COSTUMES!
THE Archies
6

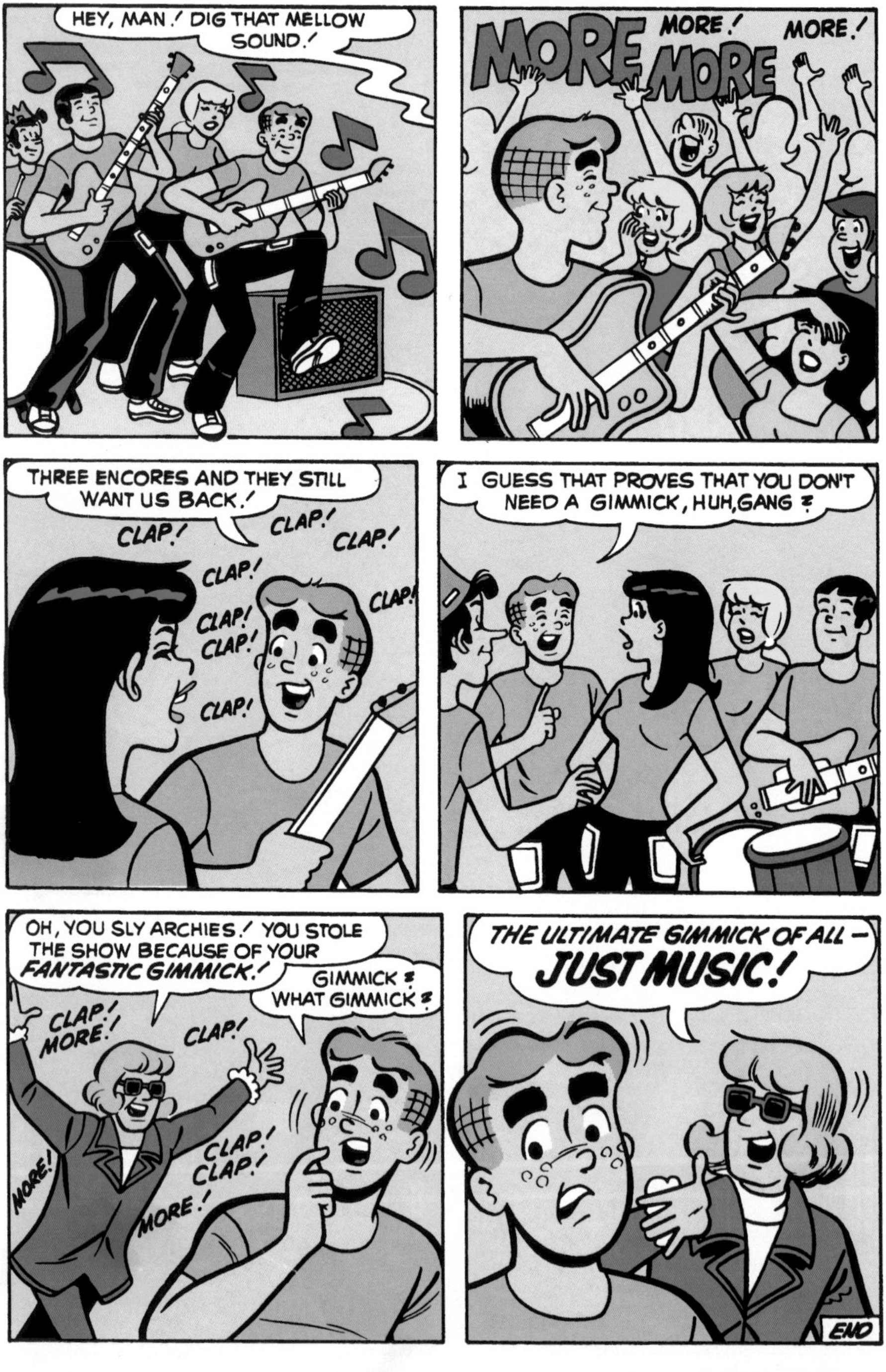
HEY, MAN! DIG THAT MELLOW SOUND!
MORE MORE! MORE MORE MORE!
THREE ENCORES AND THEY STILL WANT US BACK!
CLAP! CLAP! CLAP! CLAP! CLAP! CLAP! CLAP! CLAP!
I GUESS THAT PROVES THAT YOU DON'T NEED A GIMMICK, HUH, GANG?
OH, YOU SLY ARCHIES! YOU STOLE THE SHOW BECAUSE OF YOUR FANTASTIC GIMMICK!
GIMMICK? WHAT GIMMICK?
CLAP! MORE! CLAP! MORE! CLAP! CLAP! MORE!
THE ULTIMATE GIMMICK OF ALL — JUST MUSIC!
END

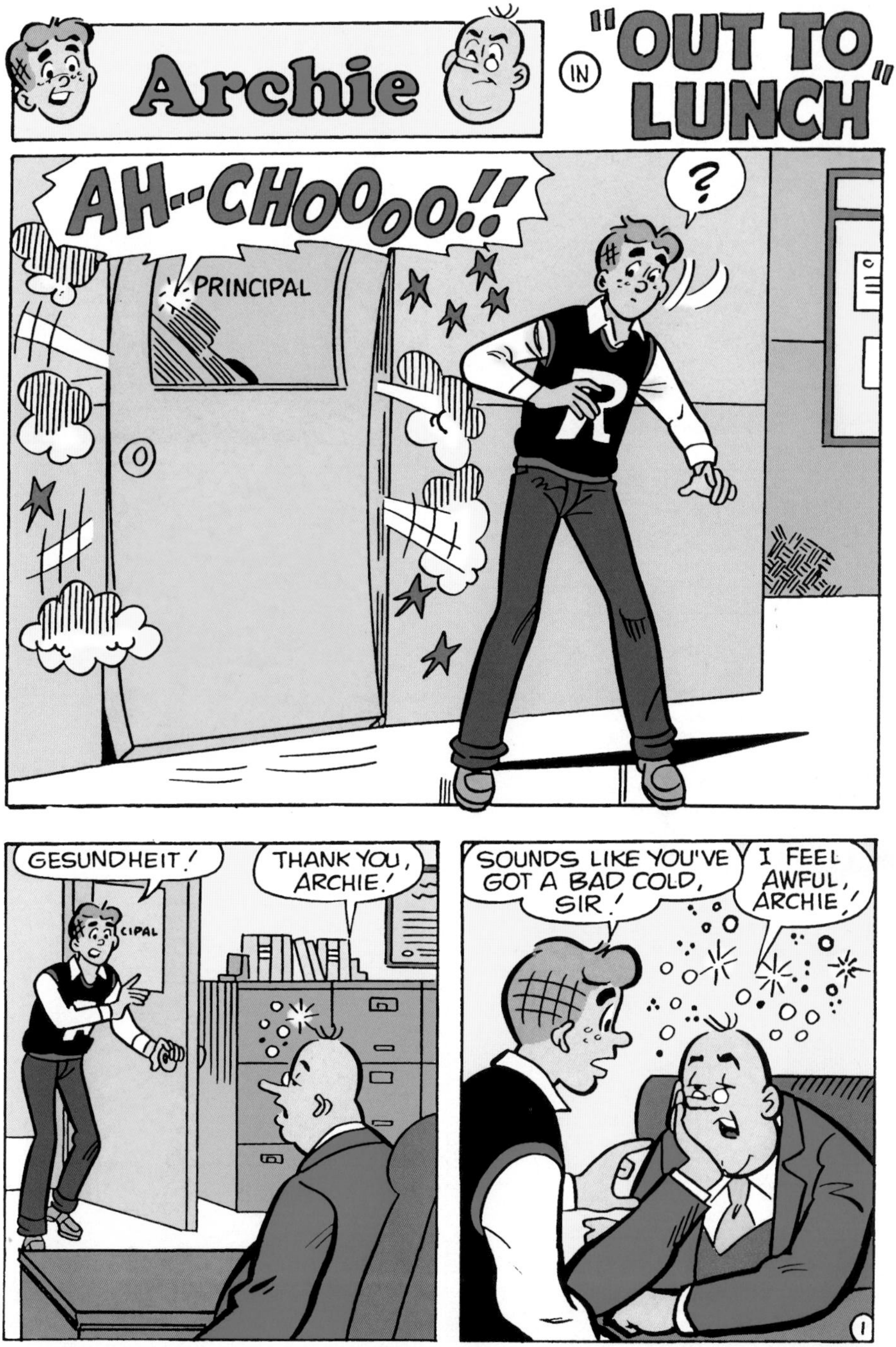
Archie
IN "OUT TO LUNCH"
AH--CHOOOOOO!!
?
PRINCIPAL
GESUNDHEIT!
THANK YOU, ARCHIE!
CIPAL
SOUNDS LIKE YOU'VE GOT A BAD COLD, SIR!
I FEEL AWFUL, ARCHIE!
1

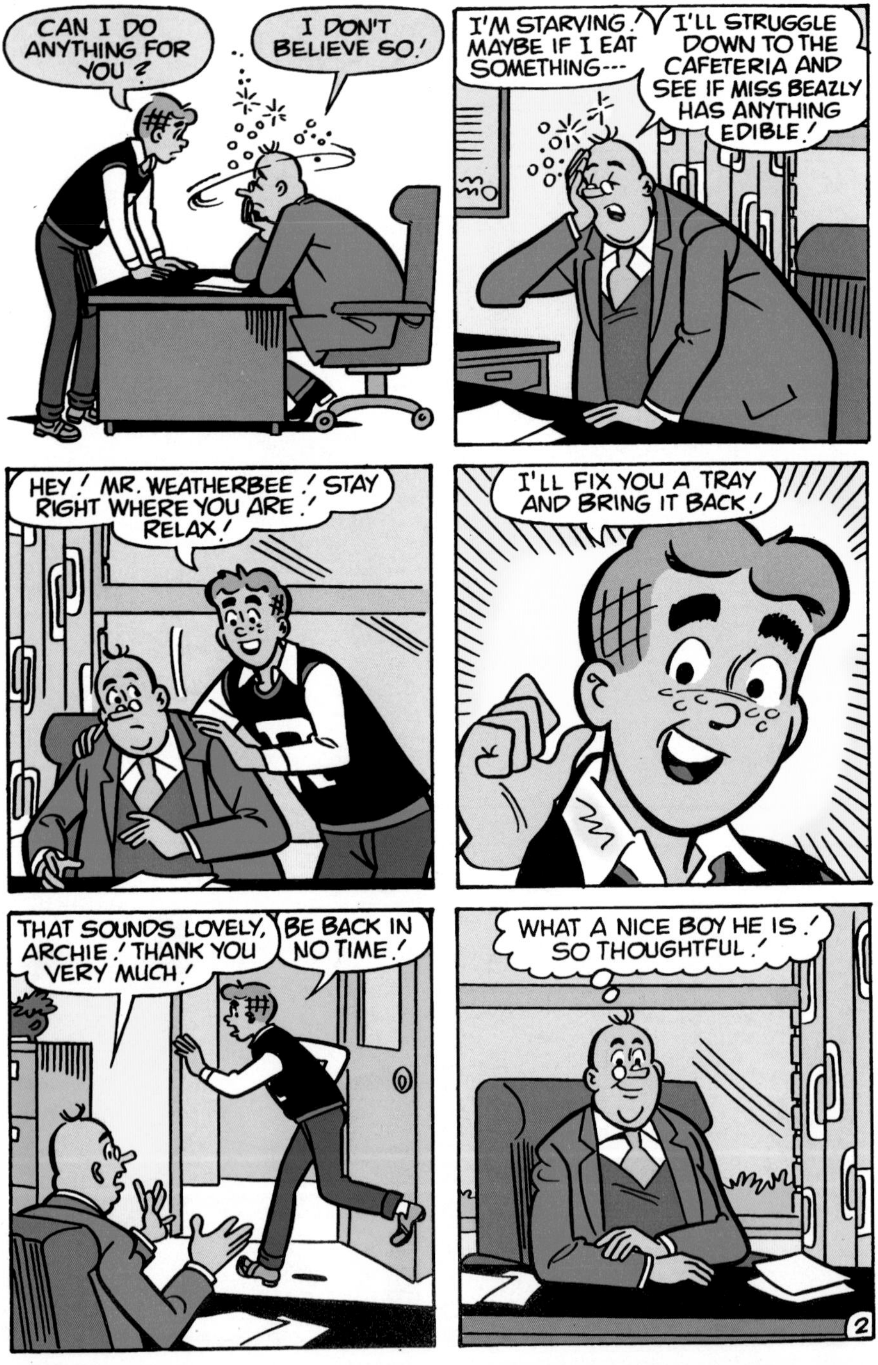
CAN I DO ANYTHING FOR YOU ?
I DON'T BELIEVE SO !
I'M STARVING ! MAYBE IF I EAT SOMETHING---
I'LL STRUGGLE DOWN TO THE CAFETERIA AND SEE IF MISS BEAZLY HAS ANYTHING EDIBLE !
HEY ! MR. WEATHERBEE ! STAY RIGHT WHERE YOU ARE ! RELAX !
I'LL FIX YOU A TRAY AND BRING IT BACK !
THAT SOUNDS LOVELY, ARCHIE ! THANK YOU VERY MUCH !
BE BACK IN NO TIME !
WHAT A NICE BOY HE IS ! SO THOUGHTFUL !
2

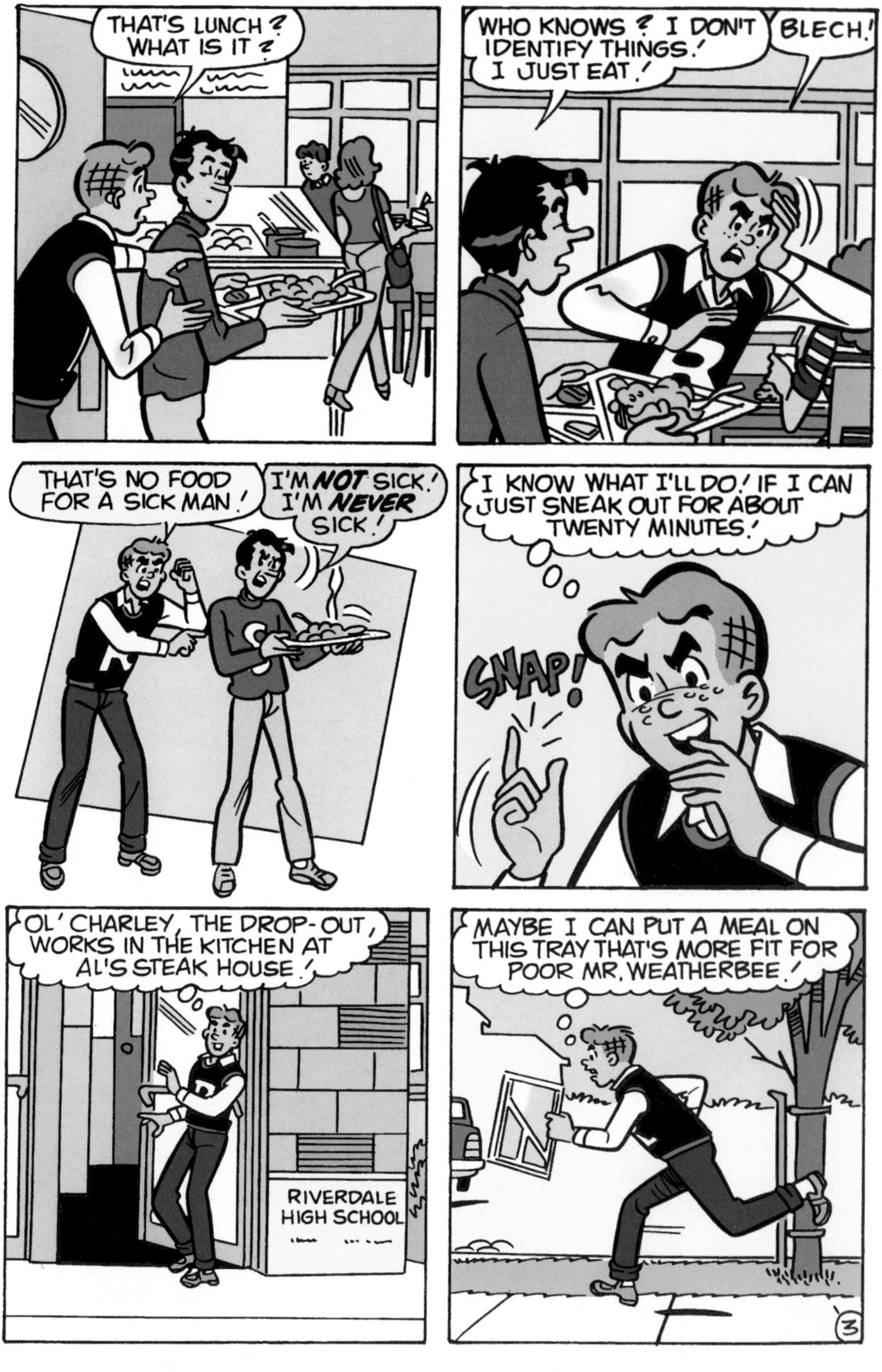
THAT'S LUNCH? WHAT IS IT?
WHO KNOWS? I DON'T IDENTIFY THINGS! I JUST EAT!
BLECH!
THAT'S NO FOOD FOR A SICK MAN!
I'M NOT SICK! I'M NEVER SICK!
I KNOW WHAT I'LL DO! IF I CAN JUST SNEAK OUT FOR ABOUT TWENTY MINUTES!
SNAP!
OL' CHARLEY, THE DROP-OUT, WORKS IN THE KITCHEN AT AL'S STEAK HOUSE!
RIVERDALE HIGH SCHOOL
MAYBE I CAN PUT A MEAL ON THIS TRAY THAT'S MORE FIT FOR POOR MR. WEATHERBEE!
3

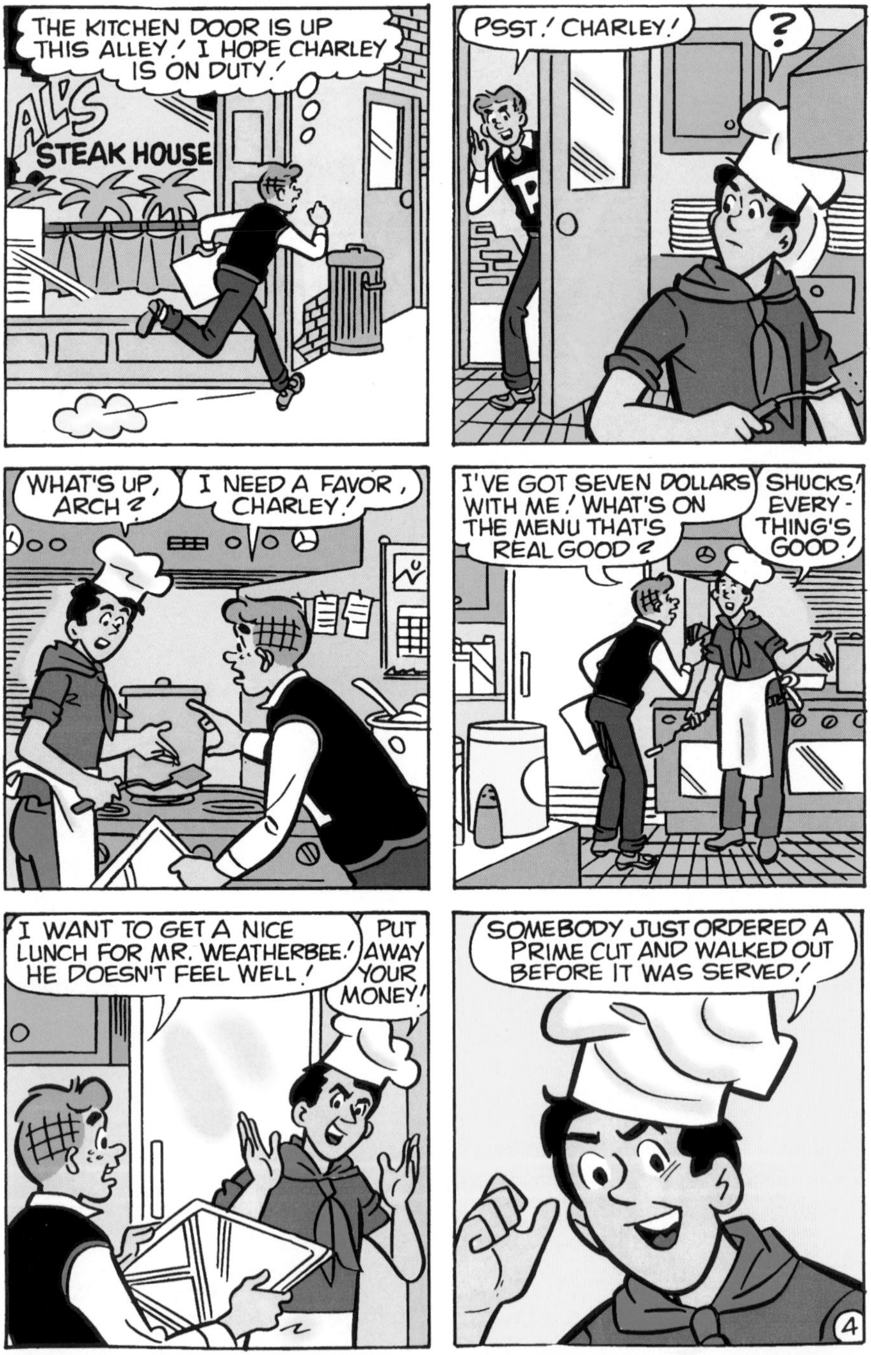
THE KITCHEN DOOR IS UP THIS ALLEY! I HOPE CHARLEY IS ON DUTY!
AL'S
STEAK HOUSE
PSST! CHARLEY!
?
WHAT'S UP, ARCH?
I NEED A FAVOR, CHARLEY!
I'VE GOT SEVEN DOLLARS WITH ME! WHAT'S ON THE MENU THAT'S REAL GOOD?
SHUCKS! EVERY-THING'S GOOD!
I WANT TO GET A NICE LUNCH FOR MR. WEATHERBEE! HE DOESN'T FEEL WELL!
PUT AWAY YOUR MONEY!
SOMEBODY JUST ORDERED A PRIME CUT AND WALKED OUT BEFORE IT WAS SERVED!
4

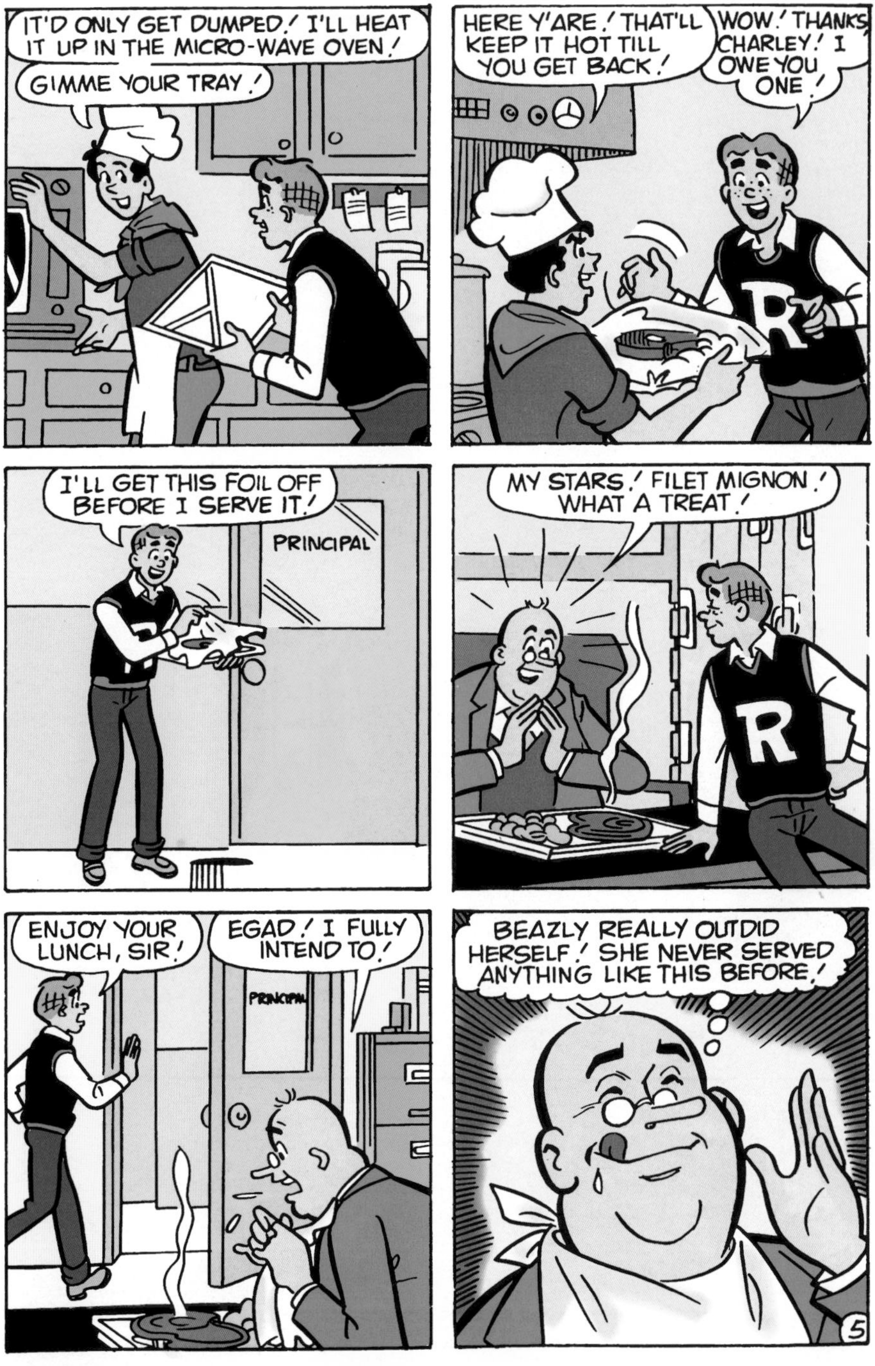
IT'D ONLY GET DUMPED! I'LL HEAT IT UP IN THE MICRO-WAVE OVEN!
GIMME YOUR TRAY!
HERE Y'ARE! THAT'LL KEEP IT HOT TILL YOU GET BACK!
WOW! THANKS, CHARLEY! I OWE YOU ONE!
I'LL GET THIS FOIL OFF BEFORE I SERVE IT!
PRINCIPAL
MY STARS! FILET MIGNON! WHAT A TREAT!
ENJOY YOUR LUNCH, SIR!
EGAD! I FULLY INTEND TO!
PRINCIPAL
BEAZLY REALLY OUTDID HERSELF! SHE NEVER SERVED ANYTHING LIKE THIS BEFORE!
5

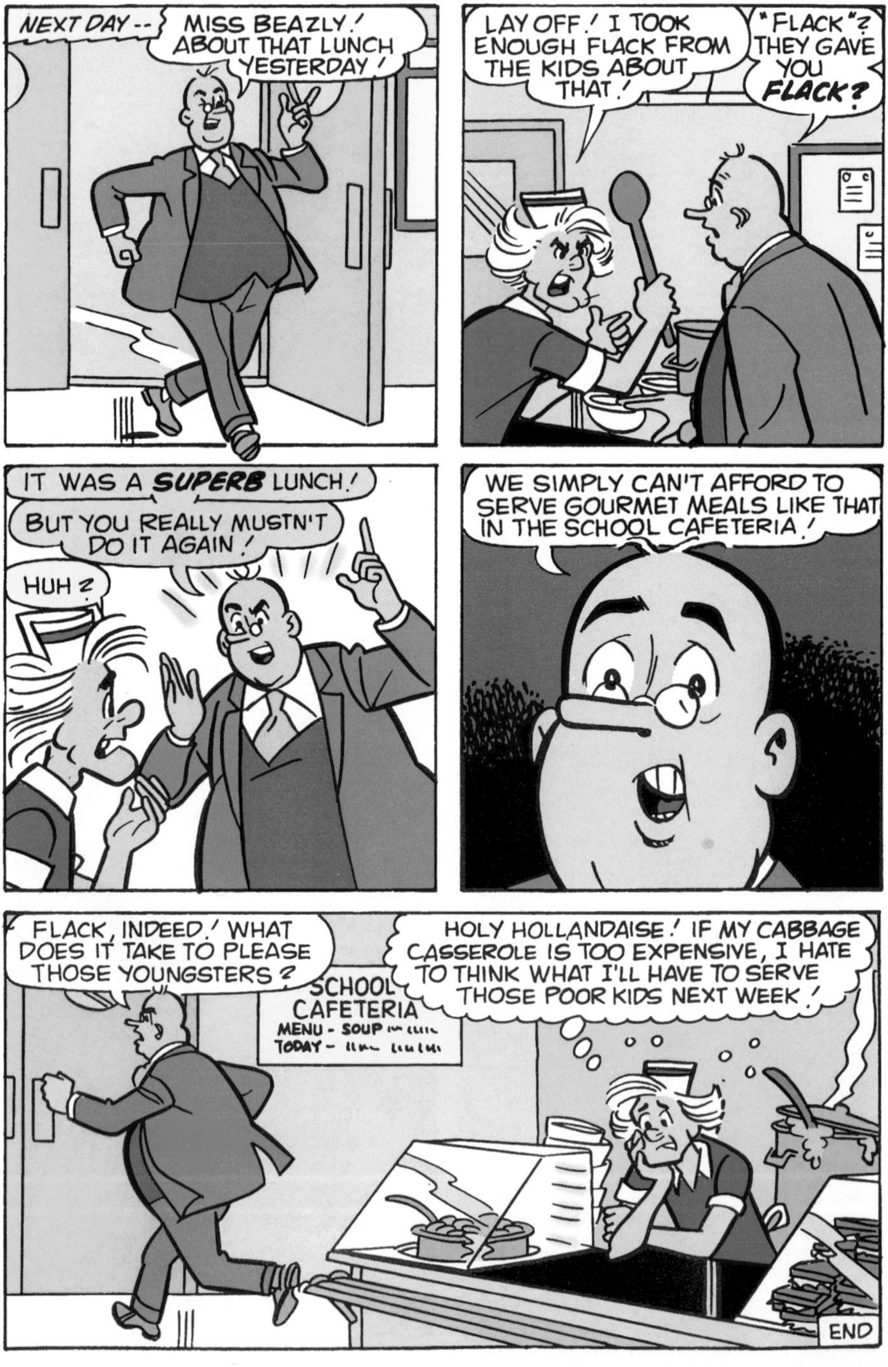
NEXT DAY --
MISS BEAZLY! ABOUT THAT LUNCH YESTERDAY!
LAY OFF! I TOOK ENOUGH FLACK FROM THE KIDS ABOUT THAT!
"FLACK"? THEY GAVE YOU FLACK?
IT WAS A SUPERB LUNCH!
BUT YOU REALLY MUSTN'T DO IT AGAIN!
HUH?
WE SIMPLY CAN'T AFFORD TO SERVE GOURMET MEALS LIKE THAT IN THE SCHOOL CAFETERIA!
FLACK, INDEED! WHAT DOES IT TAKE TO PLEASE THOSE YOUNGSTERS?
HOLY HOLLANDAISE! IF MY CABBAGE CASSEROLE IS TOO EXPENSIVE, I HATE TO THINK WHAT I'LL HAVE TO SERVE THOSE POOR KIDS NEXT WEEK!
SCHOOL CAFETERIA
MENU - SOUP
TODAY -
END

Archie in "THE JOINER"

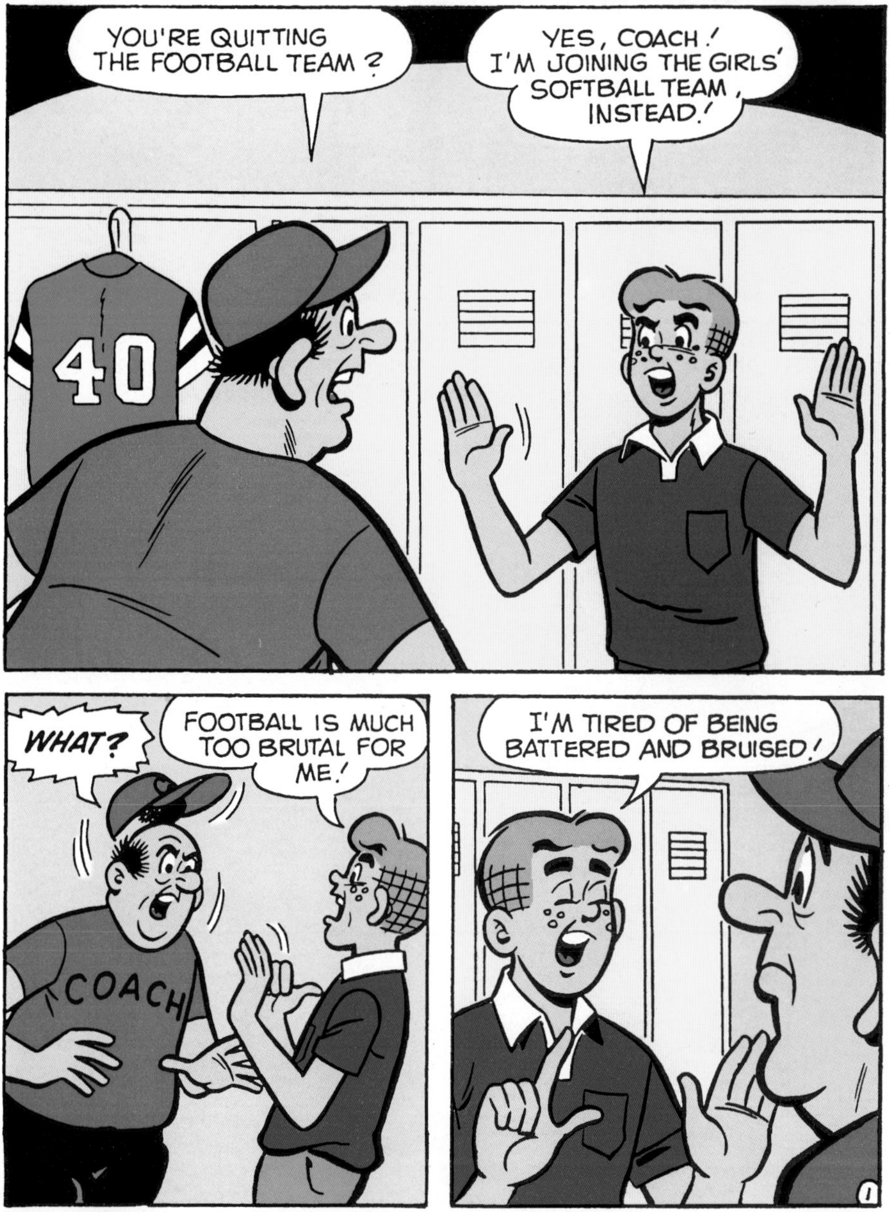
YOU'RE QUITTING THE FOOTBALL TEAM ?
YES, COACH! I'M JOINING THE GIRLS' SOFTBALL TEAM, INSTEAD!
40
WHAT?
FOOTBALL IS MUCH TOO BRUTAL FOR ME!
COACH
I'M TIRED OF BEING BATTERED AND BRUISED!

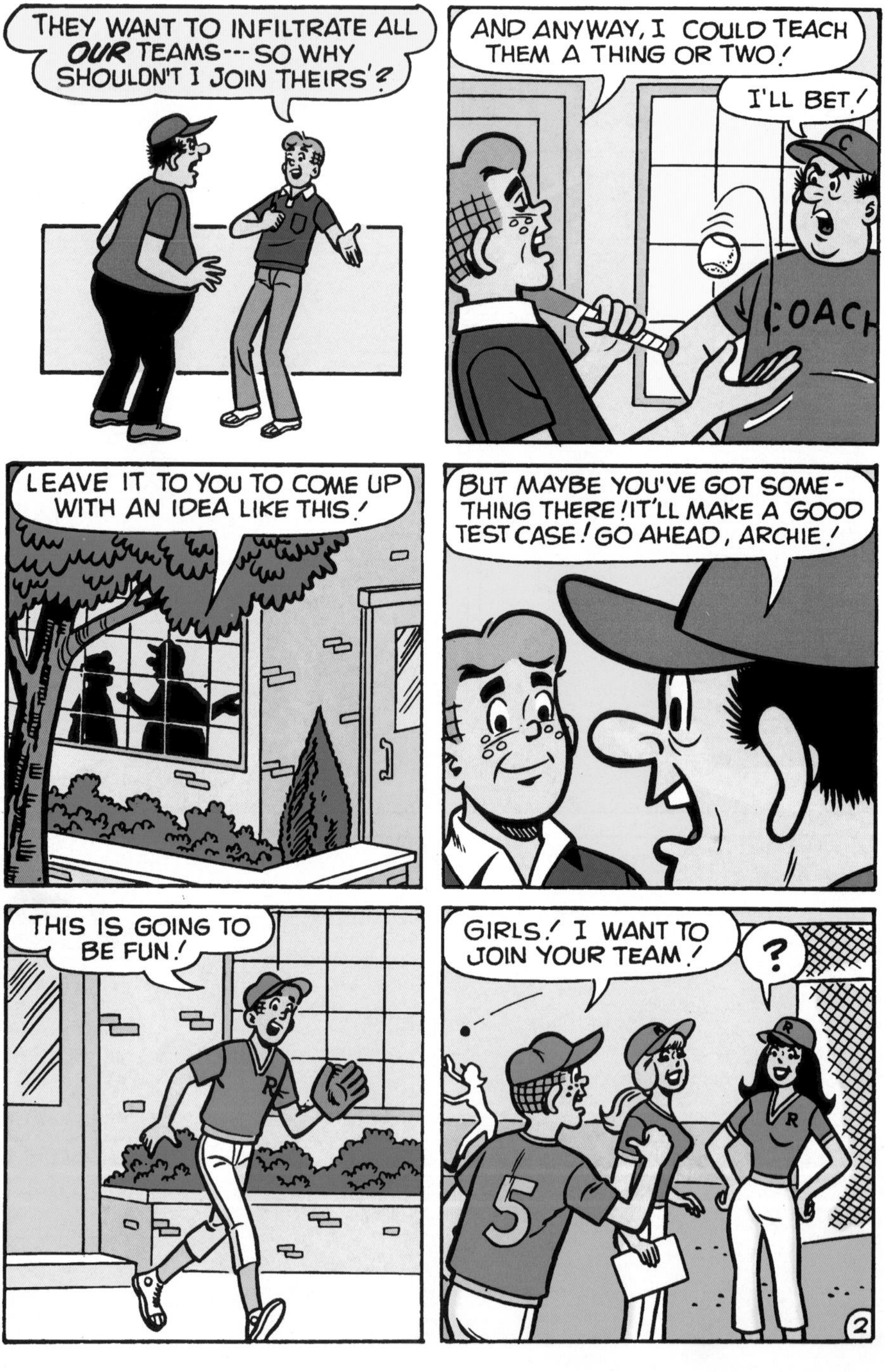
THEY WANT TO INFILTRATE ALL OUR TEAMS--- SO WHY SHOULDN'T I JOIN THEIRS'?
AND ANYWAY, I COULD TEACH THEM A THING OR TWO!
I'LL BET!
COACH
LEAVE IT TO YOU TO COME UP WITH AN IDEA LIKE THIS!
BUT MAYBE YOU'VE GOT SOME-THING THERE! IT'LL MAKE A GOOD TEST CASE! GO AHEAD, ARCHIE!
THIS IS GOING TO BE FUN!
GIRLS! I WANT TO JOIN YOUR TEAM!
?
2

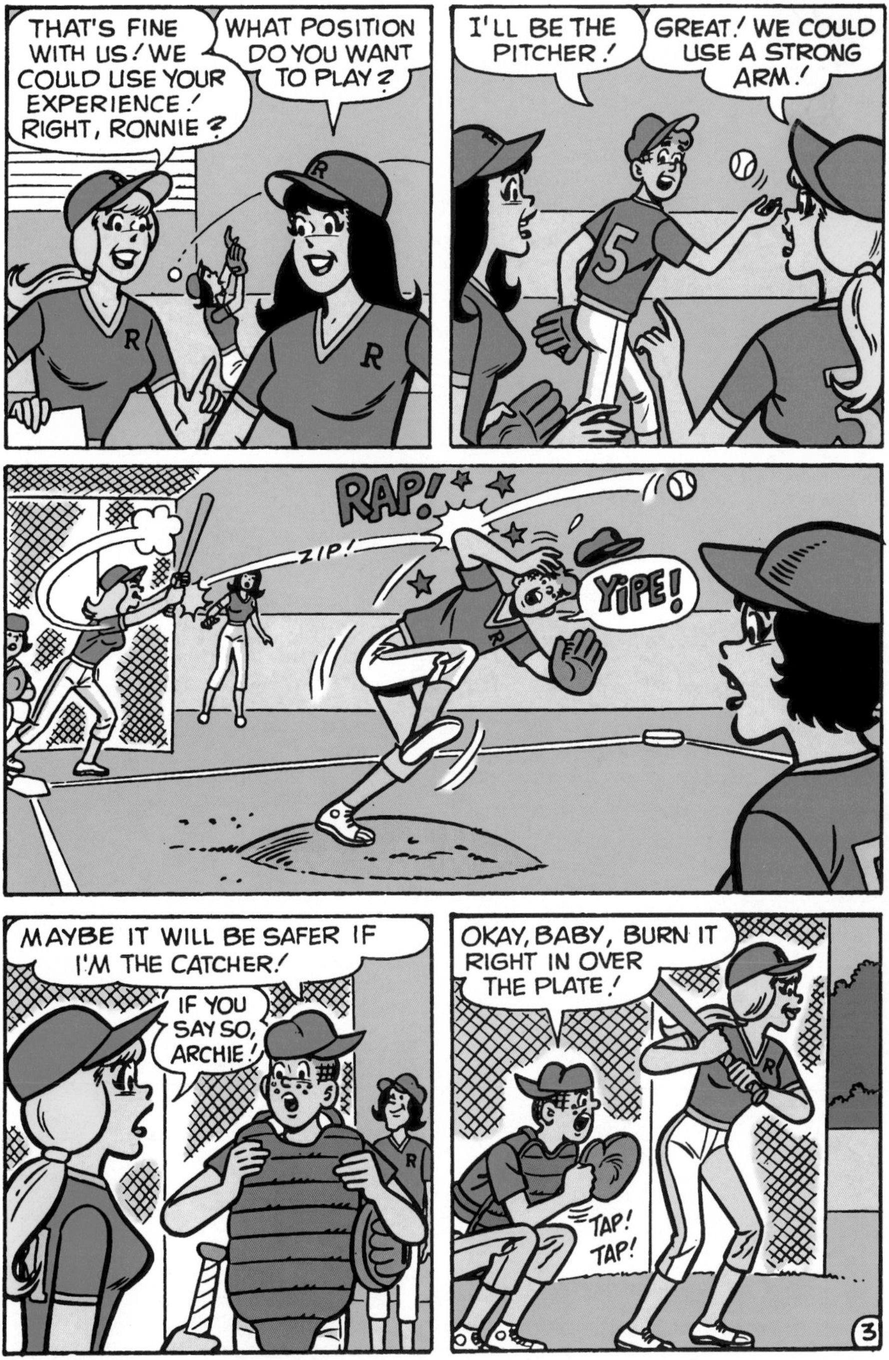
THAT'S FINE WITH US! WE COULD USE YOUR EXPERIENCE! RIGHT, RONNIE?
WHAT POSITION DO YOU WANT TO PLAY?
I'LL BE THE PITCHER!
GREAT! WE COULD USE A STRONG ARM!
RAP!
ZIP!
YIPE!
MAYBE IT WILL BE SAFER IF I'M THE CATCHER!
IF YOU SAY SO, ARCHIE!
OKAY, BABY, BURN IT RIGHT IN OVER THE PLATE!
TAP! TAP!
3

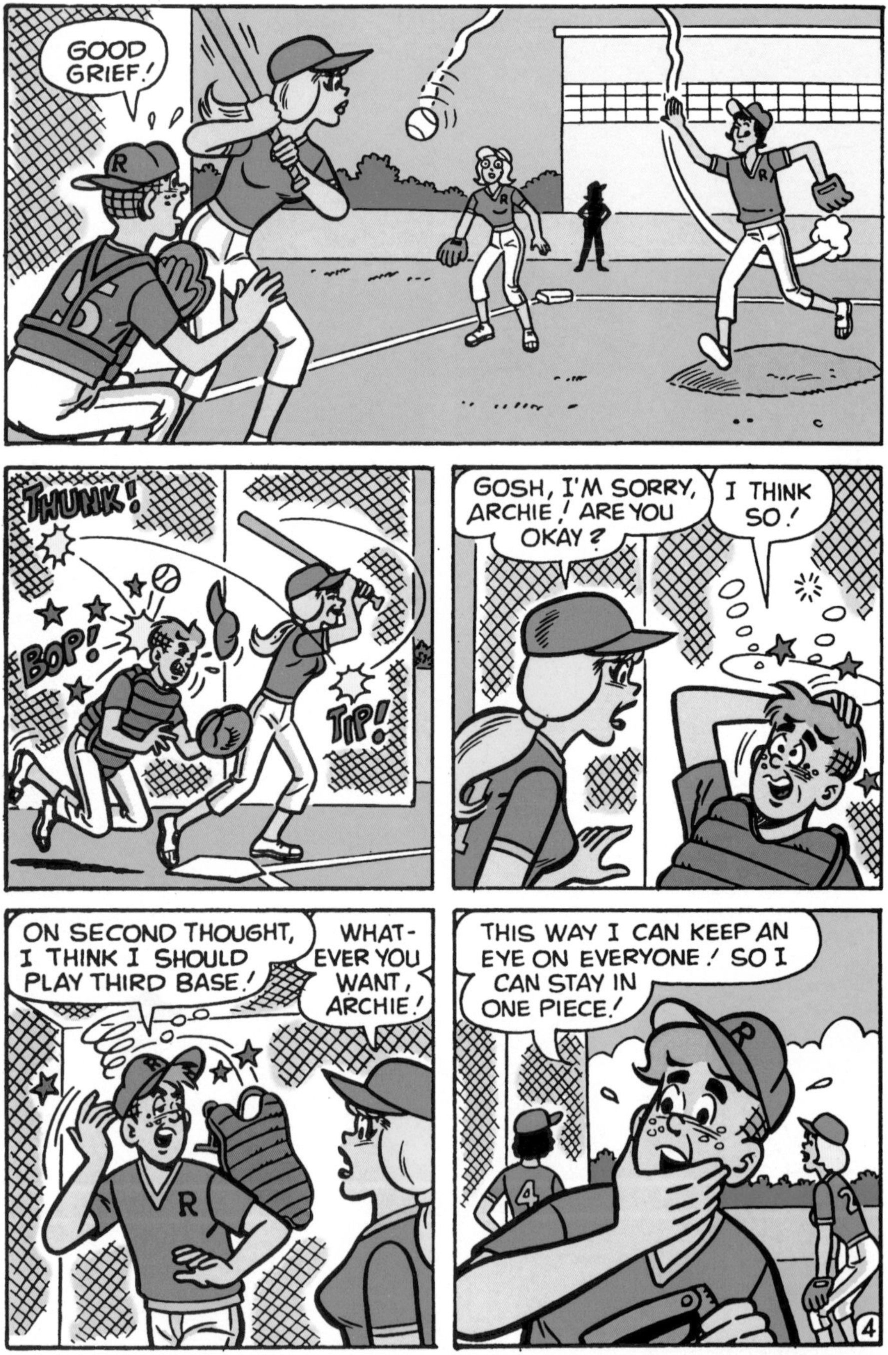
GOOD GRIEF!
THUNK!
BOP!
TIP!
GOSH, I'M SORRY, ARCHIE! ARE YOU OKAY?
I THINK SO!
ON SECOND THOUGHT, I THINK I SHOULD PLAY THIRD BASE!
WHAT-EVER YOU WANT, ARCHIE!
THIS WAY I CAN KEEP AN EYE ON EVERYONE! SO I CAN STAY IN ONE PIECE!
4

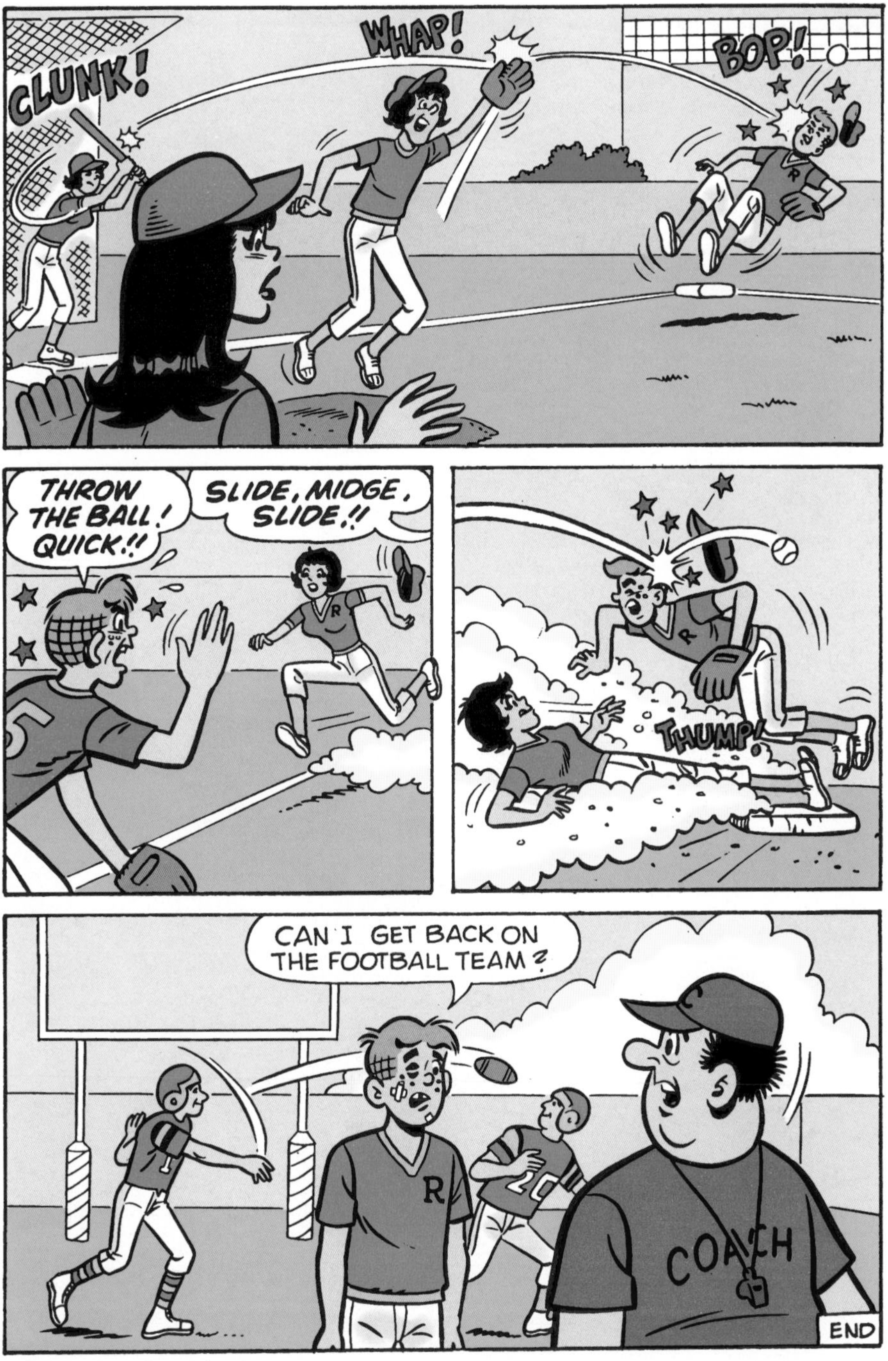
CLUNK!
WHAP!
BOP!
THROW THE BALL! QUICK!!
SLIDE, MIDGE, SLIDE!!
THUMP!
CAN I GET BACK ON THE FOOTBALL TEAM?
COACH
END

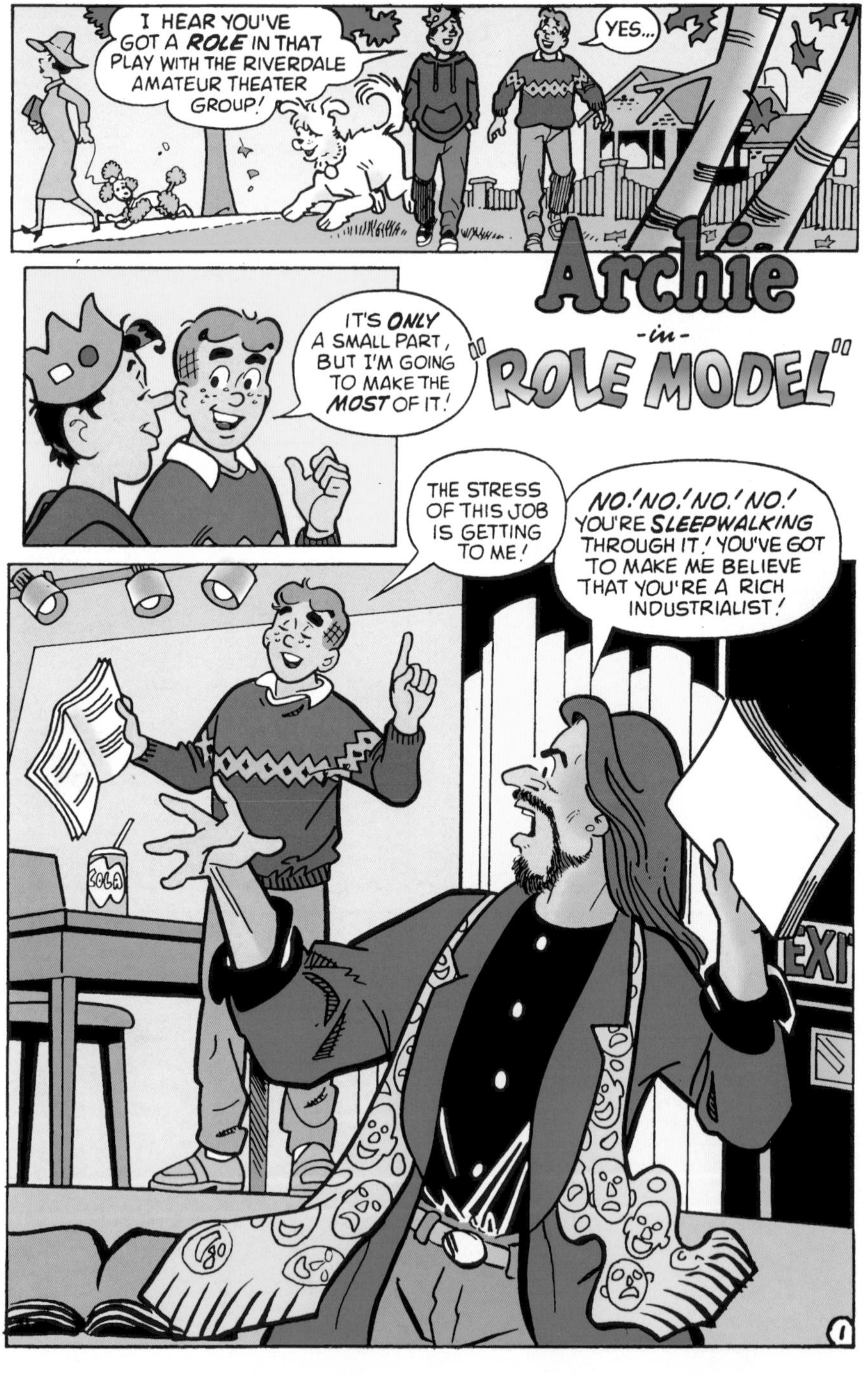
I HEAR YOU'VE GOT A ROLE IN THAT PLAY WITH THE RIVERDALE AMATEUR THEATER GROUP!
YES...
Archie
-in-
"ROLE MODEL"
IT'S ONLY A SMALL PART, BUT I'M GOING TO MAKE THE MOST OF IT!
THE STRESS OF THIS JOB IS GETTING TO ME!
NO! NO! NO! NO! YOU'RE SLEEPWALKING THROUGH IT! YOU'VE GOT TO MAKE ME BELIEVE THAT YOU'RE A RICH INDUSTRIALIST!
COLA
EXIT
1

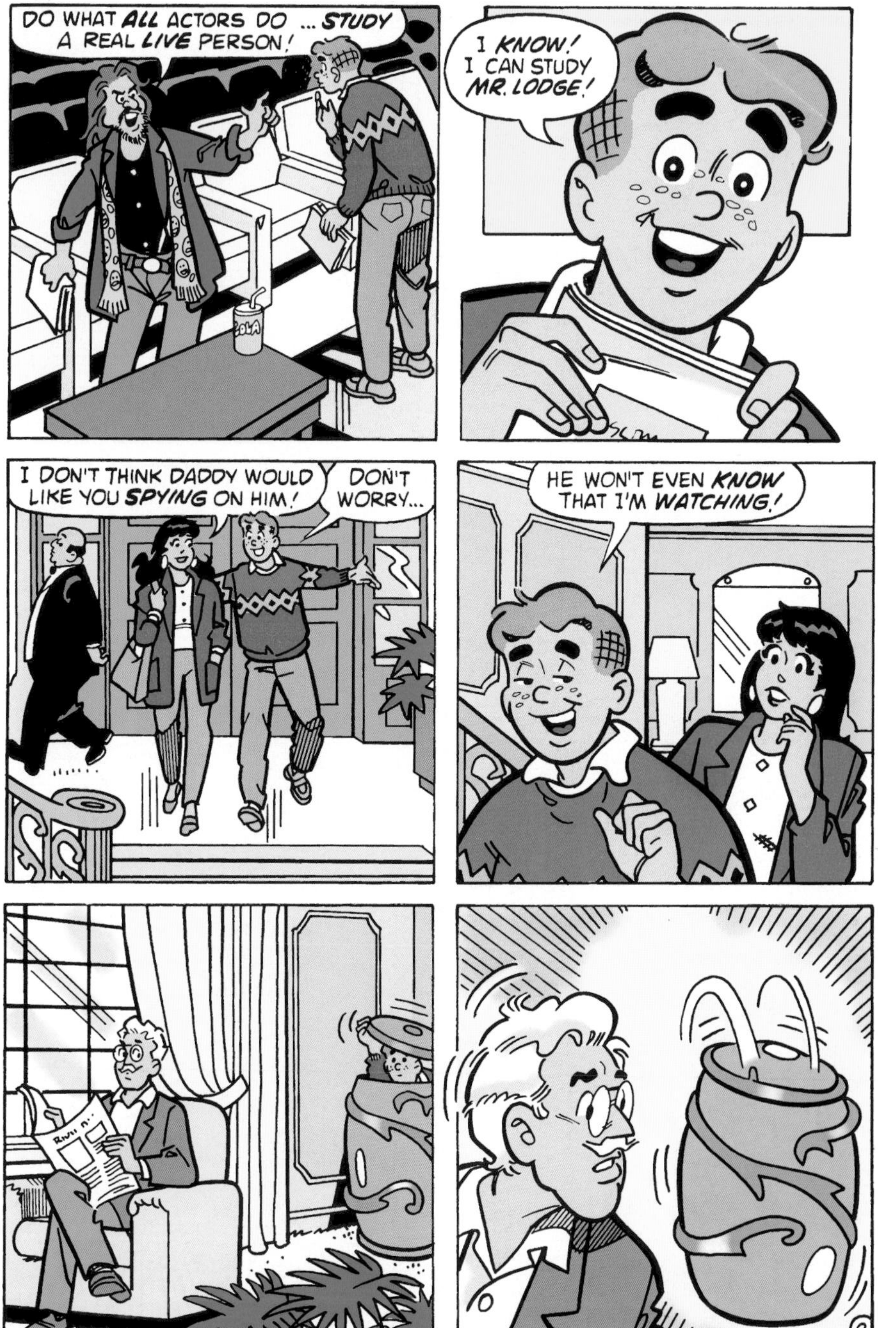
DO WHAT ALL ACTORS DO ... STUDY A REAL LIVE PERSON!
I KNOW! I CAN STUDY MR. LODGE!
I DON'T THINK DADDY WOULD LIKE YOU SPYING ON HIM!
DON'T WORRY...
HE WON'T EVEN KNOW THAT I'M WATCHING!
2

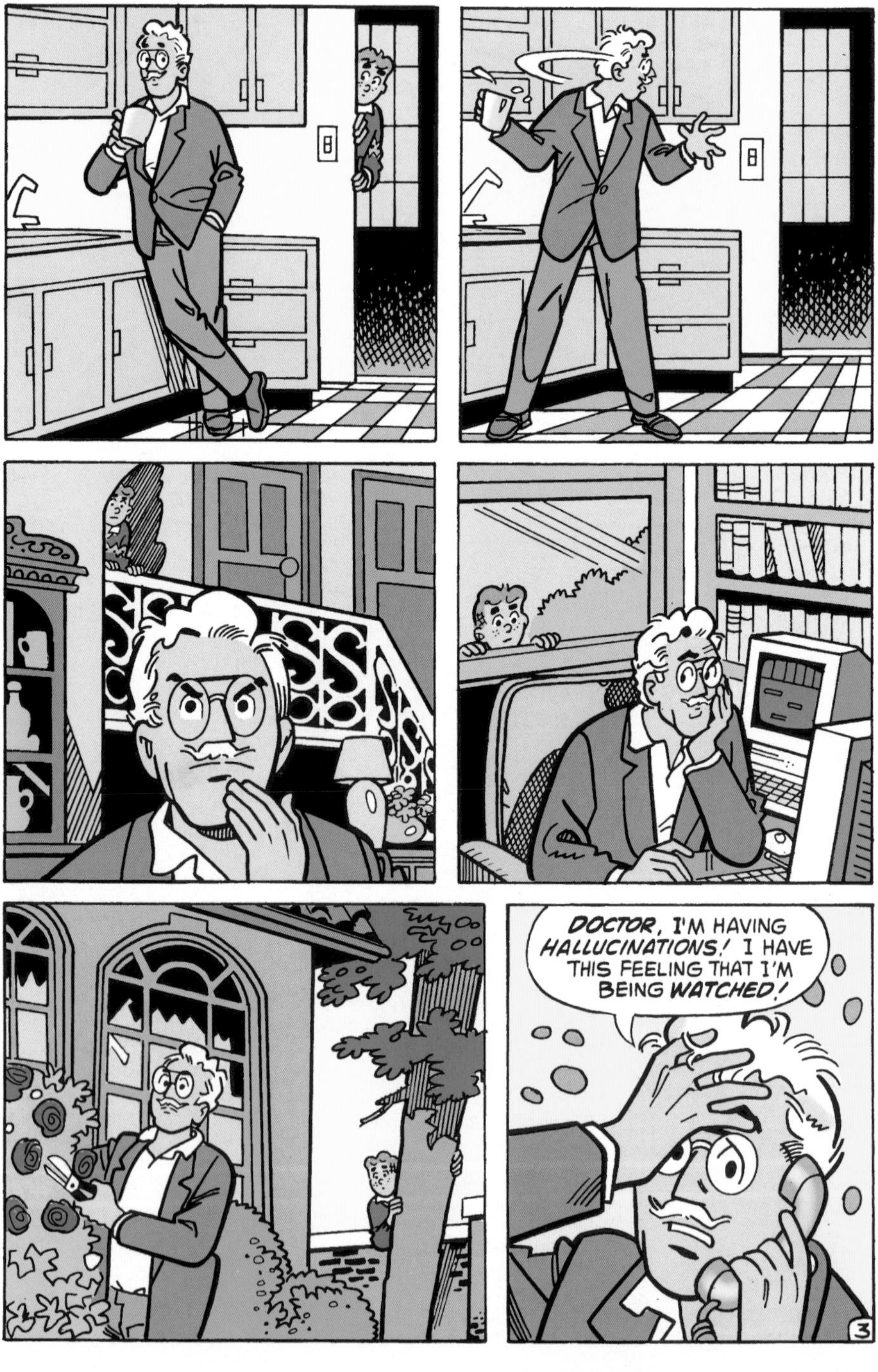
DOCTOR, I'M HAVING HALLUCINATIONS! I HAVE THIS FEELING THAT I'M BEING WATCHED!
3

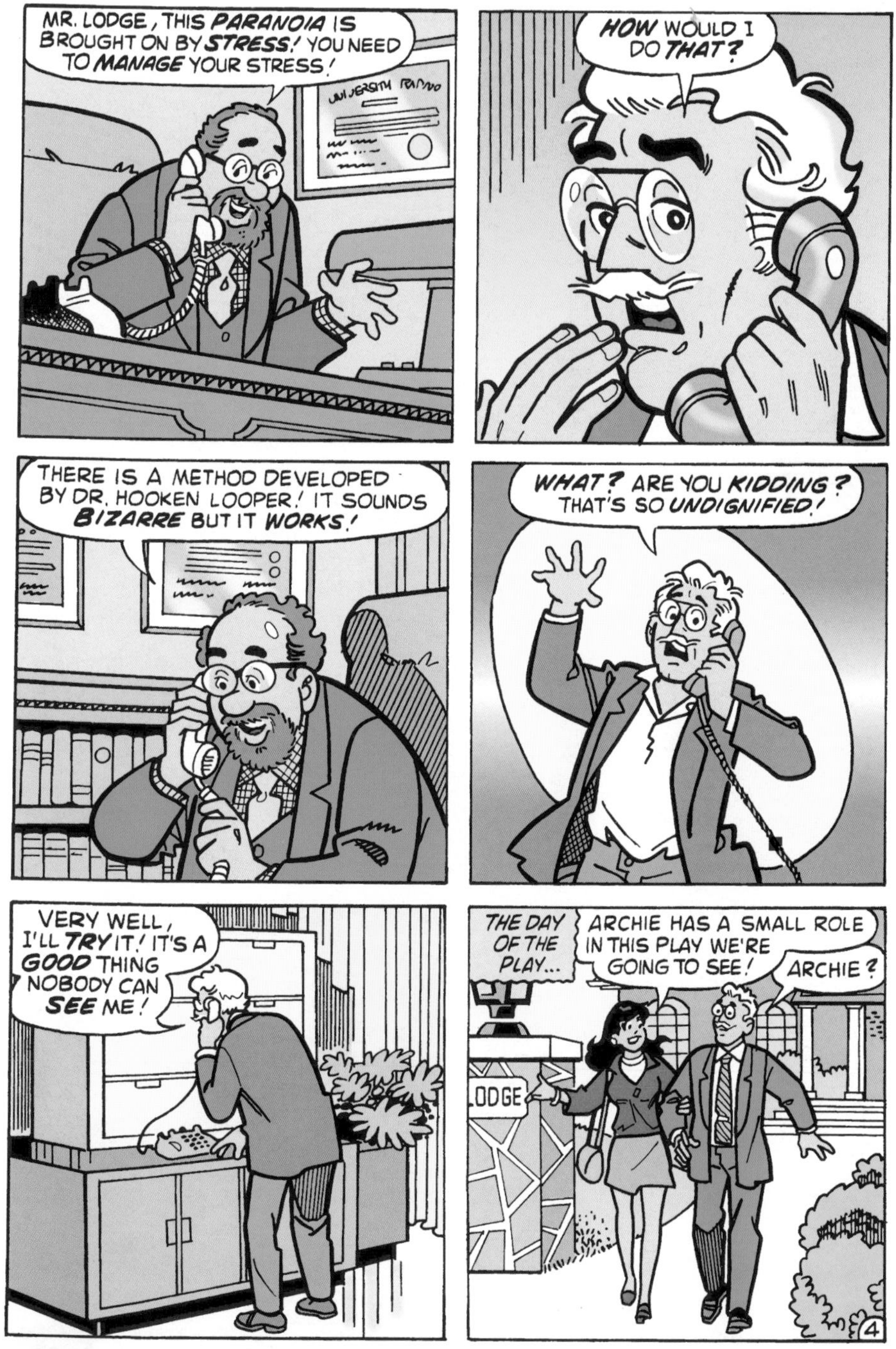
MR. LODGE, THIS PARANOIA IS BROUGHT ON BY STRESS! YOU NEED TO MANAGE YOUR STRESS!
HOW WOULD I DO THAT?
THERE IS A METHOD DEVELOPED BY DR. HOOKEN LOOPER! IT SOUNDS BIZARRE BUT IT WORKS!
WHAT? ARE YOU KIDDING? THAT'S SO UNDIGNIFIED!
VERY WELL, I'LL TRY IT! IT'S A GOOD THING NOBODY CAN SEE ME!
THE DAY OF THE PLAY...
ARCHIE HAS A SMALL ROLE IN THIS PLAY WE'RE GOING TO SEE!
ARCHIE?
LODGE
4

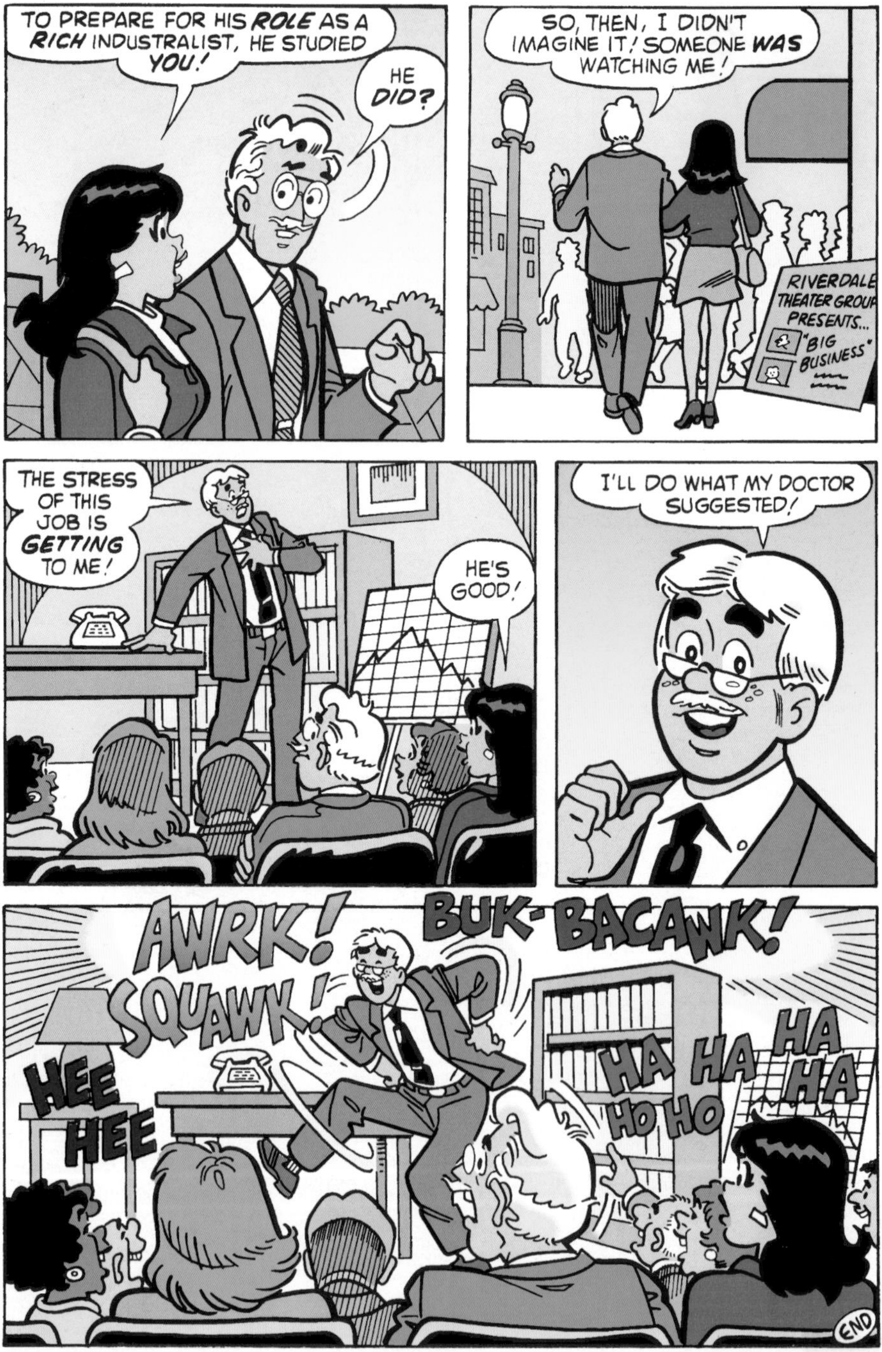
TO PREPARE FOR HIS ROLE AS A RICH INDUSTRALIST, HE STUDIED YOU!
HE DID?
SO, THEN, I DIDN'T IMAGINE IT! SOMEONE WAS WATCHING ME!
RIVERDALE THEATER GROUP PRESENTS... "BIG BUSINESS"
THE STRESS OF THIS JOB IS GETTING TO ME!
HE'S GOOD!
I'LL DO WHAT MY DOCTOR SUGGESTED!
AWRK!
BUK-BACAWK!
SQUAWK!
HEE HEE
HA HA HA HA HA
HO HO
END

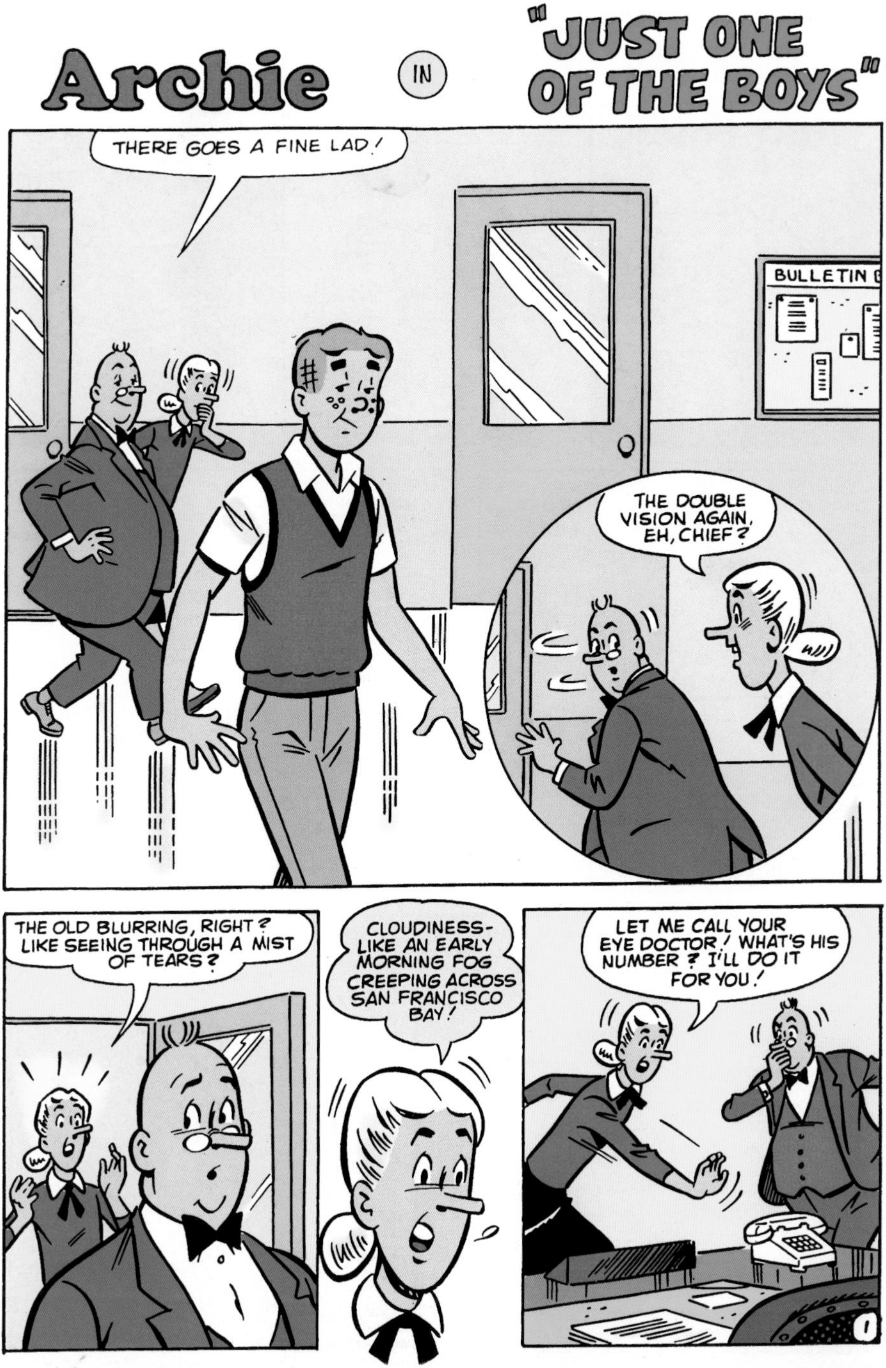
Archie IN "JUST ONE OF THE BOYS"
THERE GOES A FINE LAD!
BULLETIN B
THE DOUBLE VISION AGAIN, EH, CHIEF?
THE OLD BLURRING, RIGHT? LIKE SEEING THROUGH A MIST OF TEARS?
CLOUDINESS- LIKE AN EARLY MORNING FOG CREEPING ACROSS SAN FRANCISCO BAY!
LET ME CALL YOUR EYE DOCTOR! WHAT'S HIS NUMBER? I'LL DO IT FOR YOU!
1

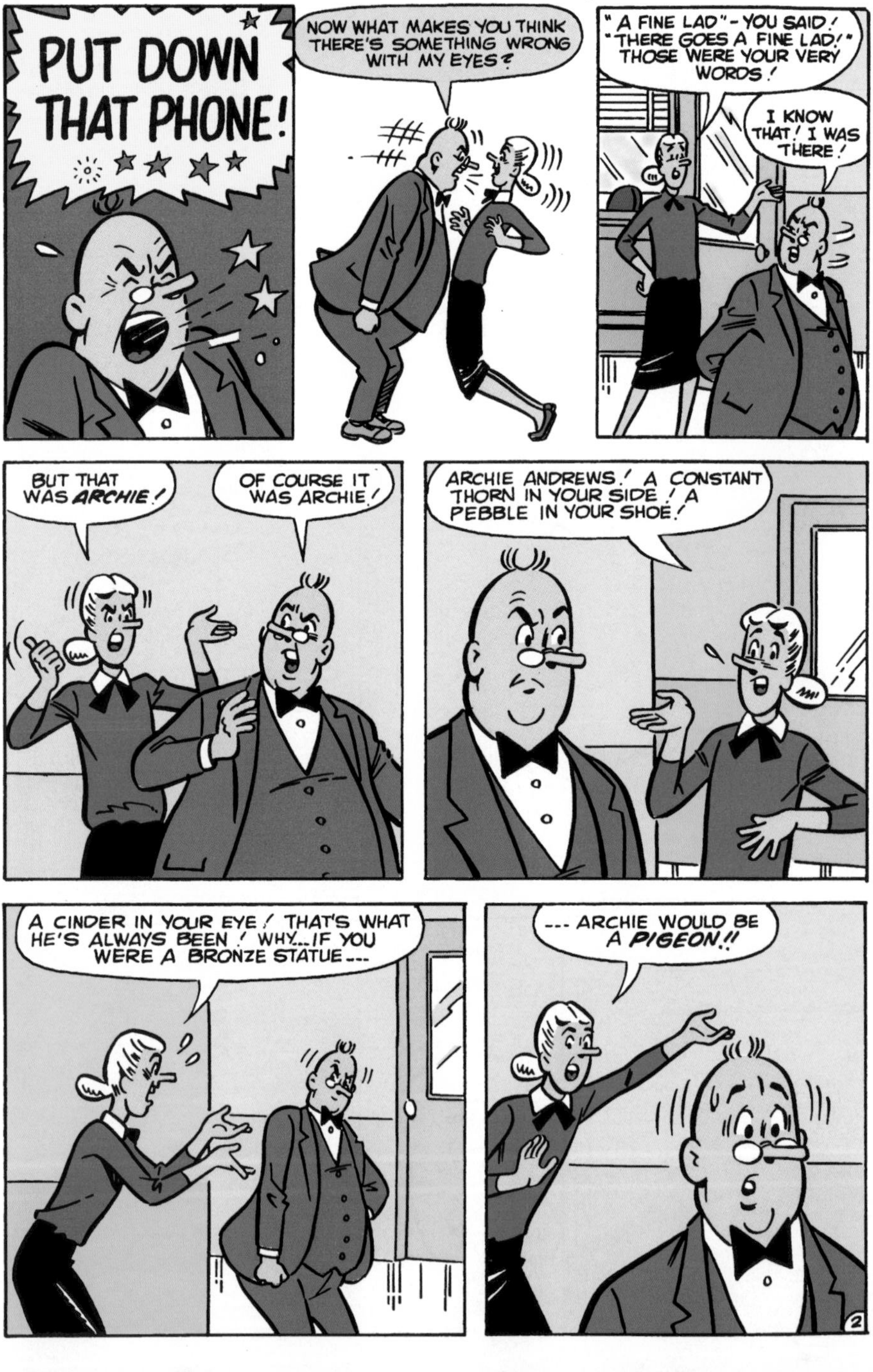
PUT DOWN THAT PHONE!
NOW WHAT MAKES YOU THINK THERE'S SOMETHING WRONG WITH MY EYES?
"A FINE LAD" - YOU SAID! "THERE GOES A FINE LAD!" THOSE WERE YOUR VERY WORDS!
I KNOW THAT! I WAS THERE!
BUT THAT WAS ARCHIE!
OF COURSE IT WAS ARCHIE!
ARCHIE ANDREWS! A CONSTANT THORN IN YOUR SIDE! A PEBBLE IN YOUR SHOE!
A CINDER IN YOUR EYE! THAT'S WHAT HE'S ALWAYS BEEN! WHY...IF YOU WERE A BRONZE STATUE---
---ARCHIE WOULD BE A PIGEON!!
2

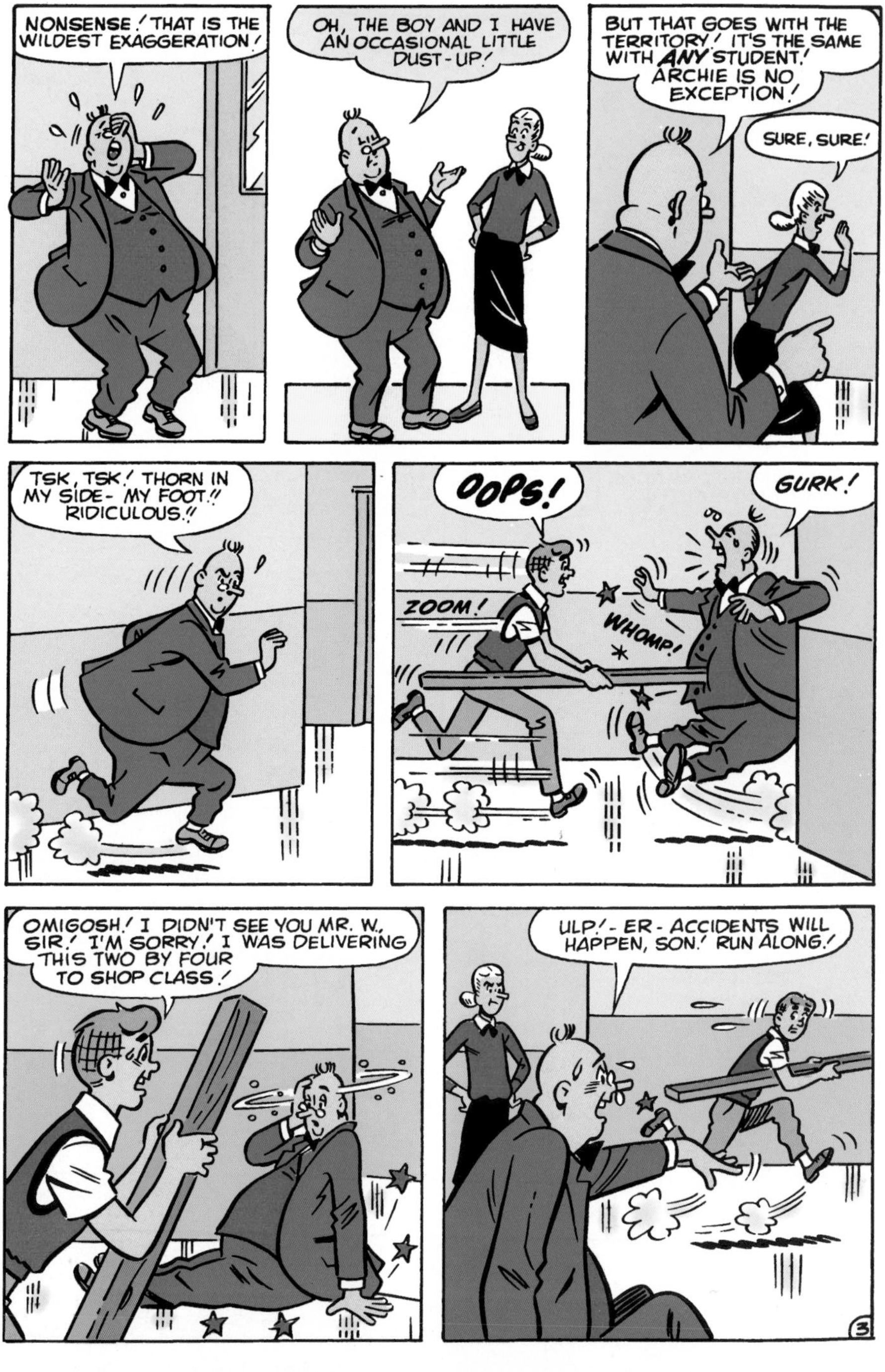
NONSENSE! THAT IS THE WILDEST EXAGGERATION!
OH, THE BOY AND I HAVE AN OCCASIONAL LITTLE DUST-UP!
BUT THAT GOES WITH THE TERRITORY! IT'S THE SAME WITH ANY STUDENT! ARCHIE IS NO EXCEPTION!
SURE, SURE!
TSK, TSK! THORN IN MY SIDE- MY FOOT!! RIDICULOUS!!
OOPS!
GURK!
ZOOM!
WHOMP!
OMIGOSH! I DIDN'T SEE YOU MR. W., SIR! I'M SORRY! I WAS DELIVERING THIS TWO BY FOUR TO SHOP CLASS!
ULP! - ER - ACCIDENTS WILL HAPPEN, SON! RUN ALONG!
3

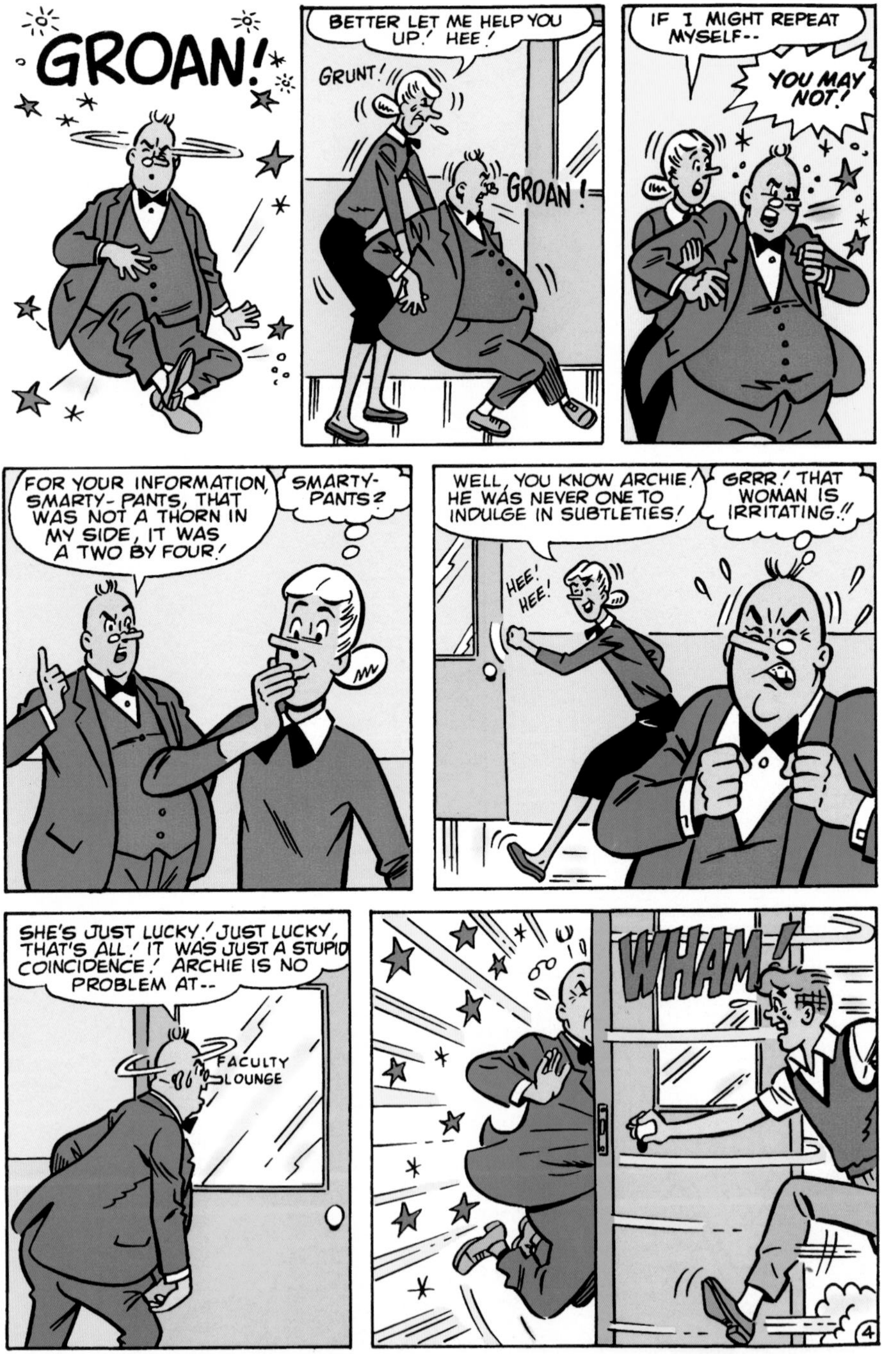
GROAN!
BETTER LET ME HELP YOU UP! HEE!
GRUNT!
GROAN!
IF I MIGHT REPEAT MYSELF--
YOU MAY NOT!
FOR YOUR INFORMATION, SMARTY-PANTS, THAT WAS NOT A THORN IN MY SIDE, IT WAS A TWO BY FOUR!
SMARTY-PANTS?
WELL, YOU KNOW ARCHIE! HE WAS NEVER ONE TO INDULGE IN SUBTLETIES!
HEE! HEE!
GRRR! THAT WOMAN IS IRRITATING!!
SHE'S JUST LUCKY! JUST LUCKY, THAT'S ALL! IT WAS JUST A STUPID COINCIDENCE! ARCHIE IS NO PROBLEM AT--
FACULTY LOUNGE
WHAM!
4

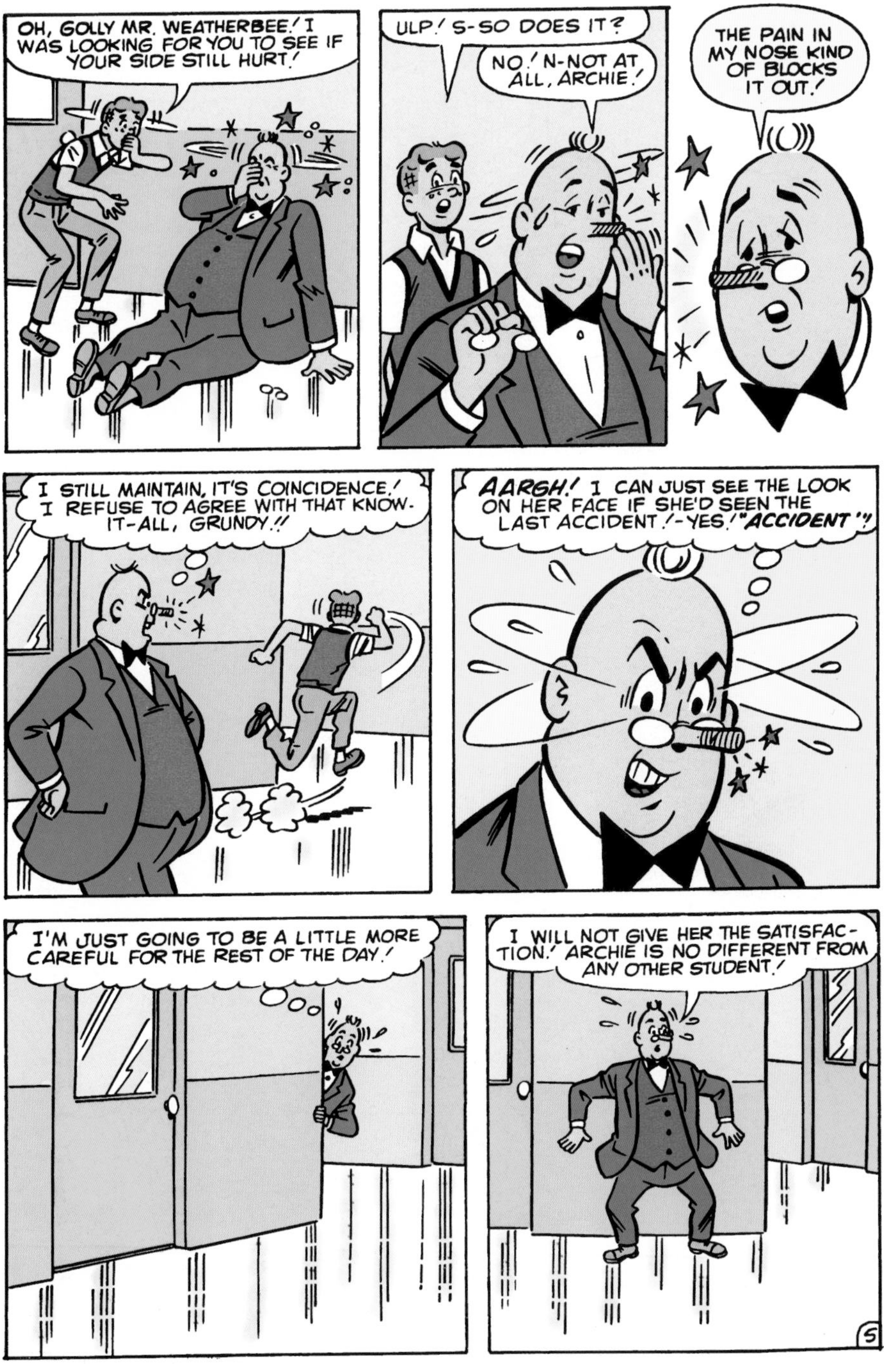
OH, GOLLY MR. WEATHERBEE! I WAS LOOKING FOR YOU TO SEE IF YOUR SIDE STILL HURT!
ULP! S-SO DOES IT?
NO! N-NOT AT ALL, ARCHIE!
THE PAIN IN MY NOSE KIND OF BLOCKS IT OUT!
I STILL MAINTAIN, IT'S COINCIDENCE! I REFUSE TO AGREE WITH THAT KNOW-IT-ALL, GRUNDY!!
AARGH! I CAN JUST SEE THE LOOK ON HER FACE IF SHE'D SEEN THE LAST ACCIDENT!-YES!"ACCIDENT"!!
I'M JUST GOING TO BE A LITTLE MORE CAREFUL FOR THE REST OF THE DAY!
I WILL NOT GIVE HER THE SATISFACTION! ARCHIE IS NO DIFFERENT FROM ANY OTHER STUDENT!
5

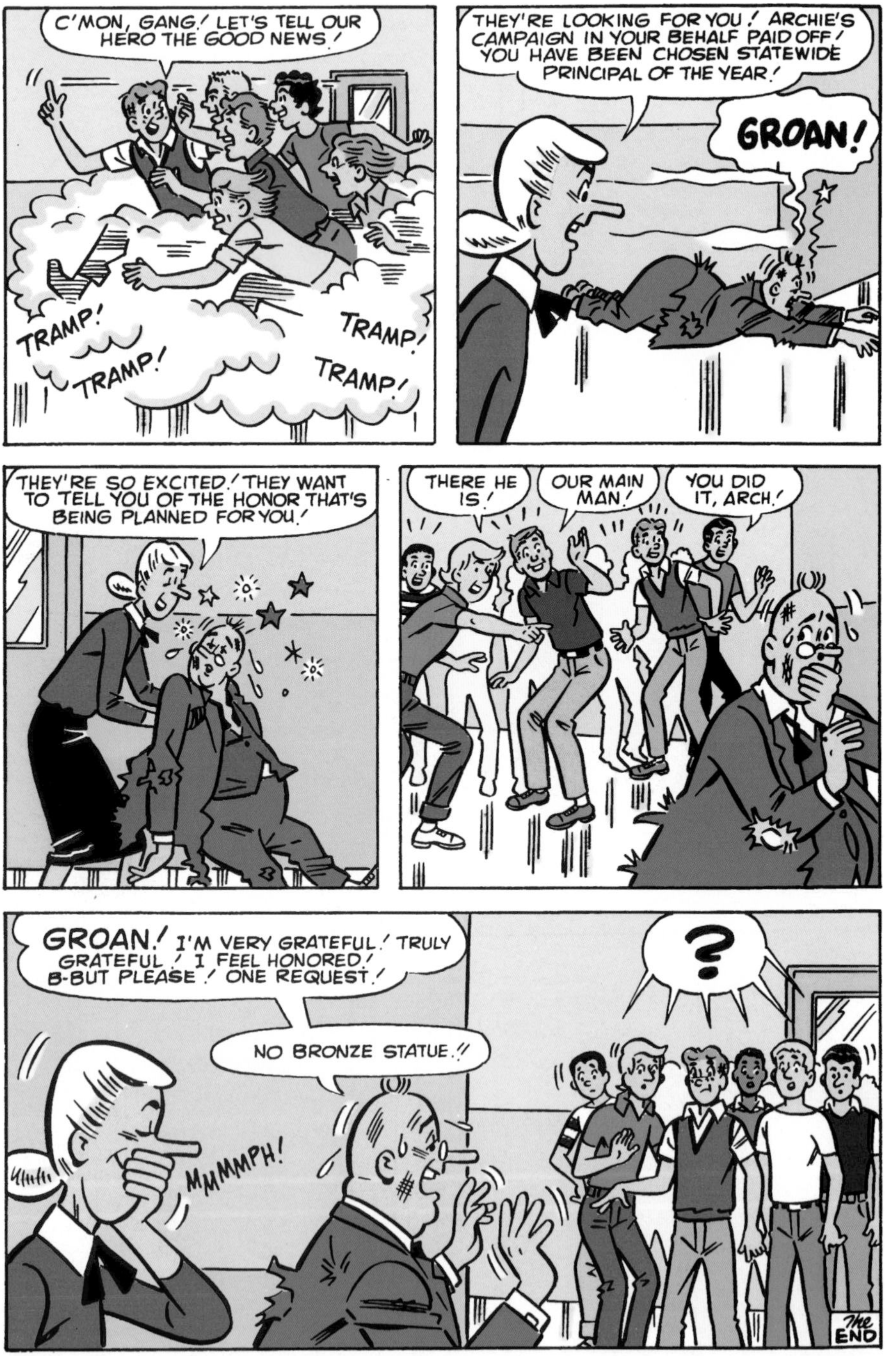

C'MON, GANG! LET'S TELL OUR HERO THE GOOD NEWS!
TRAMP! TRAMP! TRAMP! TRAMP!
THEY'RE LOOKING FOR YOU! ARCHIE'S CAMPAIGN IN YOUR BEHALF PAID OFF! YOU HAVE BEEN CHOSEN STATEWIDE PRINCIPAL OF THE YEAR!
GROAN!
THEY'RE SO EXCITED! THEY WANT TO TELL YOU OF THE HONOR THAT'S BEING PLANNED FOR YOU!
THERE HE IS!
OUR MAIN MAN!
YOU DID IT, ARCH!
GROAN! I'M VERY GRATEFUL! TRULY GRATEFUL! I FEEL HONORED! B-BUT PLEASE! ONE REQUEST!
NO BRONZE STATUE!!
?
MMMMPH!
The END

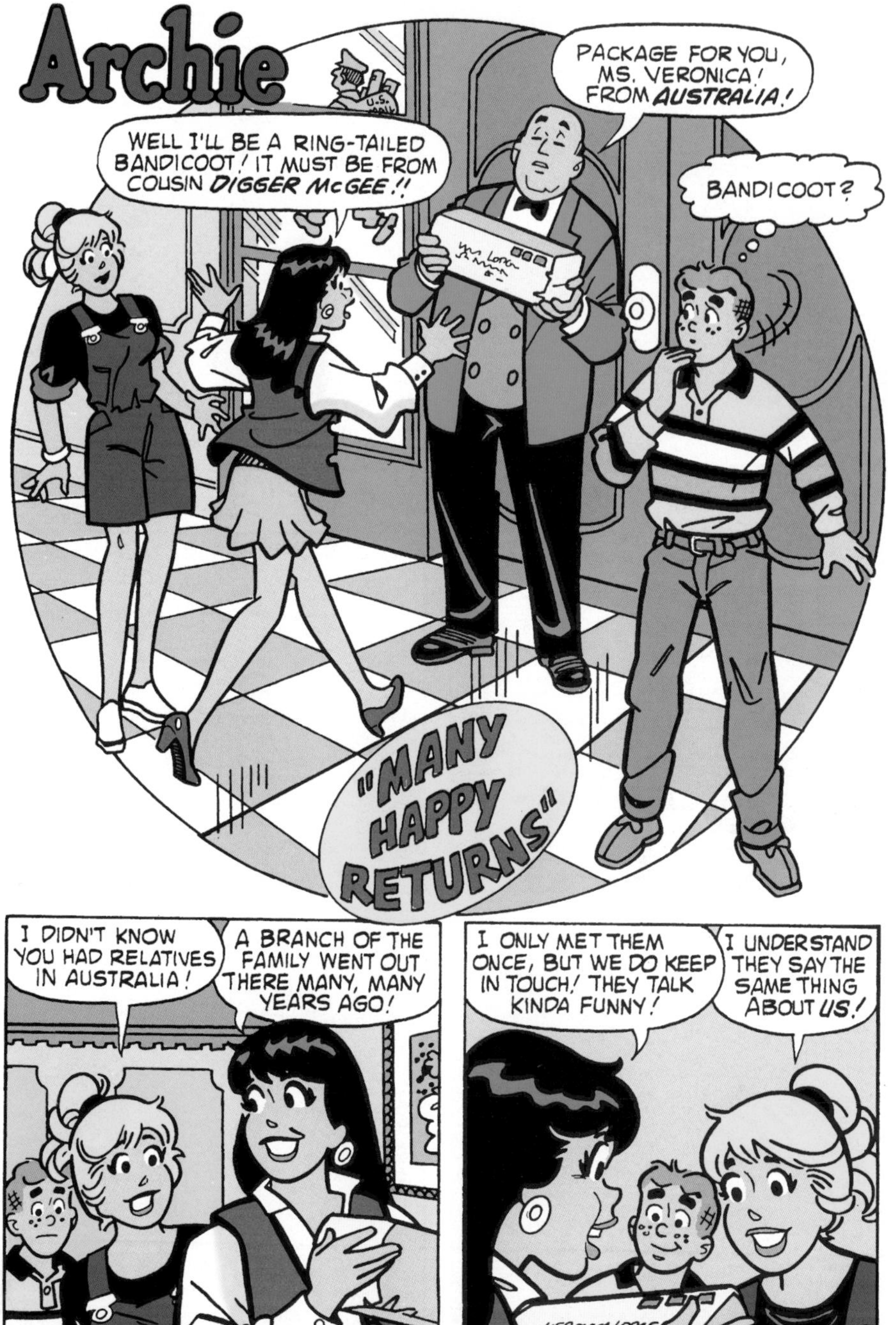
Archie
PACKAGE FOR YOU, MS. VERONICA! FROM AUSTRALIA!
WELL I'LL BE A RING-TAILED BANDICOOT! IT MUST BE FROM COUSIN DIGGER McGEE!!
BANDICOOT?
"MANY HAPPY RETURNS"
I DIDN'T KNOW YOU HAD RELATIVES IN AUSTRALIA!
A BRANCH OF THE FAMILY WENT OUT THERE MANY, MANY YEARS AGO!
I ONLY MET THEM ONCE, BUT WE DO KEEP IN TOUCH! THEY TALK KINDA FUNNY!
I UNDERSTAND THEY SAY THE SAME THING ABOUT US!
1

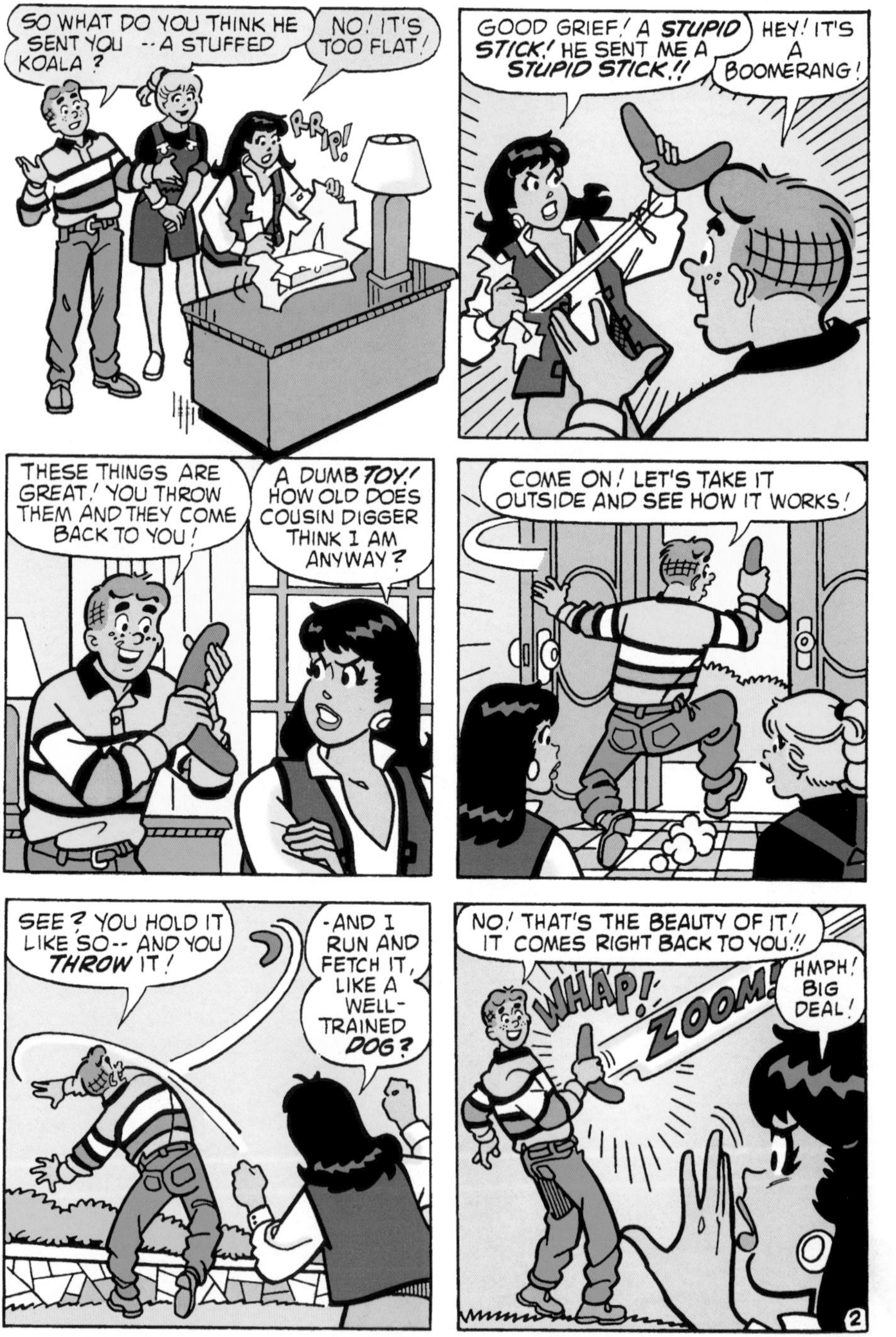
SO WHAT DO YOU THINK HE SENT YOU -- A STUFFED KOALA ?
NO! IT'S TOO FLAT!
R-R-RIP!
GOOD GRIEF! A STUPID STICK! HE SENT ME A STUPID STICK!!
HEY! IT'S A BOOMERANG!
THESE THINGS ARE GREAT! YOU THROW THEM AND THEY COME BACK TO YOU!
A DUMB TOY! HOW OLD DOES COUSIN DIGGER THINK I AM ANYWAY?
COME ON! LET'S TAKE IT OUTSIDE AND SEE HOW IT WORKS!
SEE? YOU HOLD IT LIKE SO-- AND YOU THROW IT!
-AND I RUN AND FETCH IT, LIKE A WELL-TRAINED DOG?
NO! THAT'S THE BEAUTY OF IT! IT COMES RIGHT BACK TO YOU!!
WHAP!
ZOOM!
HMPH! BIG DEAL!
2

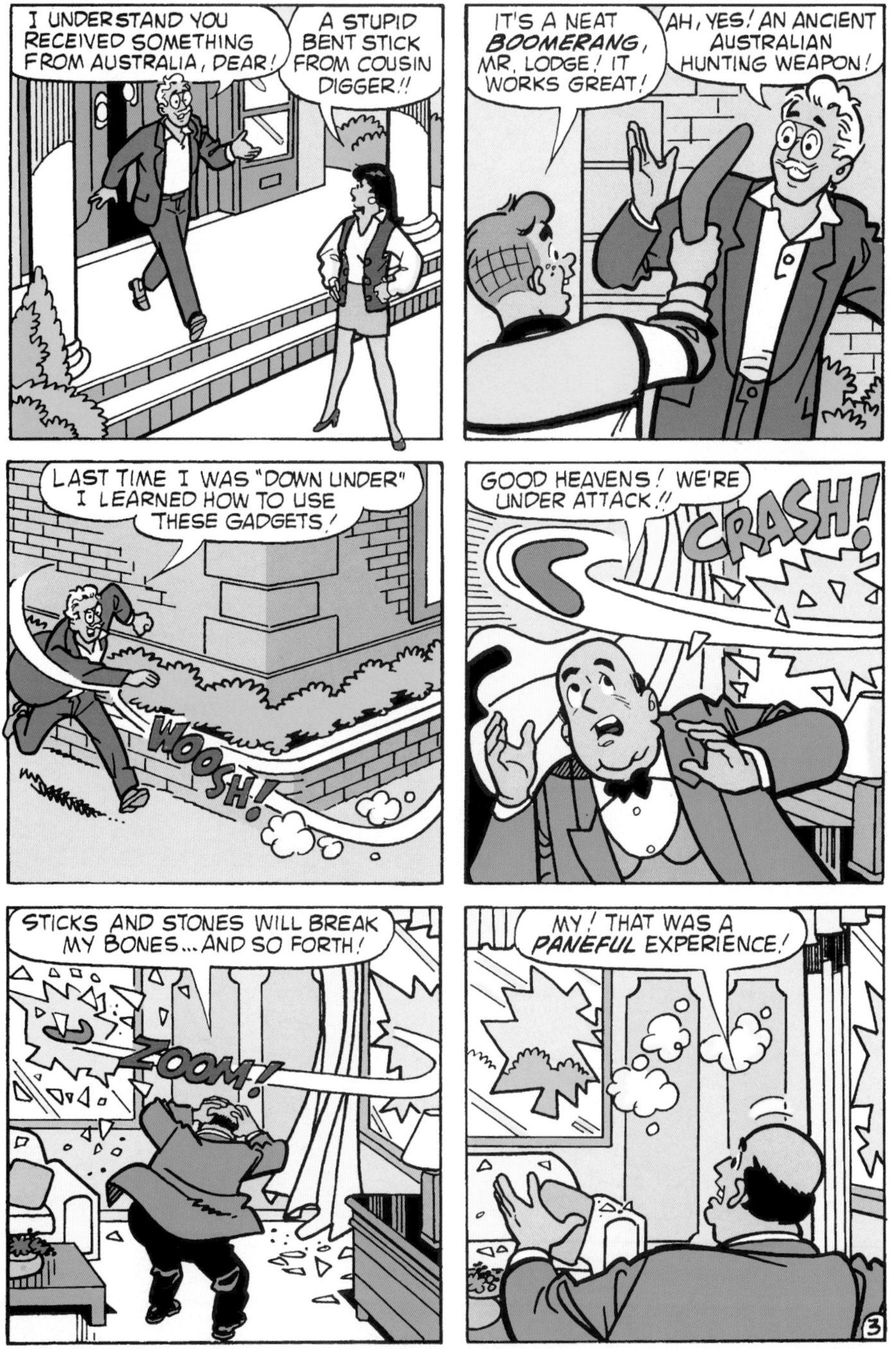
I UNDERSTAND YOU RECEIVED SOMETHING FROM AUSTRALIA, DEAR!
A STUPID BENT STICK FROM COUSIN DIGGER!!
IT'S A NEAT BOOMERANG, MR. LODGE! IT WORKS GREAT!
AH, YES! AN ANCIENT AUSTRALIAN HUNTING WEAPON!
LAST TIME I WAS "DOWN UNDER" I LEARNED HOW TO USE THESE GADGETS!
WOOSH!
GOOD HEAVENS! WE'RE UNDER ATTACK!!
CRASH!
STICKS AND STONES WILL BREAK MY BONES... AND SO FORTH!
ZOOM!
MY! THAT WAS A PANEFUL EXPERIENCE!
3

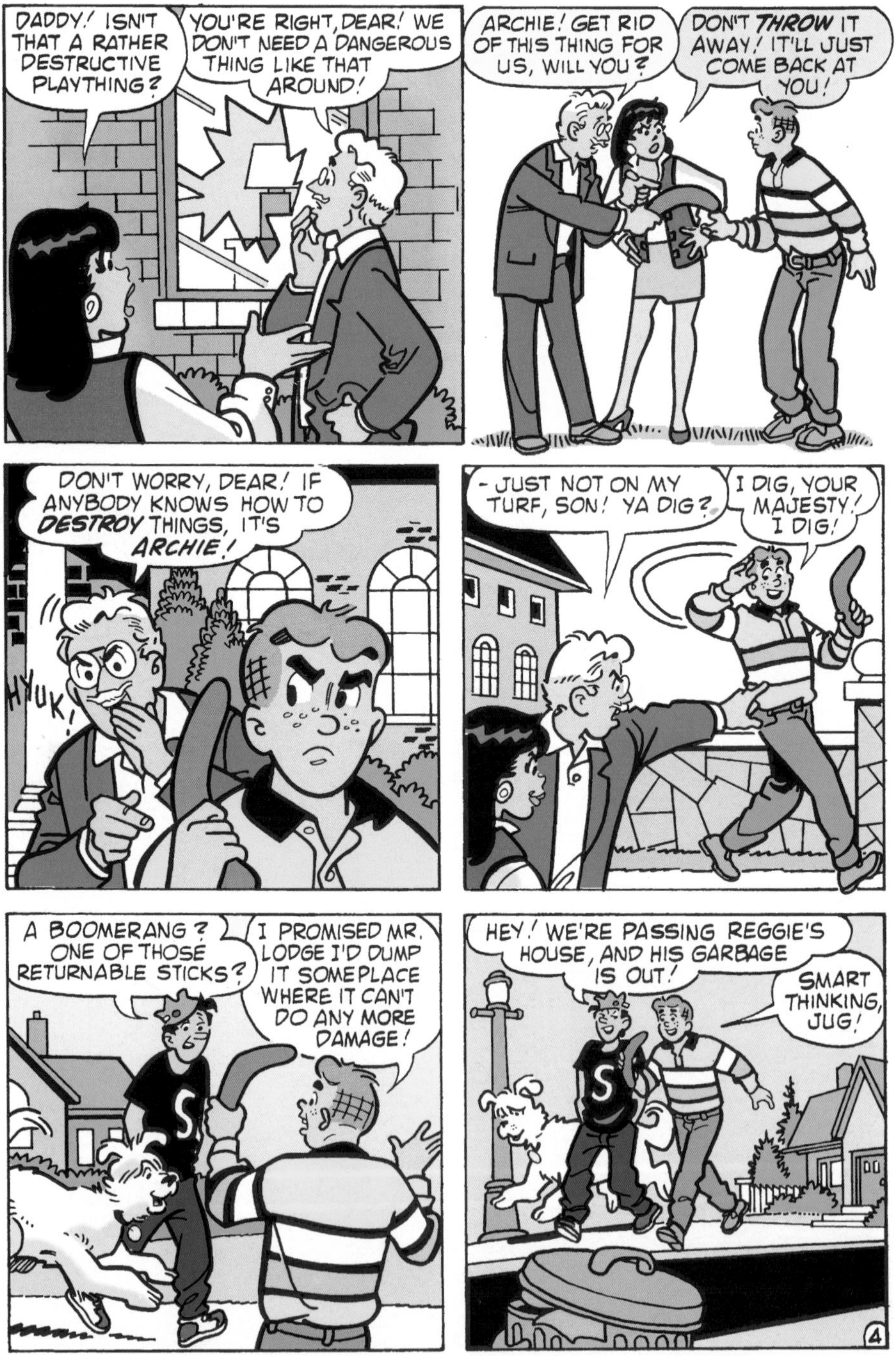

DADDY! ISN'T THAT A RATHER DESTRUCTIVE PLAYTHING?
YOU'RE RIGHT, DEAR! WE DON'T NEED A DANGEROUS THING LIKE THAT AROUND!
ARCHIE! GET RID OF THIS THING FOR US, WILL YOU?
DON'T THROW IT AWAY! IT'LL JUST COME BACK AT YOU!
DON'T WORRY, DEAR! IF ANYBODY KNOWS HOW TO DESTROY THINGS, IT'S ARCHIE!
HYUK!
- JUST NOT ON MY TURF, SON! YA DIG?
I DIG, YOUR MAJESTY! I DIG!
A BOOMERANG? ONE OF THOSE RETURNABLE STICKS?
I PROMISED MR. LODGE I'D DUMP IT SOMEPLACE WHERE IT CAN'T DO ANY MORE DAMAGE!
HEY! WE'RE PASSING REGGIE'S HOUSE, AND HIS GARBAGE IS OUT!
SMART THINKING, JUG!
4

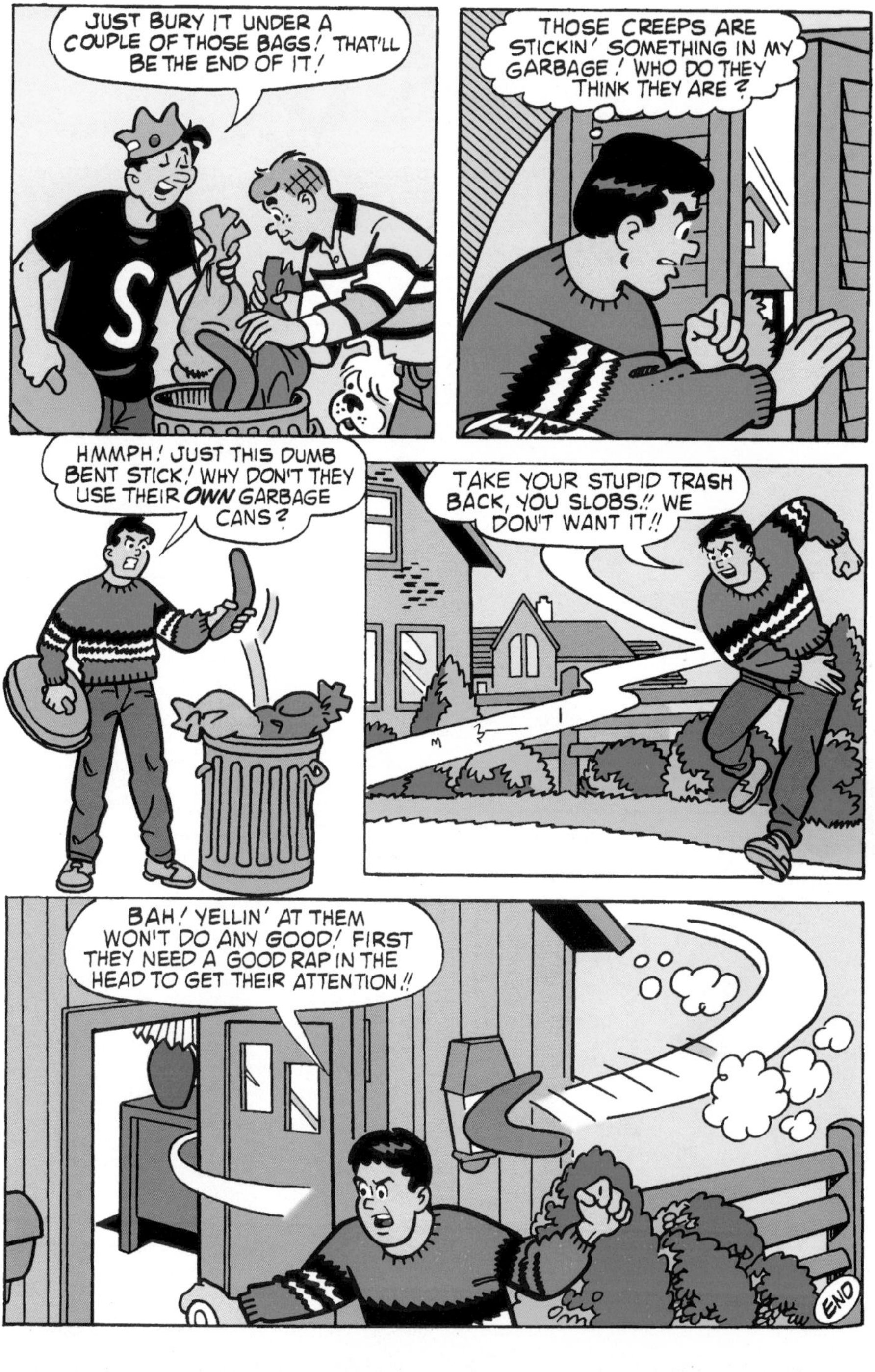
JUST BURY IT UNDER A COUPLE OF THOSE BAGS! THAT'LL BE THE END OF IT!
THOSE CREEPS ARE STICKIN' SOMETHING IN MY GARBAGE! WHO DO THEY THINK THEY ARE?
HMMPH! JUST THIS DUMB BENT STICK! WHY DON'T THEY USE THEIR OWN GARBAGE CANS?
TAKE YOUR STUPID TRASH BACK, YOU SLOBS!! WE DON'T WANT IT!!
BAH! YELLIN' AT THEM WON'T DO ANY GOOD! FIRST THEY NEED A GOOD RAP IN THE HEAD TO GET THEIR ATTENTION!!
END

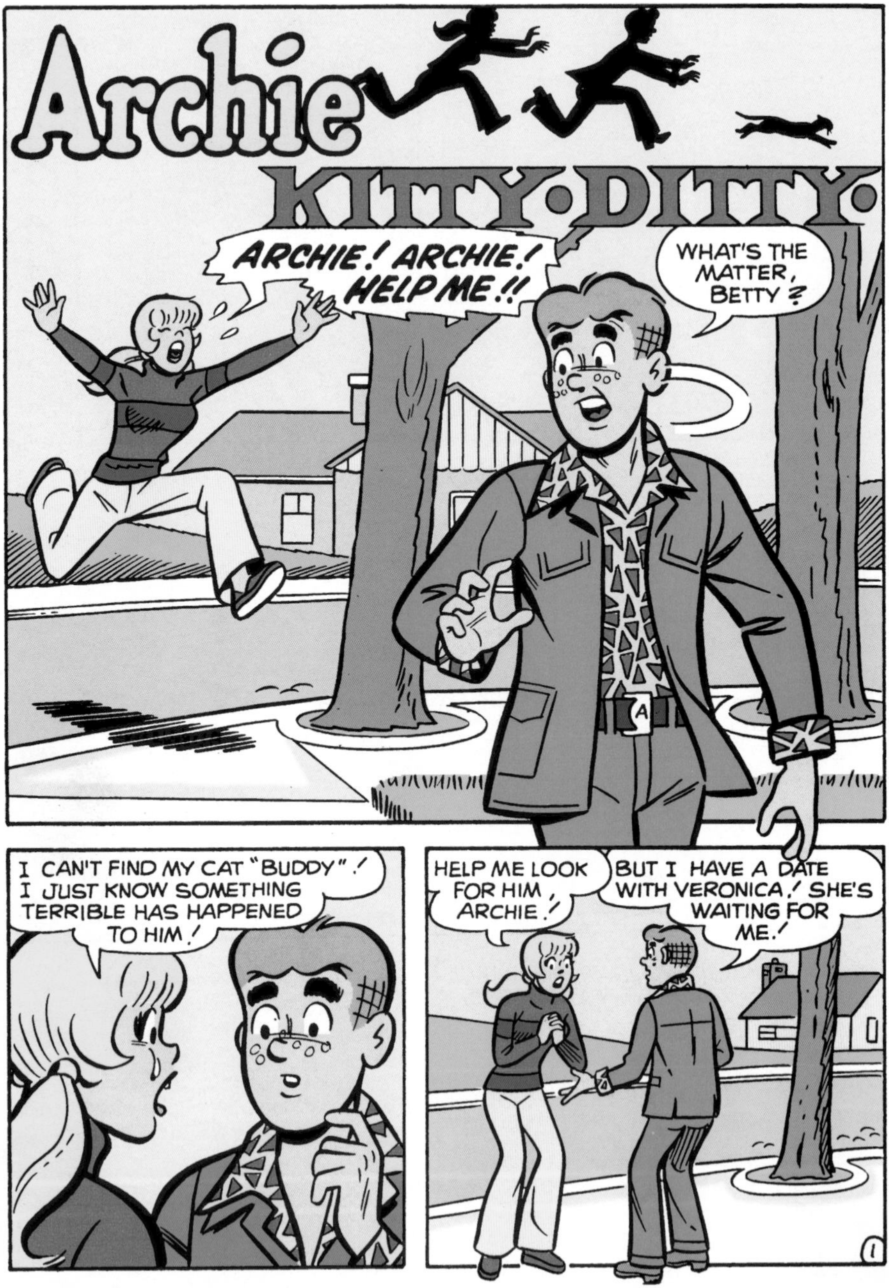
Archie
KITTY•DITTY•
ARCHIE! ARCHIE! HELP ME!!
WHAT'S THE MATTER, BETTY?
I CAN'T FIND MY CAT "BUDDY"! I JUST KNOW SOMETHING TERRIBLE HAS HAPPENED TO HIM!
HELP ME LOOK FOR HIM, ARCHIE!
BUT I HAVE A DATE WITH VERONICA! SHE'S WAITING FOR ME!
1

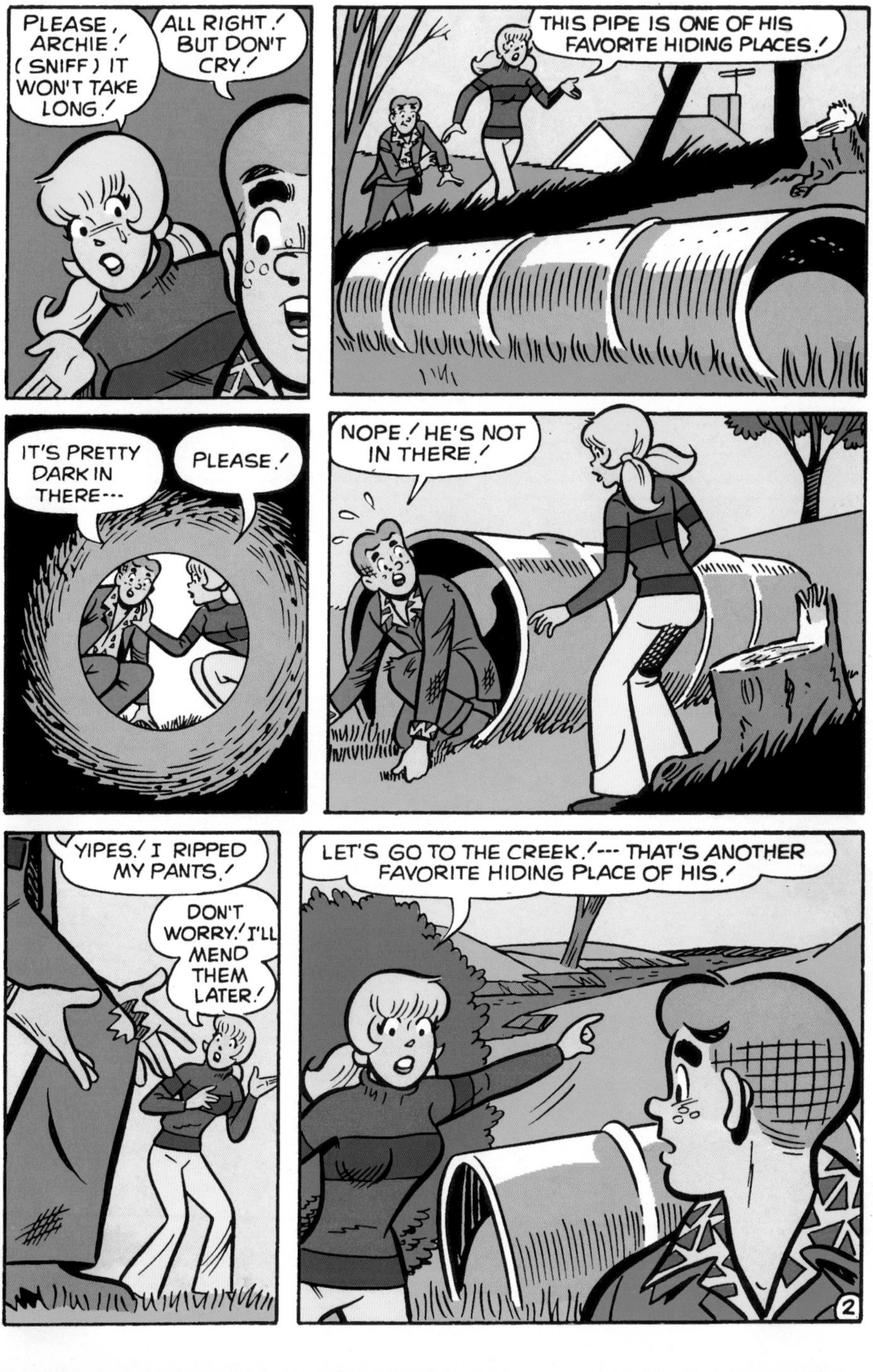
PLEASE, ARCHIE.! (SNIFF) IT WON'T TAKE LONG.!
ALL RIGHT.! BUT DON'T CRY.!
THIS PIPE IS ONE OF HIS FAVORITE HIDING PLACES.!
IT'S PRETTY DARK IN THERE---
PLEASE.!
NOPE.! HE'S NOT IN THERE.!
YIPES.! I RIPPED MY PANTS.!
DON'T WORRY.! I'LL MEND THEM LATER.!
LET'S GO TO THE CREEK.!--- THAT'S ANOTHER FAVORITE HIDING PLACE OF HIS.!
2

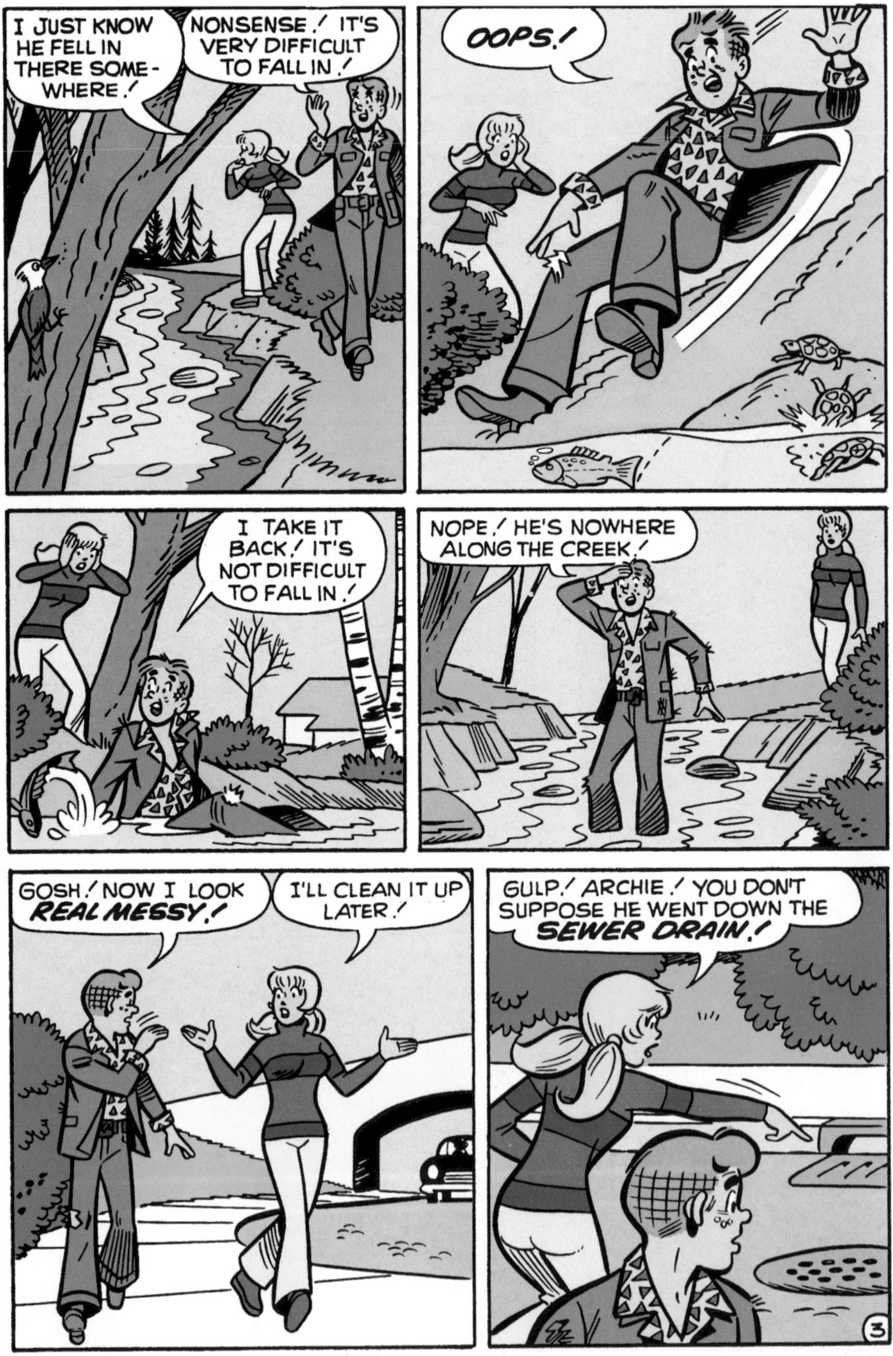
I JUST KNOW HE FELL IN THERE SOME-WHERE!
NONSENSE! IT'S VERY DIFFICULT TO FALL IN!
OOPS!
I TAKE IT BACK! IT'S NOT DIFFICULT TO FALL IN!
NOPE! HE'S NOWHERE ALONG THE CREEK!
GOSH! NOW I LOOK REAL MESSY!
I'LL CLEAN IT UP LATER!
GULP! ARCHIE! YOU DON'T SUPPOSE HE WENT DOWN THE SEWER DRAIN!
3

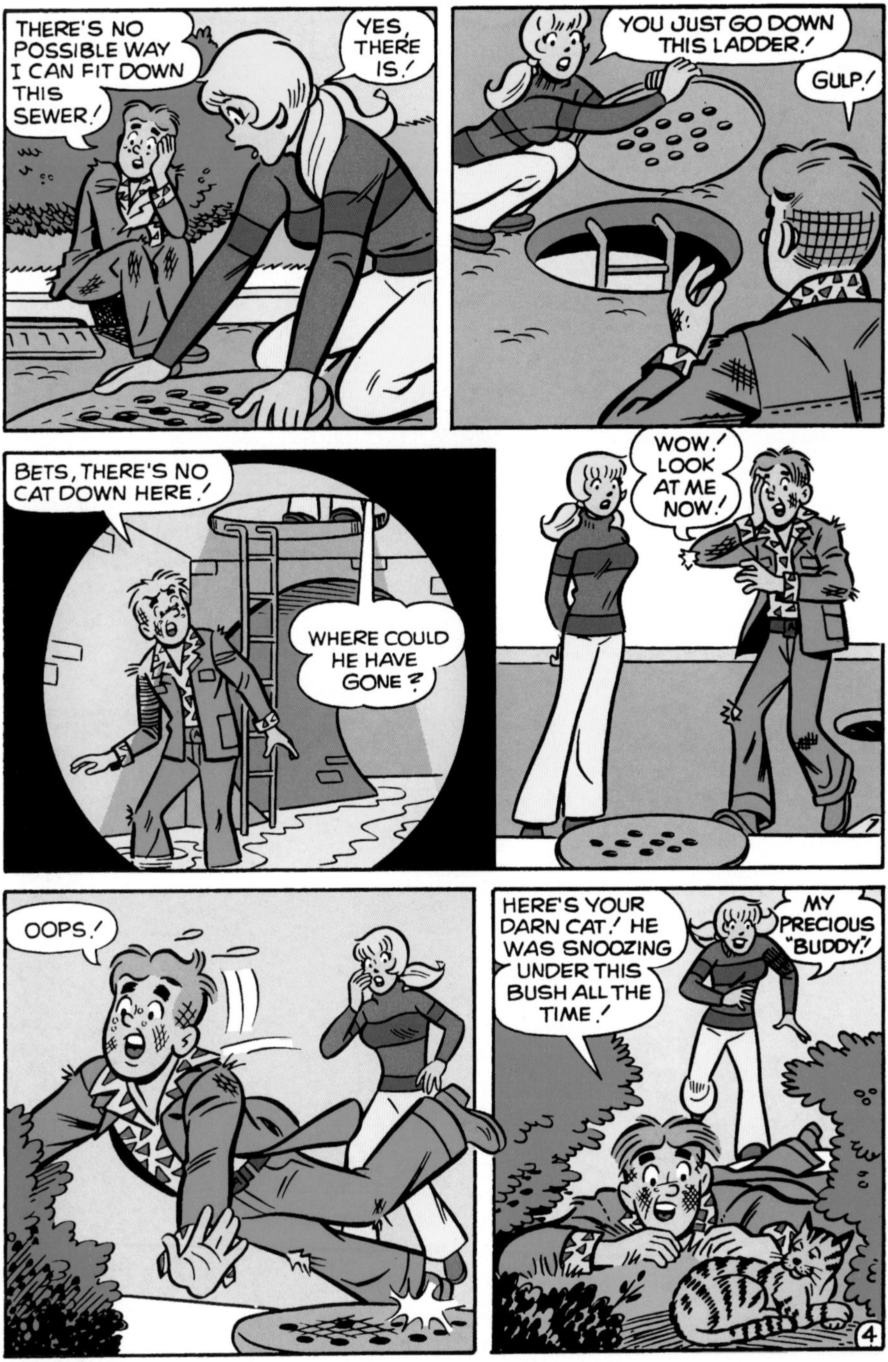
THERE'S NO POSSIBLE WAY I CAN FIT DOWN THIS SEWER!
YES, THERE IS!
YOU JUST GO DOWN THIS LADDER!
GULP!
BETS, THERE'S NO CAT DOWN HERE!
WHERE COULD HE HAVE GONE?
WOW! LOOK AT ME NOW!
OOPS!
HERE'S YOUR DARN CAT! HE WAS SNOOZING UNDER THIS BUSH ALL THE TIME!
MY PRECIOUS "BUDDY"!
4

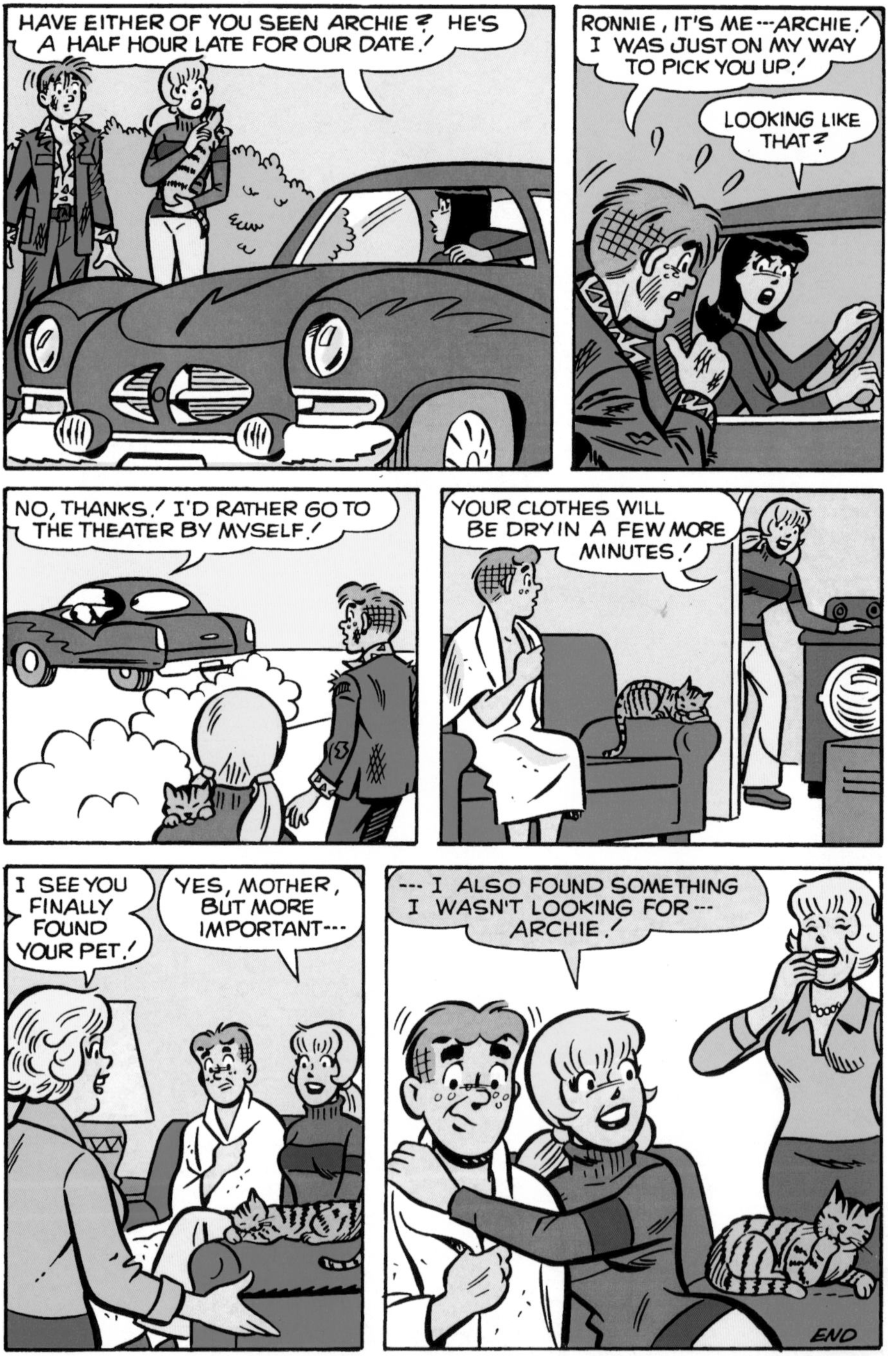
HAVE EITHER OF YOU SEEN ARCHIE? HE'S A HALF HOUR LATE FOR OUR DATE!
RONNIE, IT'S ME---ARCHIE! I WAS JUST ON MY WAY TO PICK YOU UP!
LOOKING LIKE THAT?
NO, THANKS! I'D RATHER GO TO THE THEATER BY MYSELF!
YOUR CLOTHES WILL BE DRY IN A FEW MORE MINUTES!
I SEE YOU FINALLY FOUND YOUR PET!
YES, MOTHER, BUT MORE IMPORTANT---
--- I ALSO FOUND SOMETHING I WASN'T LOOKING FOR--- ARCHIE!
END

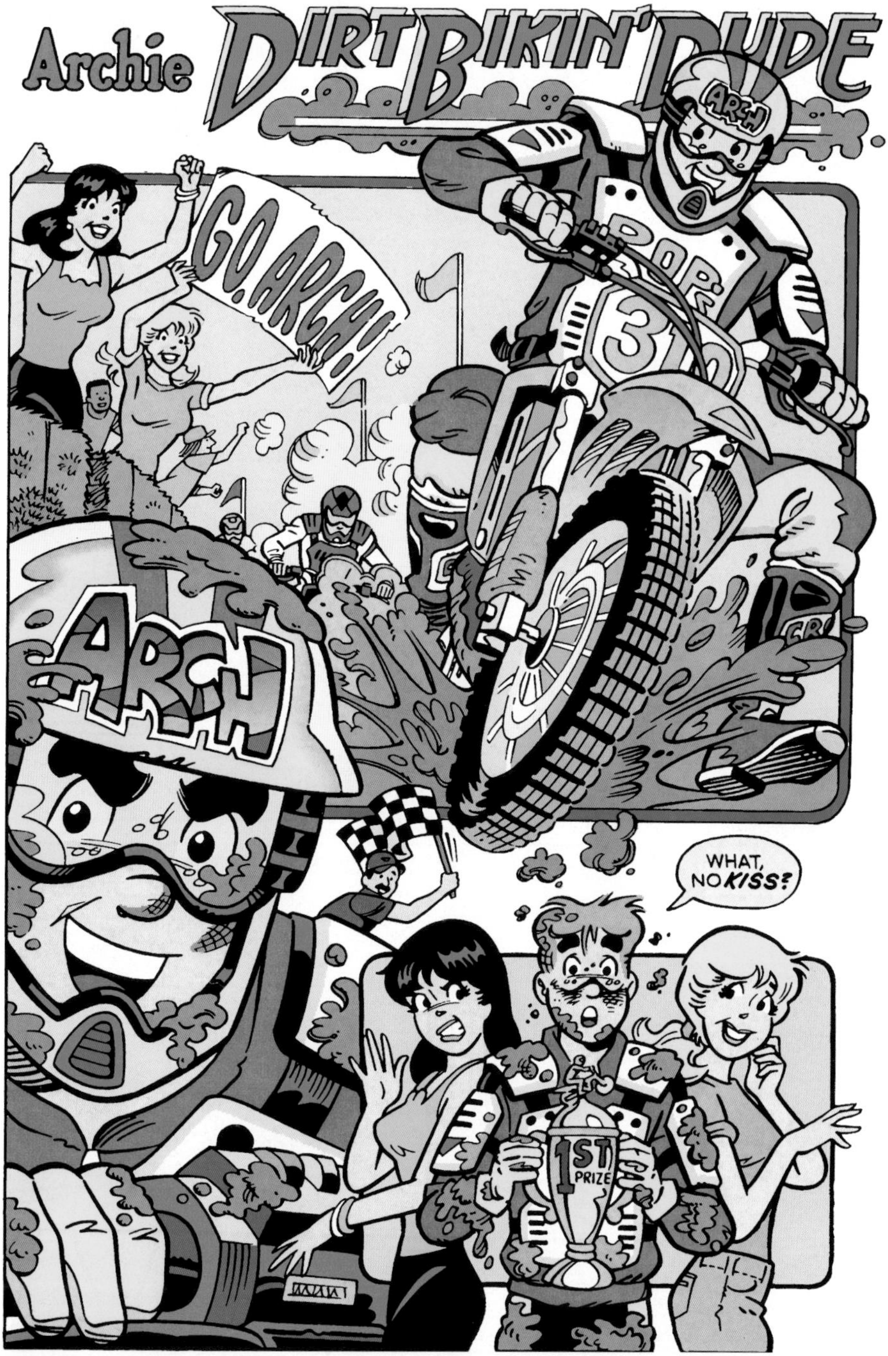
Archie
DIRT BIKIN' DUDE
GO, ARCH!
ARCH
ARCH
3
1ST PRIZE
WHAT, NO KISS?

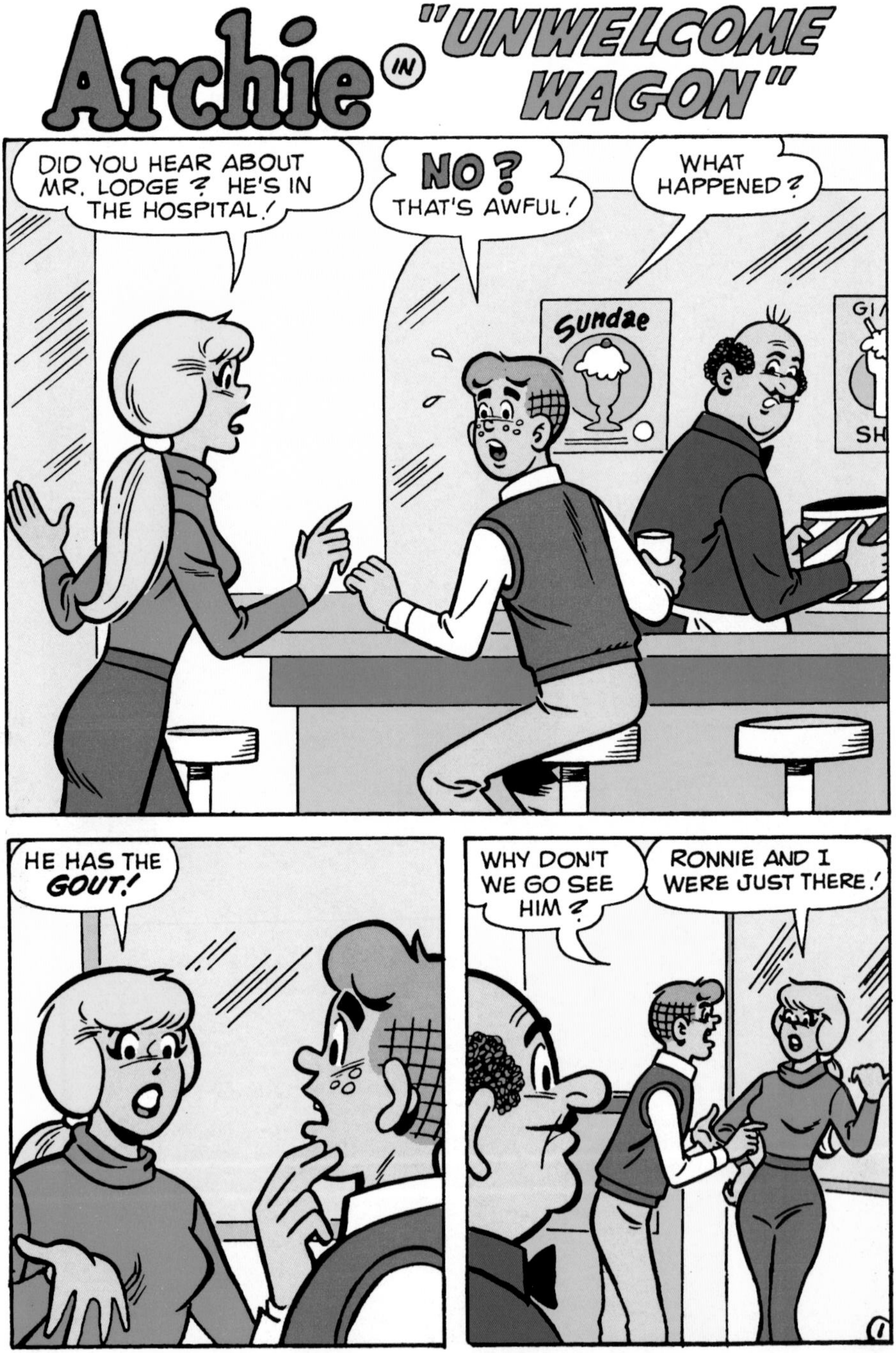
Archie
IN
"UNWELCOME WAGON"
DID YOU HEAR ABOUT MR. LODGE? HE'S IN THE HOSPITAL!
NO? THAT'S AWFUL!
WHAT HAPPENED?
Sundae
HE HAS THE GOUT!
WHY DON'T WE GO SEE HIM?
RONNIE AND I WERE JUST THERE!
1

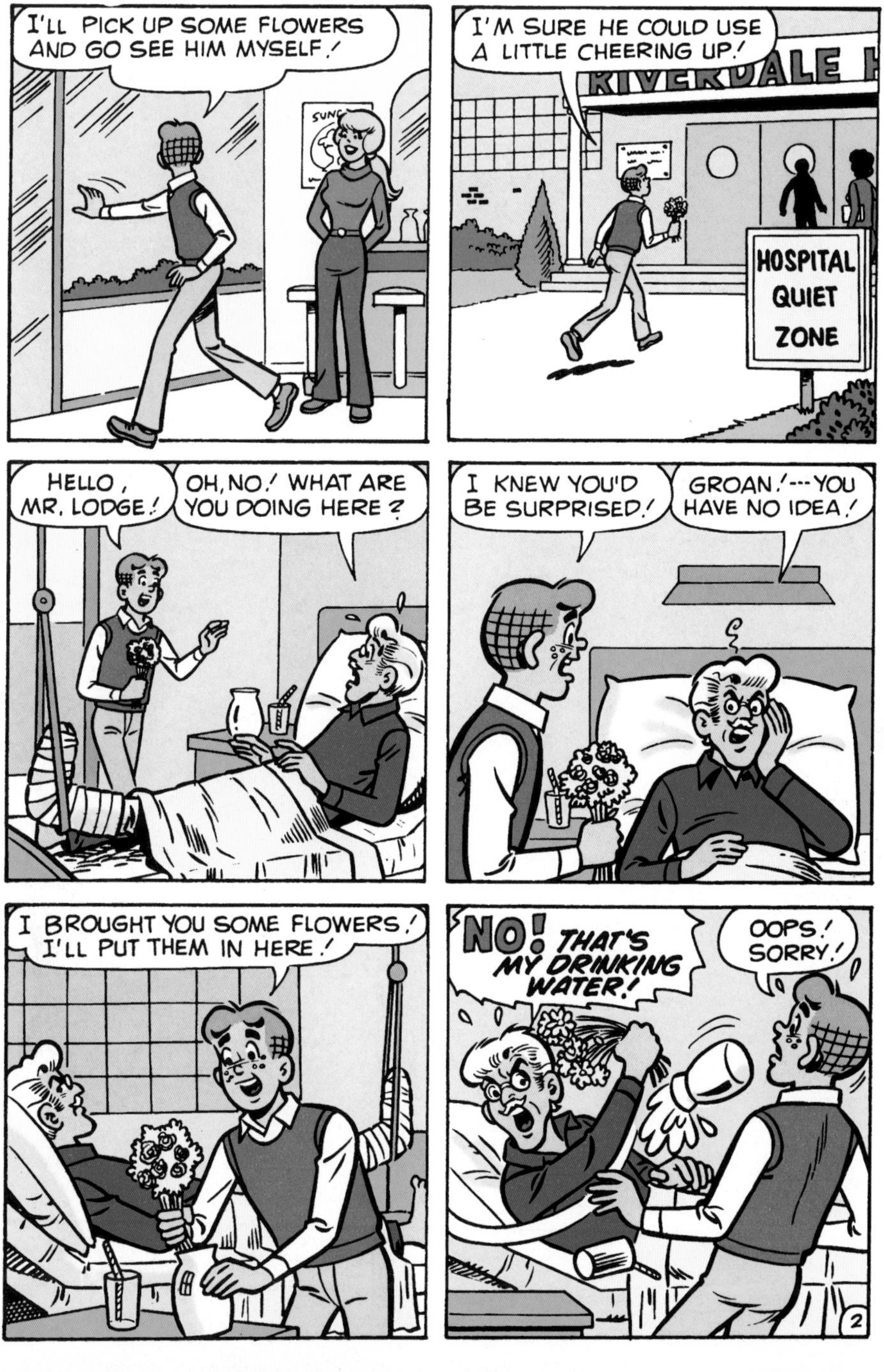
I'LL PICK UP SOME FLOWERS AND GO SEE HIM MYSELF!
I'M SURE HE COULD USE A LITTLE CHEERING UP!
RIVERDALE H
HOSPITAL QUIET ZONE
HELLO, MR. LODGE!
OH, NO! WHAT ARE YOU DOING HERE?
I KNEW YOU'D BE SURPRISED!
GROAN!---YOU HAVE NO IDEA!
I BROUGHT YOU SOME FLOWERS! I'LL PUT THEM IN HERE!
NO! THAT'S MY DRINKING WATER!
OOPS! SORRY!
2

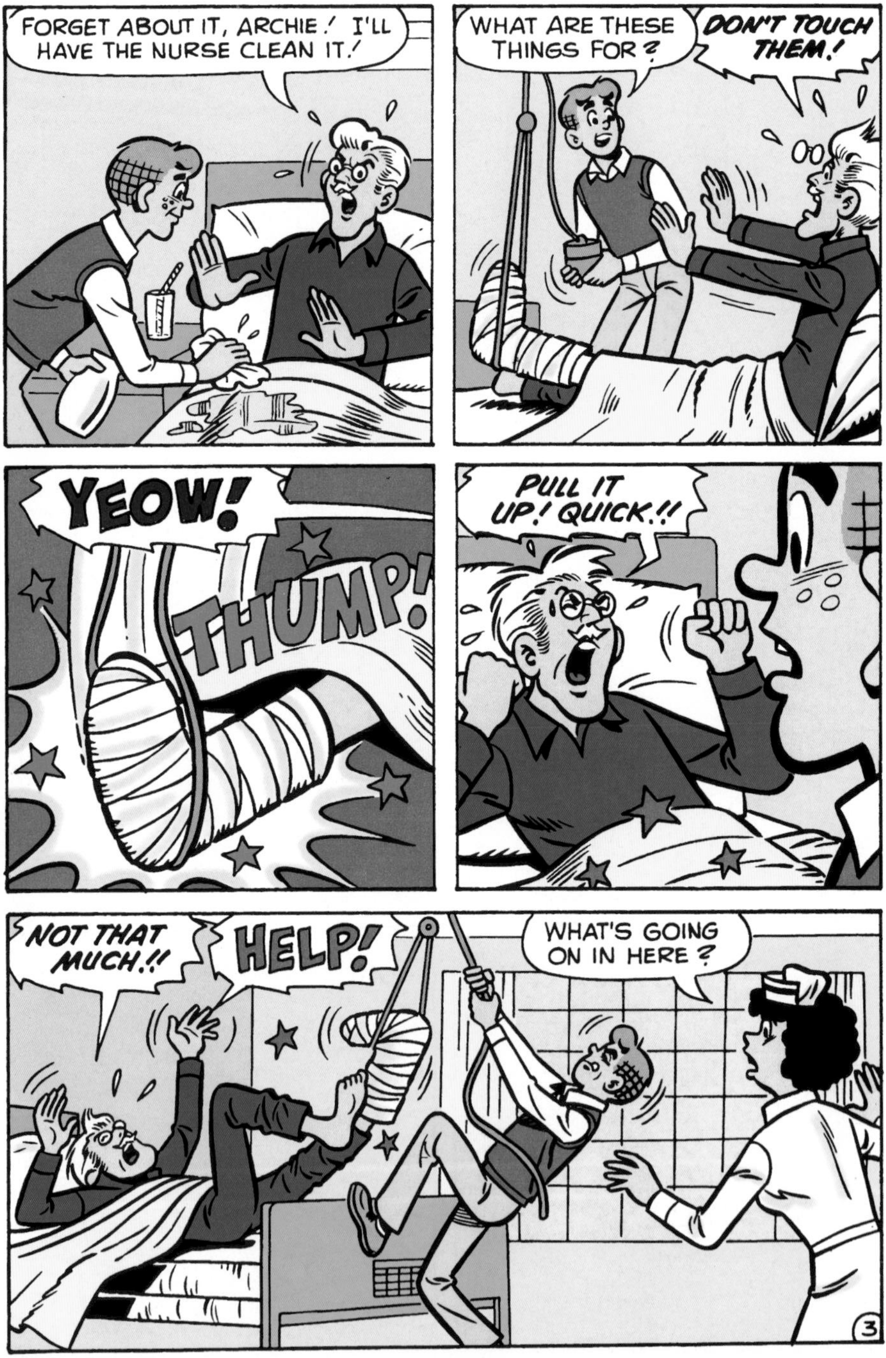
FORGET ABOUT IT, ARCHIE! I'LL HAVE THE NURSE CLEAN IT!
WHAT ARE THESE THINGS FOR?
DON'T TOUCH THEM!
YEOW!
THUMP!
PULL IT UP! QUICK!!
NOT THAT MUCH!!
HELP!
WHAT'S GOING ON IN HERE?
3

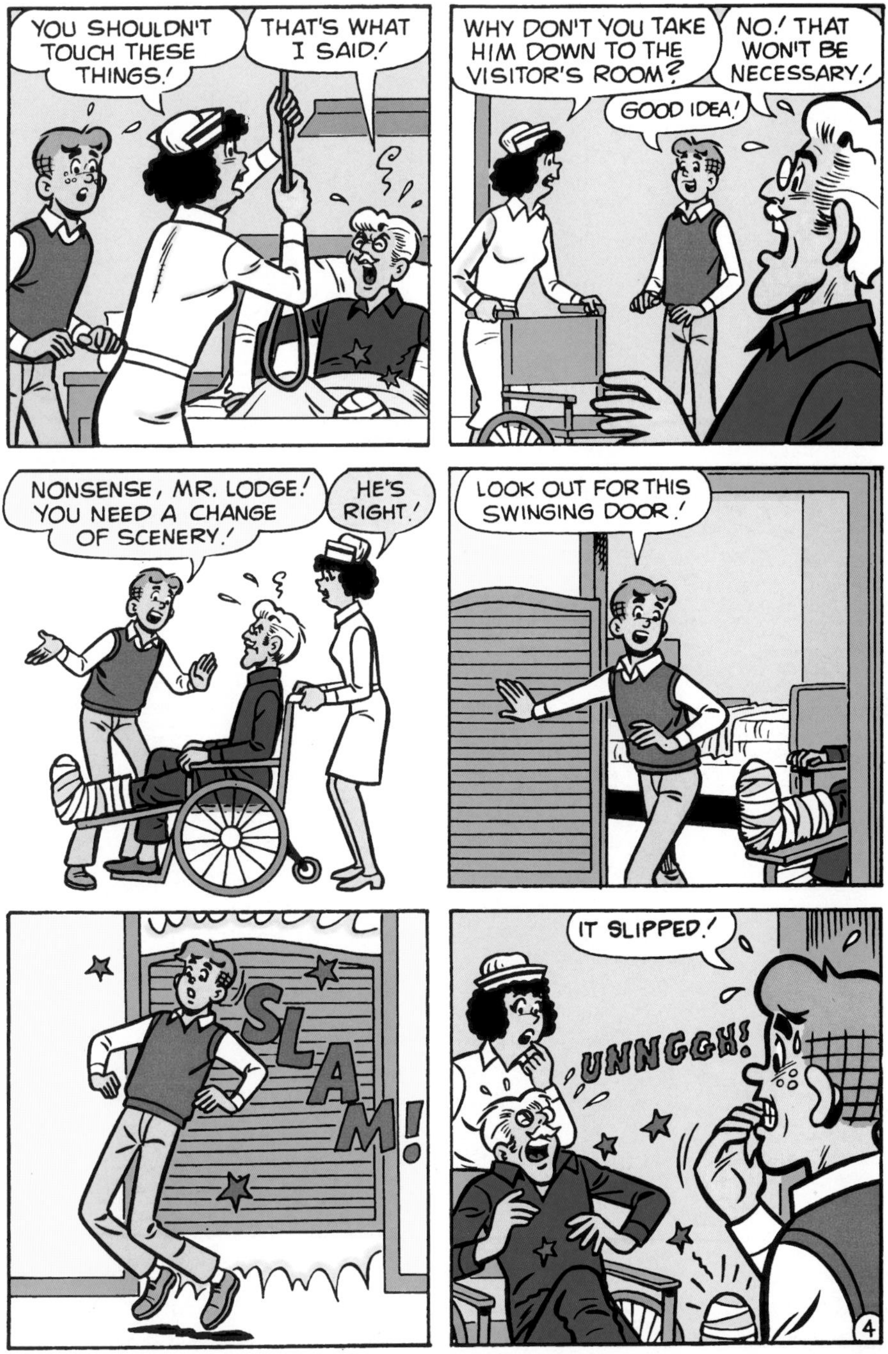
YOU SHOULDN'T TOUCH THESE THINGS!
THAT'S WHAT I SAID!
WHY DON'T YOU TAKE HIM DOWN TO THE VISITOR'S ROOM?
NO! THAT WON'T BE NECESSARY!
GOOD IDEA!
NONSENSE, MR. LODGE! YOU NEED A CHANGE OF SCENERY!
HE'S RIGHT!
LOOK OUT FOR THIS SWINGING DOOR!
SLAM!
IT SLIPPED!
UNNGGH!

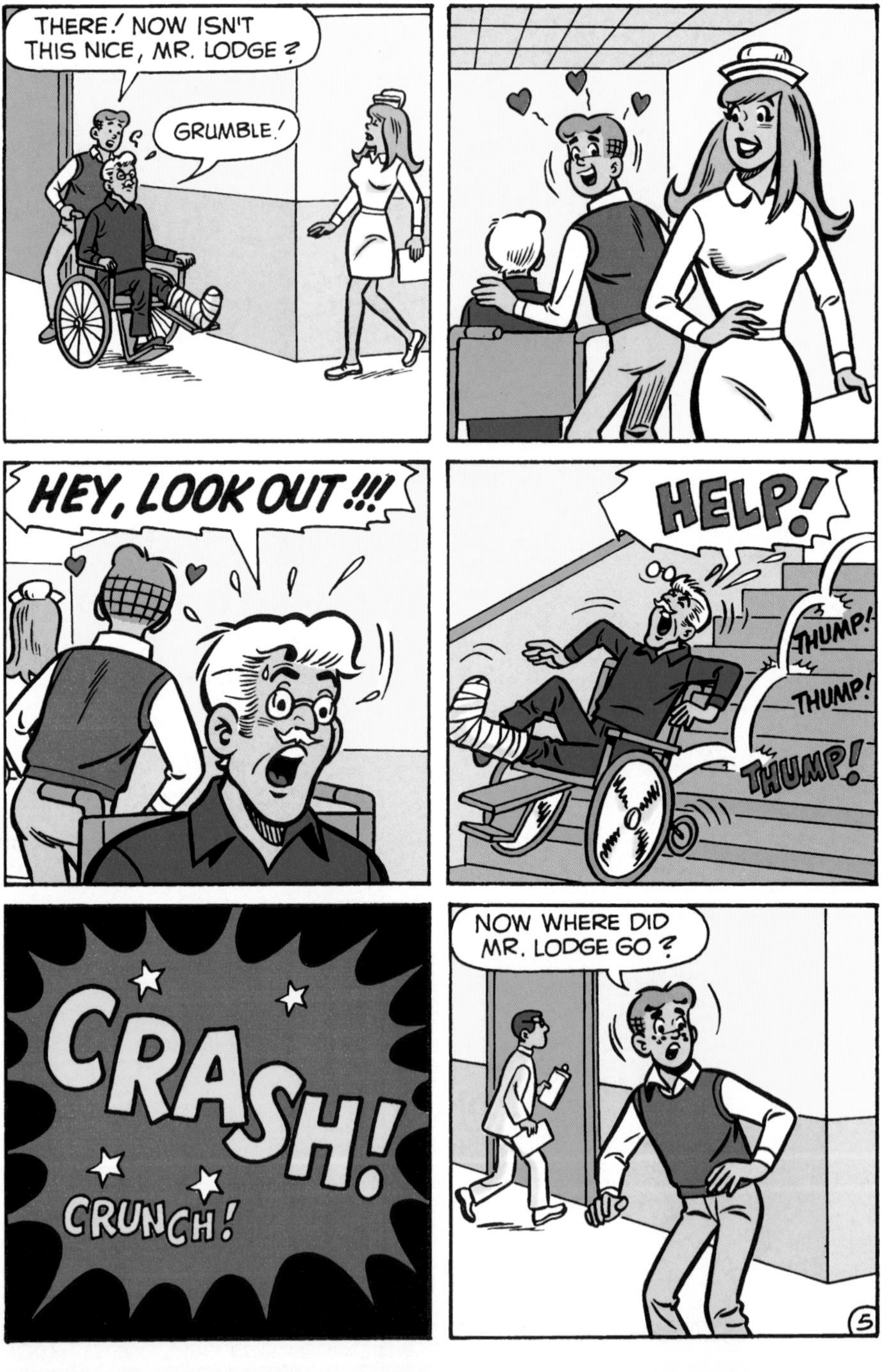
THERE! NOW ISN'T THIS NICE, MR. LODGE ?
GRUMBLE!
HEY, LOOK OUT !!!
HELP!
THUMP!
THUMP!
THUMP!
CRASH!
CRUNCH!
NOW WHERE DID MR. LODGE GO ?
5

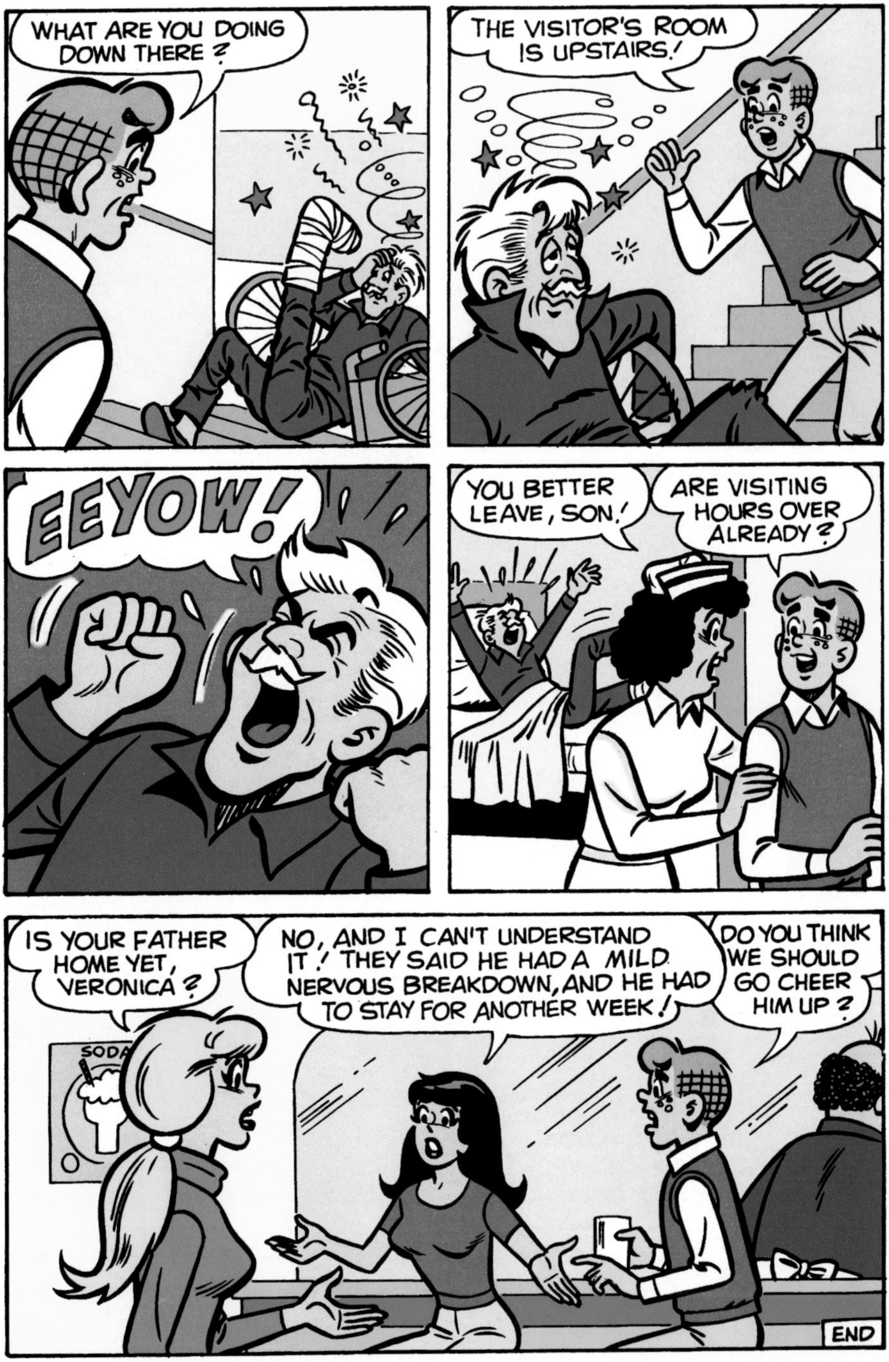
WHAT ARE YOU DOING DOWN THERE ?
THE VISITOR'S ROOM IS UPSTAIRS!
EEYOW!
YOU BETTER LEAVE, SON!
ARE VISITING HOURS OVER ALREADY ?
IS YOUR FATHER HOME YET, VERONICA ?
NO, AND I CAN'T UNDERSTAND IT! THEY SAID HE HAD A MILD NERVOUS BREAKDOWN, AND HE HAD TO STAY FOR ANOTHER WEEK!
DO YOU THINK WE SHOULD GO CHEER HIM UP ?
SODA
END

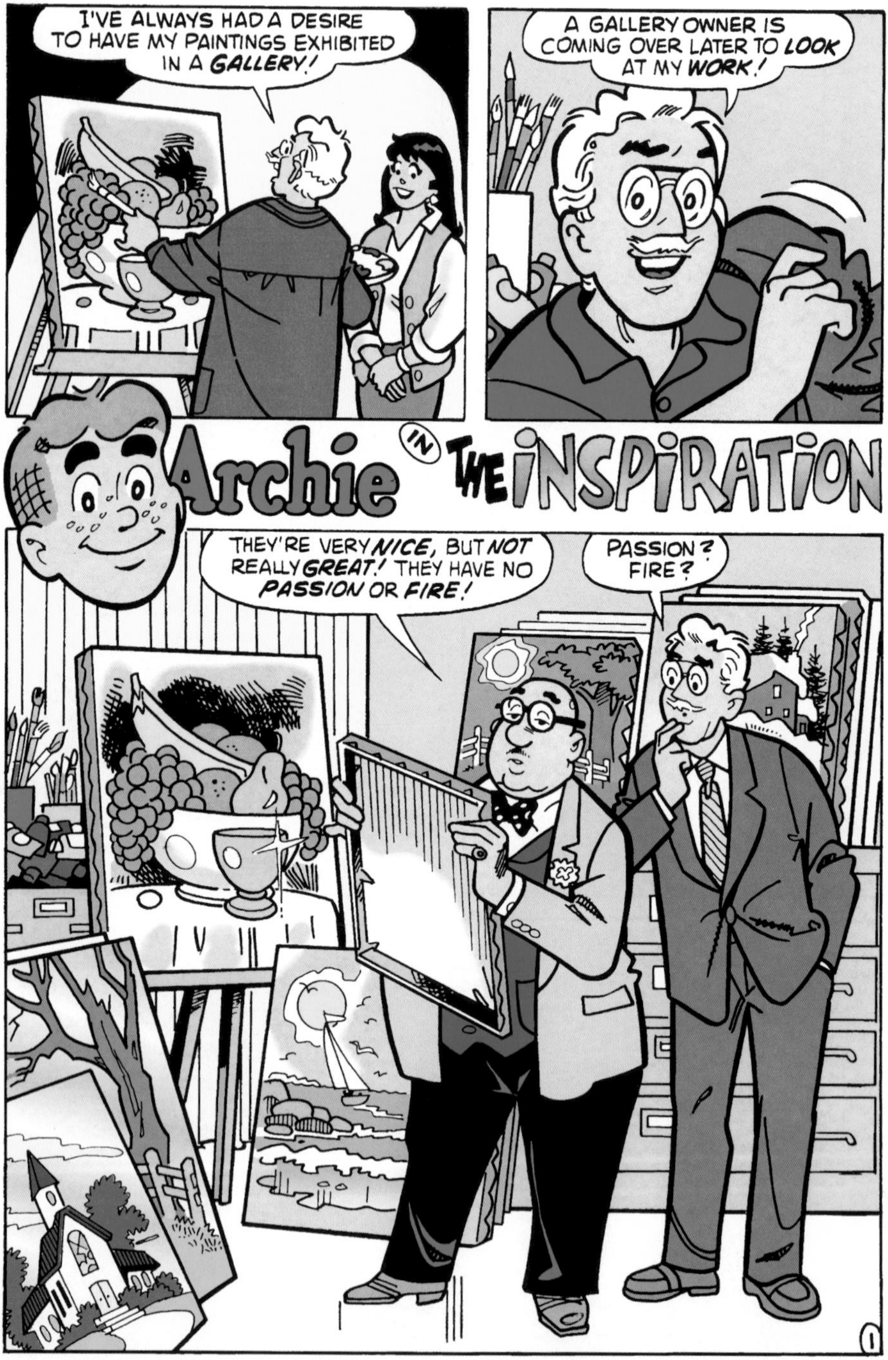
I'VE ALWAYS HAD A DESIRE TO HAVE MY PAINTINGS EXHIBITED IN A GALLERY!
A GALLERY OWNER IS COMING OVER LATER TO LOOK AT MY WORK!
Archie IN THE INSPIRATION
THEY'RE VERY NICE, BUT NOT REALLY GREAT! THEY HAVE NO PASSION OR FIRE!
PASSION? FIRE?
1

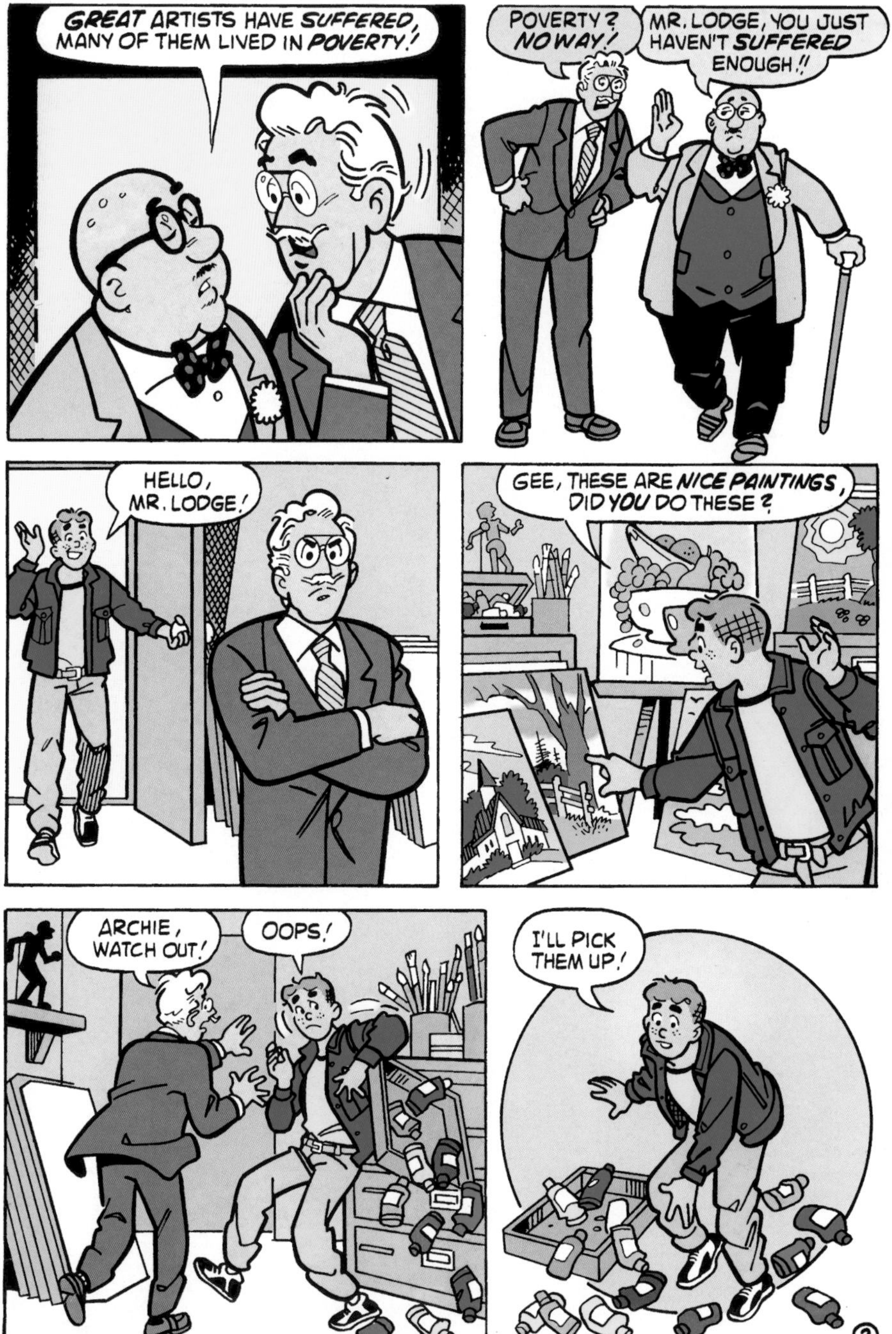
GREAT ARTISTS HAVE SUFFERED, MANY OF THEM LIVED IN POVERTY!
POVERTY? NO WAY!
MR. LODGE, YOU JUST HAVEN'T SUFFERED ENOUGH!!
HELLO, MR. LODGE!
GEE, THESE ARE NICE PAINTINGS, DID YOU DO THESE?
ARCHIE, WATCH OUT!
OOPS!
I'LL PICK THEM UP!
2

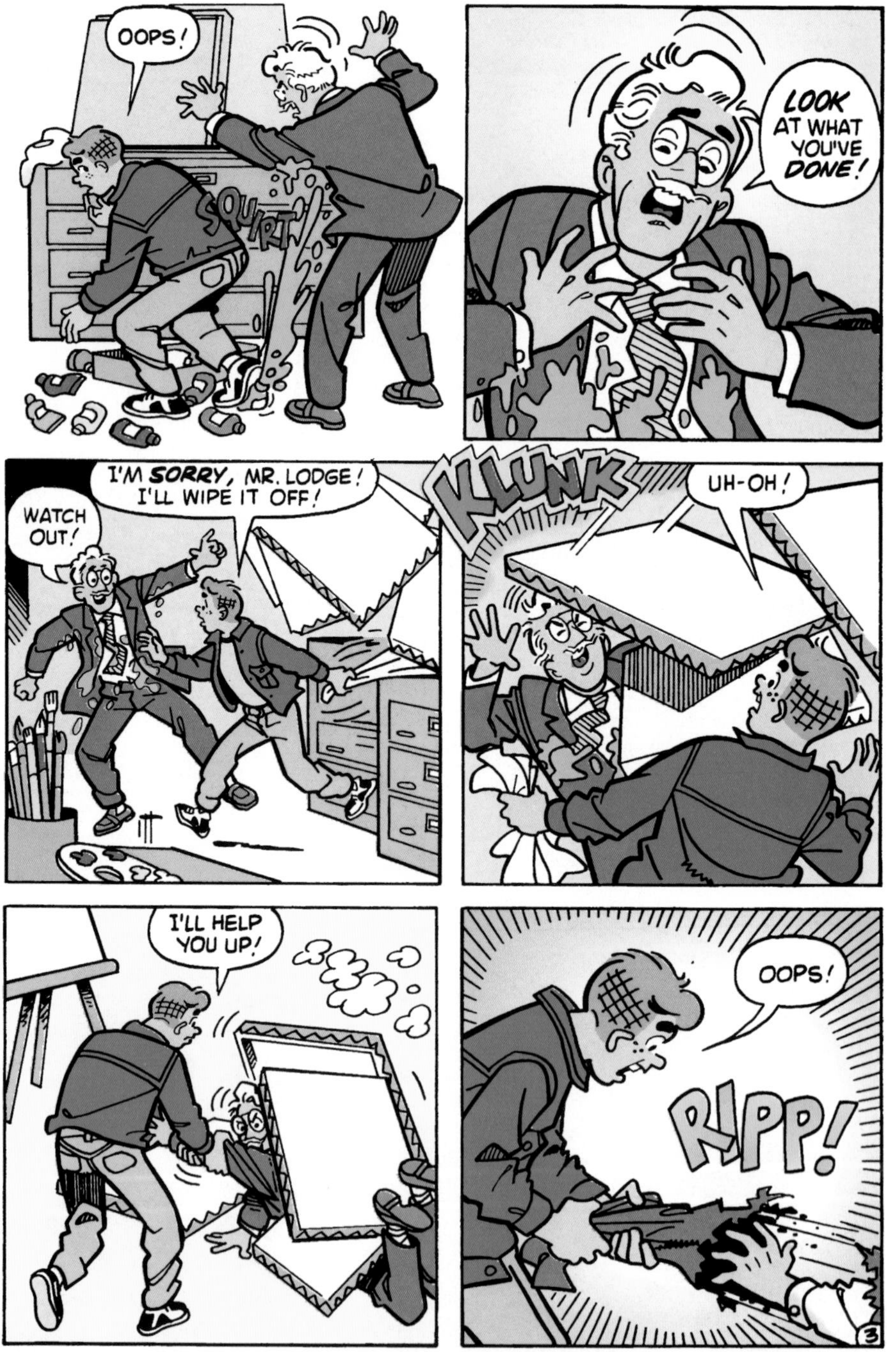
OOPS!
SQUIRT
LOOK AT WHAT YOU'VE DONE!
WATCH OUT!
I'M SORRY, MR. LODGE! I'LL WIPE IT OFF!
KLUNK
UH-OH!
I'LL HELP YOU UP!
OOPS!
RIPP!
3

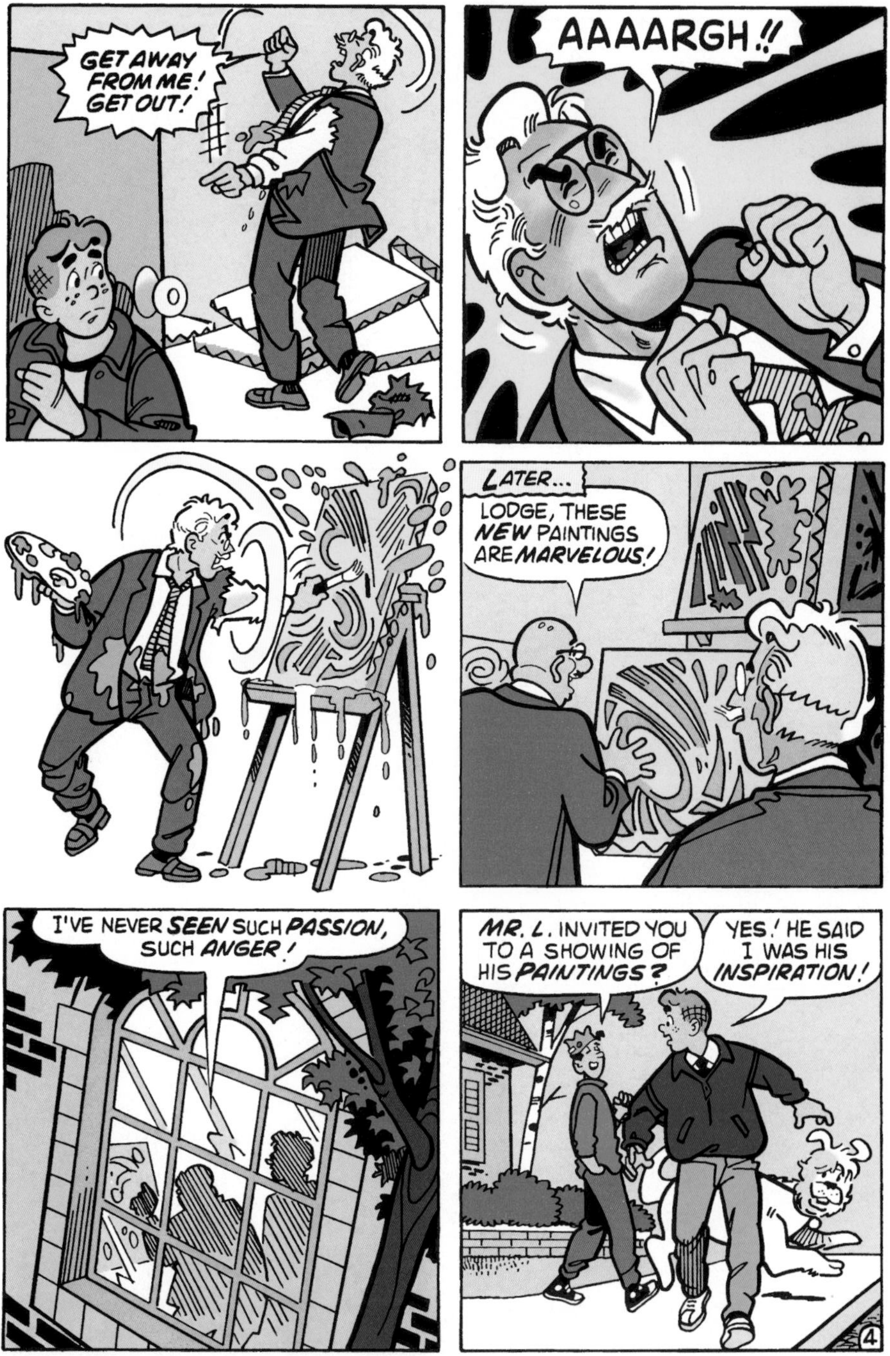
GET AWAY FROM ME! GET OUT!
AAAARGH!!
LATER...
LODGE, THESE NEW PAINTINGS ARE MARVELOUS!
I'VE NEVER SEEN SUCH PASSION, SUCH ANGER!
MR. L. INVITED YOU TO A SHOWING OF HIS PAINTINGS?
YES! HE SAID I WAS HIS INSPIRATION!
4

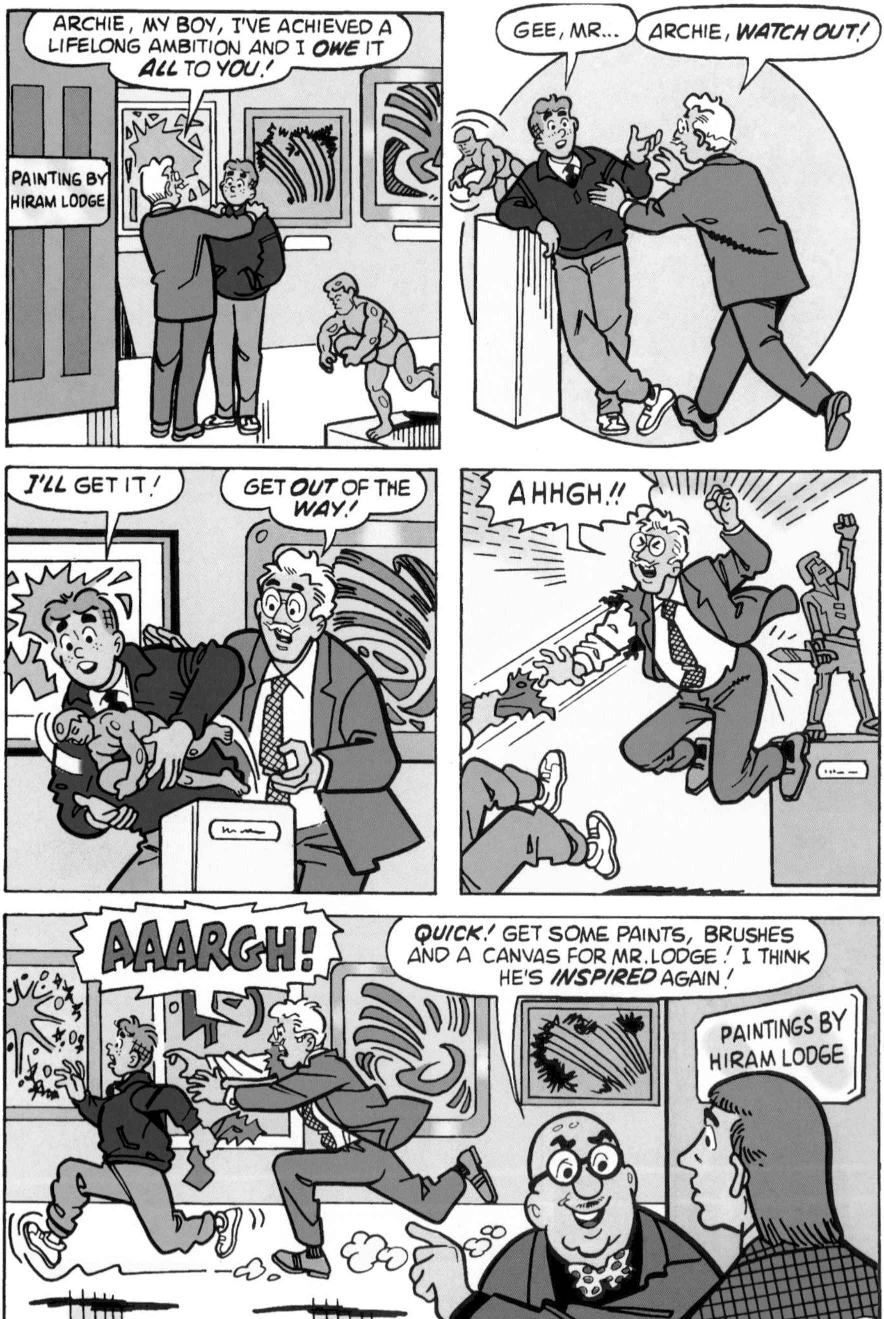
ARCHIE, MY BOY, I'VE ACHIEVED A LIFELONG AMBITION AND I OWE IT ALL TO YOU!
PAINTING BY HIRAM LODGE
GEE, MR...
ARCHIE, WATCH OUT!
I'LL GET IT!
GET OUT OF THE WAY!
AHHGH!!
AAARGH!
QUICK! GET SOME PAINTS, BRUSHES AND A CANVAS FOR MR. LODGE! I THINK HE'S INSPIRED AGAIN!
PAINTINGS BY HIRAM LODGE
END

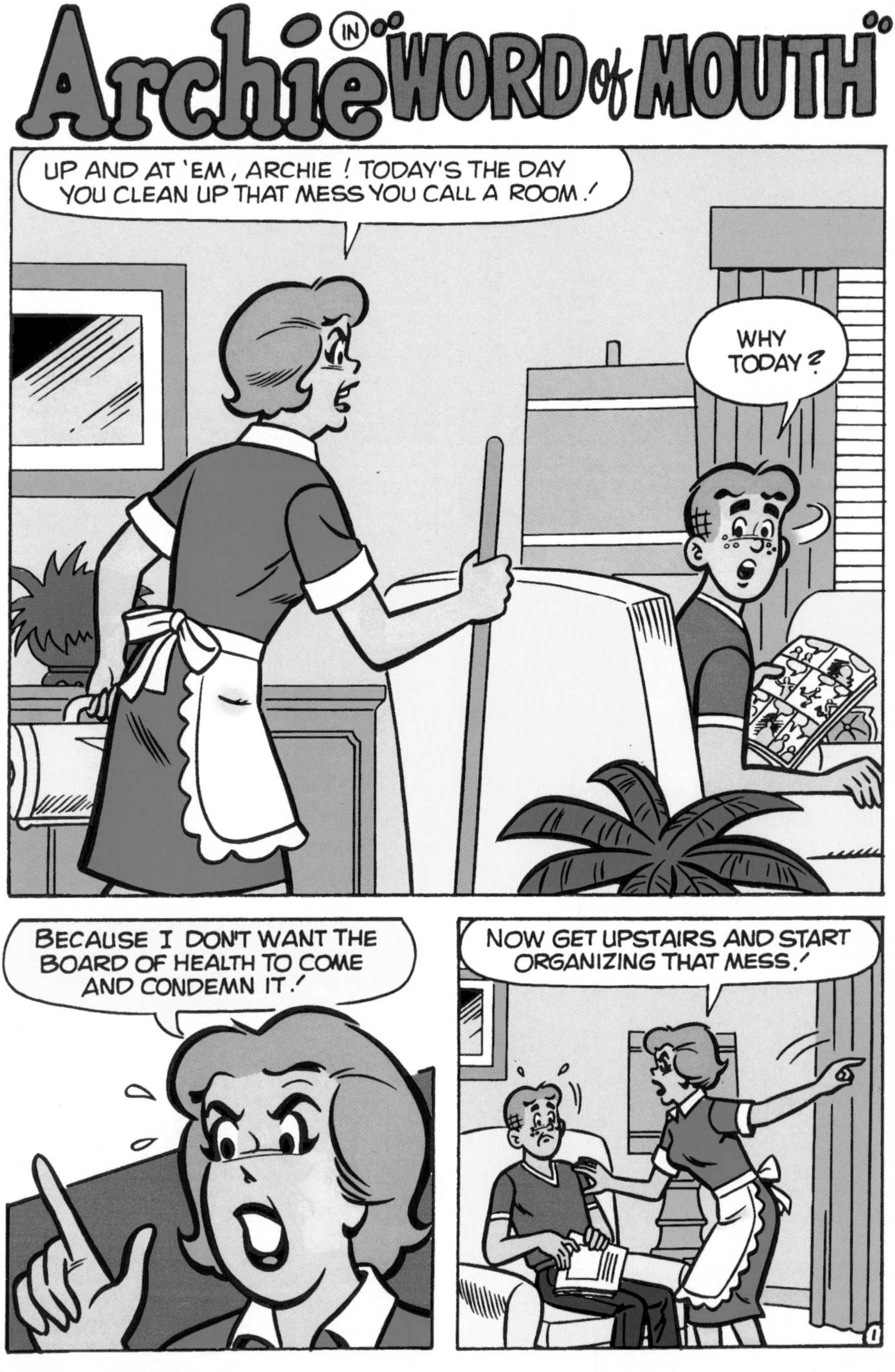
Archie IN WORD of MOUTH
UP AND AT 'EM, ARCHIE! TODAY'S THE DAY YOU CLEAN UP THAT MESS YOU CALL A ROOM!
WHY TODAY?
BECAUSE I DON'T WANT THE BOARD OF HEALTH TO COME AND CONDEMN IT!
NOW GET UPSTAIRS AND START ORGANIZING THAT MESS!
1

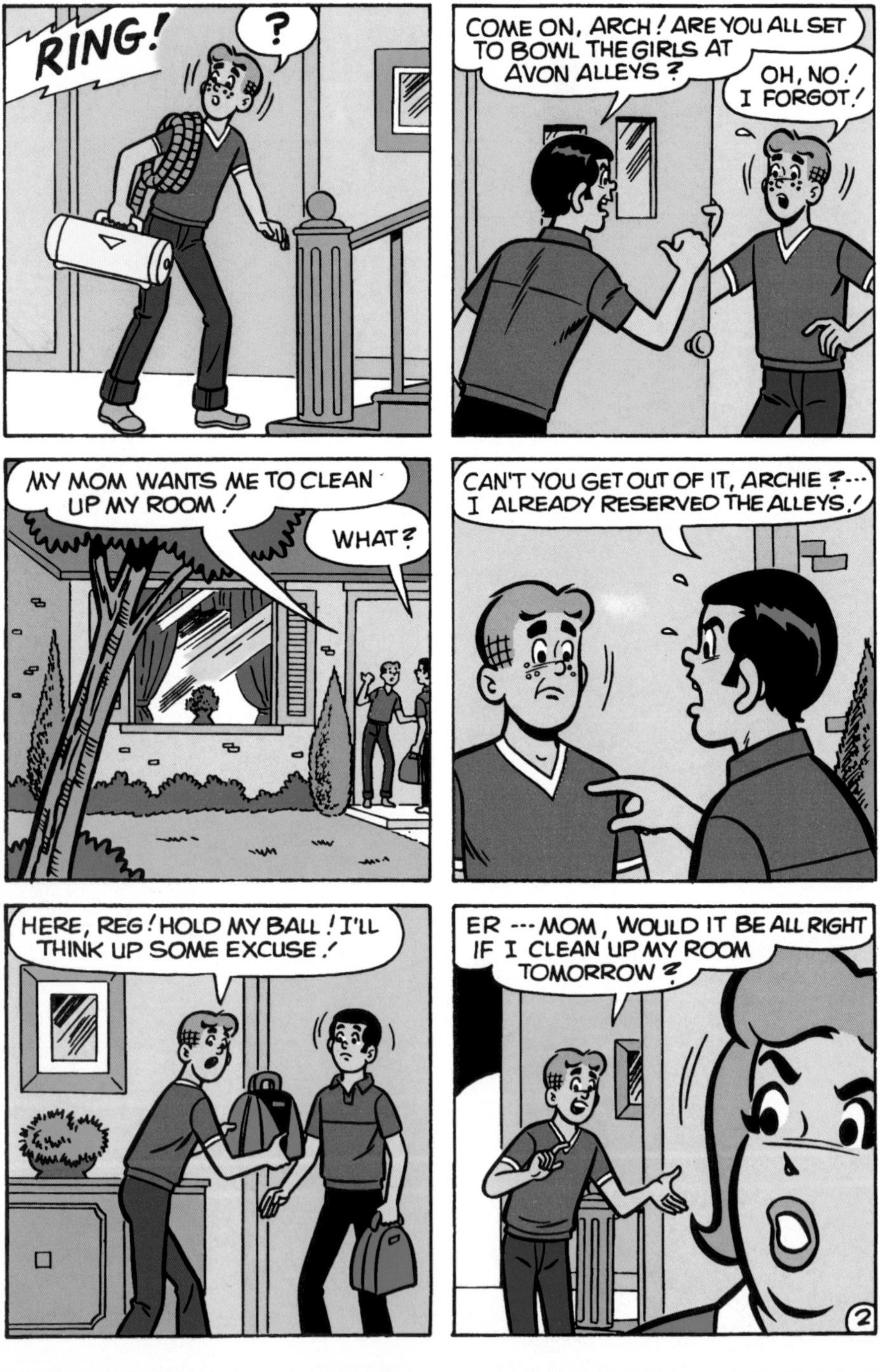
RING!
?
COME ON, ARCH! ARE YOU ALL SET TO BOWL THE GIRLS AT AVON ALLEYS?
OH, NO! I FORGOT!
MY MOM WANTS ME TO CLEAN UP MY ROOM!
WHAT?
CAN'T YOU GET OUT OF IT, ARCHIE?... I ALREADY RESERVED THE ALLEYS!
HERE, REG! HOLD MY BALL! I'LL THINK UP SOME EXCUSE!
ER --- MOM, WOULD IT BE ALL RIGHT IF I CLEAN UP MY ROOM TOMORROW?
2

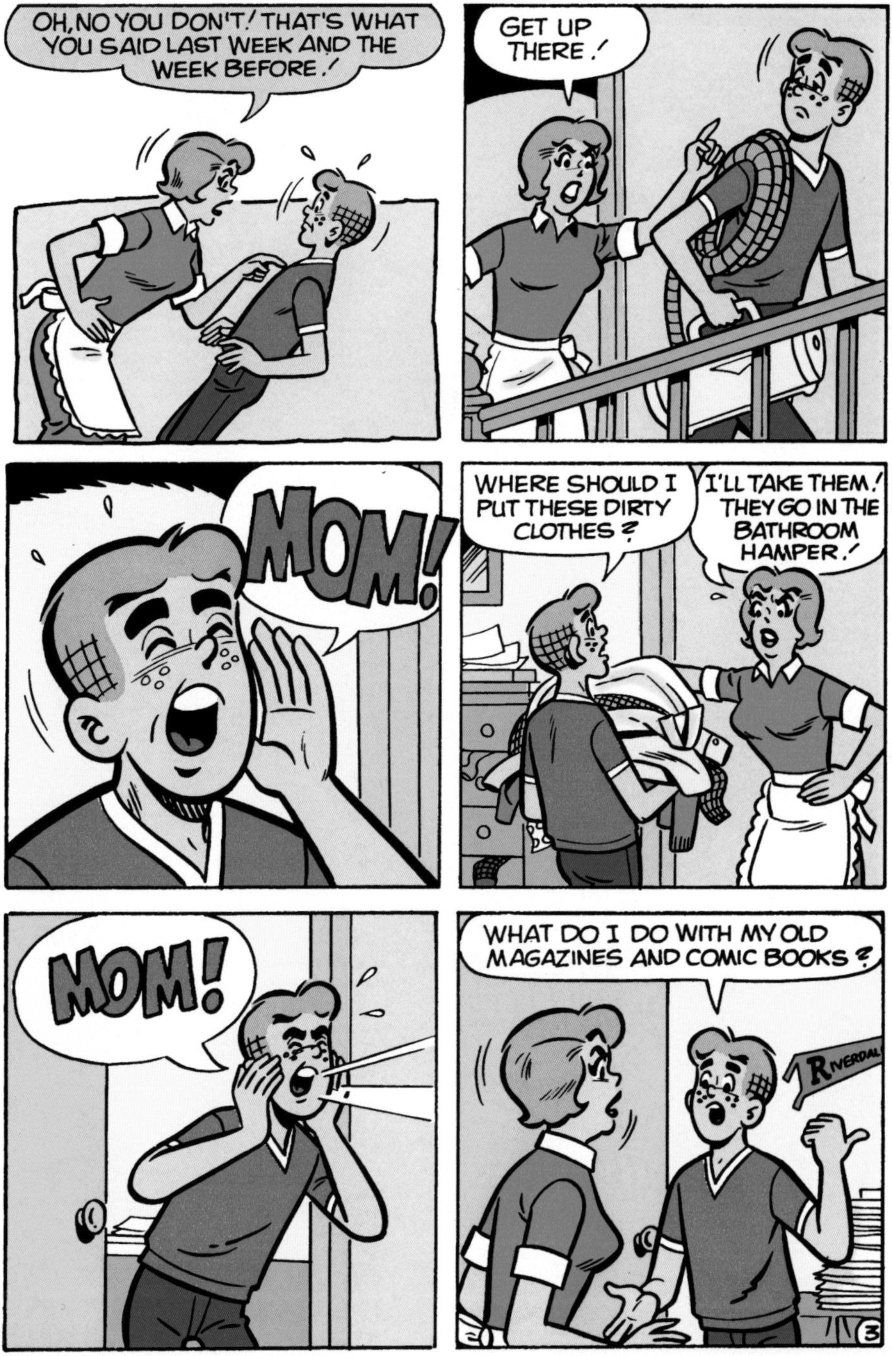
OH, NO YOU DON'T! THAT'S WHAT YOU SAID LAST WEEK AND THE WEEK BEFORE!
GET UP THERE!
MOM!
WHERE SHOULD I PUT THESE DIRTY CLOTHES?
I'LL TAKE THEM! THEY GO IN THE BATHROOM HAMPER!
MOM!
WHAT DO I DO WITH MY OLD MAGAZINES AND COMIC BOOKS?
RIVERDALE
3

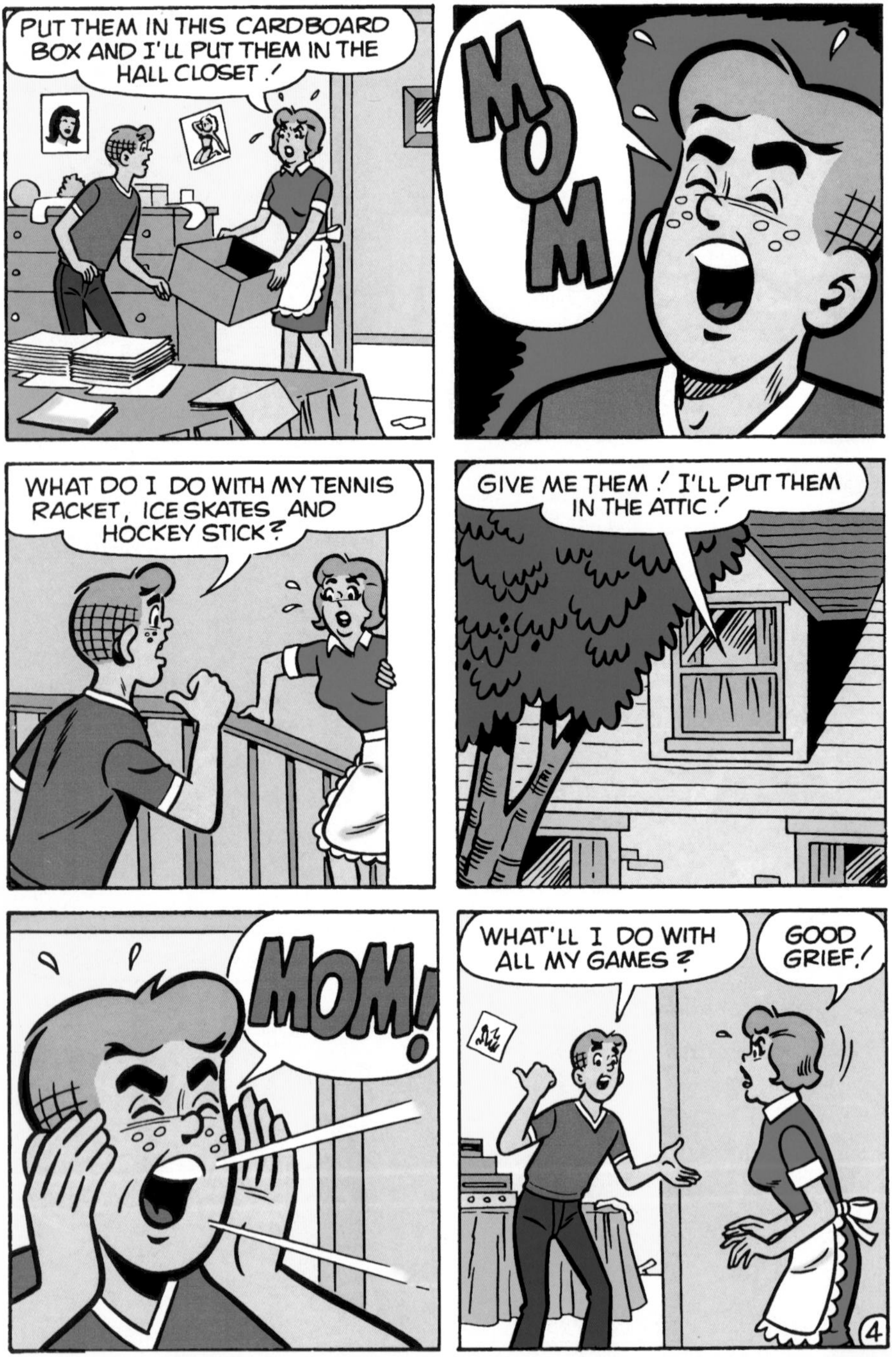
PUT THEM IN THIS CARDBOARD BOX AND I'LL PUT THEM IN THE HALL CLOSET!
MOM
WHAT DO I DO WITH MY TENNIS RACKET, ICE SKATES AND HOCKEY STICK?
GIVE ME THEM! I'LL PUT THEM IN THE ATTIC!
MOM!
WHAT'LL I DO WITH ALL MY GAMES?
GOOD GRIEF!
4

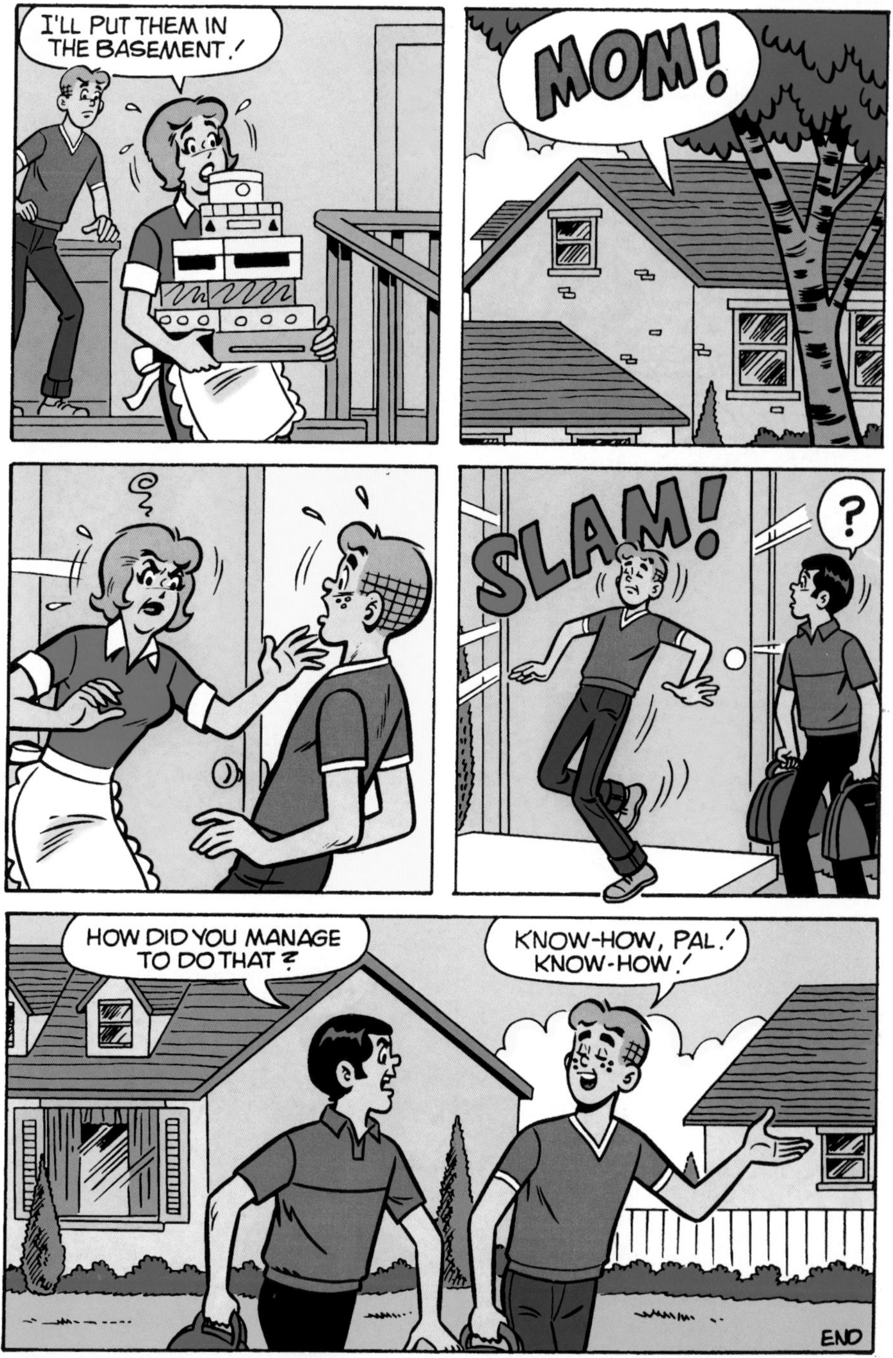
I'LL PUT THEM IN THE BASEMENT!
MOM!
SLAM!
?
HOW DID YOU MANAGE TO DO THAT?
KNOW-HOW, PAL! KNOW-HOW!
END

Archie in "SURE LURE"

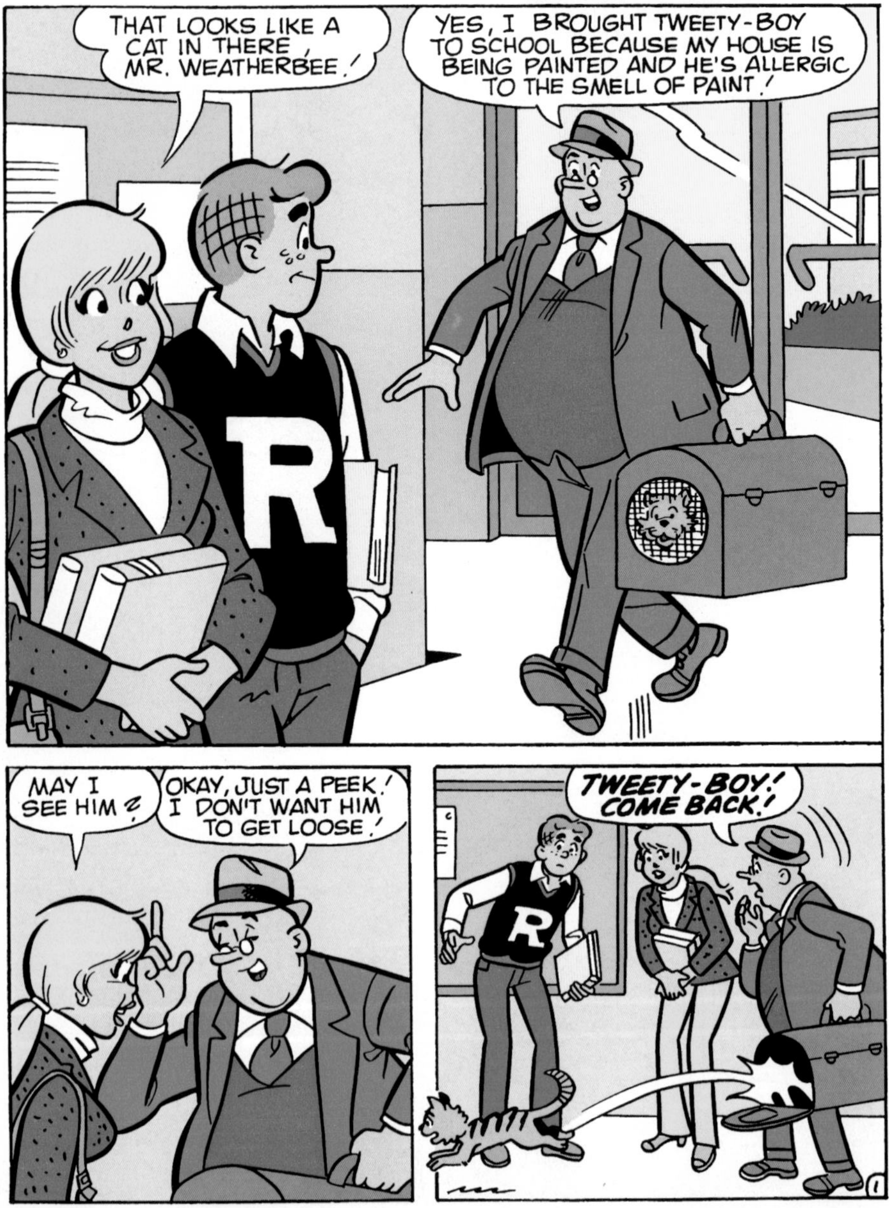
THAT LOOKS LIKE A CAT IN THERE, MR. WEATHERBEE.!
YES, I BROUGHT TWEETY-BOY TO SCHOOL BECAUSE MY HOUSE IS BEING PAINTED AND HE'S ALLERGIC TO THE SMELL OF PAINT.!
MAY I SEE HIM?
OKAY, JUST A PEEK.! I DON'T WANT HIM TO GET LOOSE.!
TWEETY-BOY! COME BACK!
1

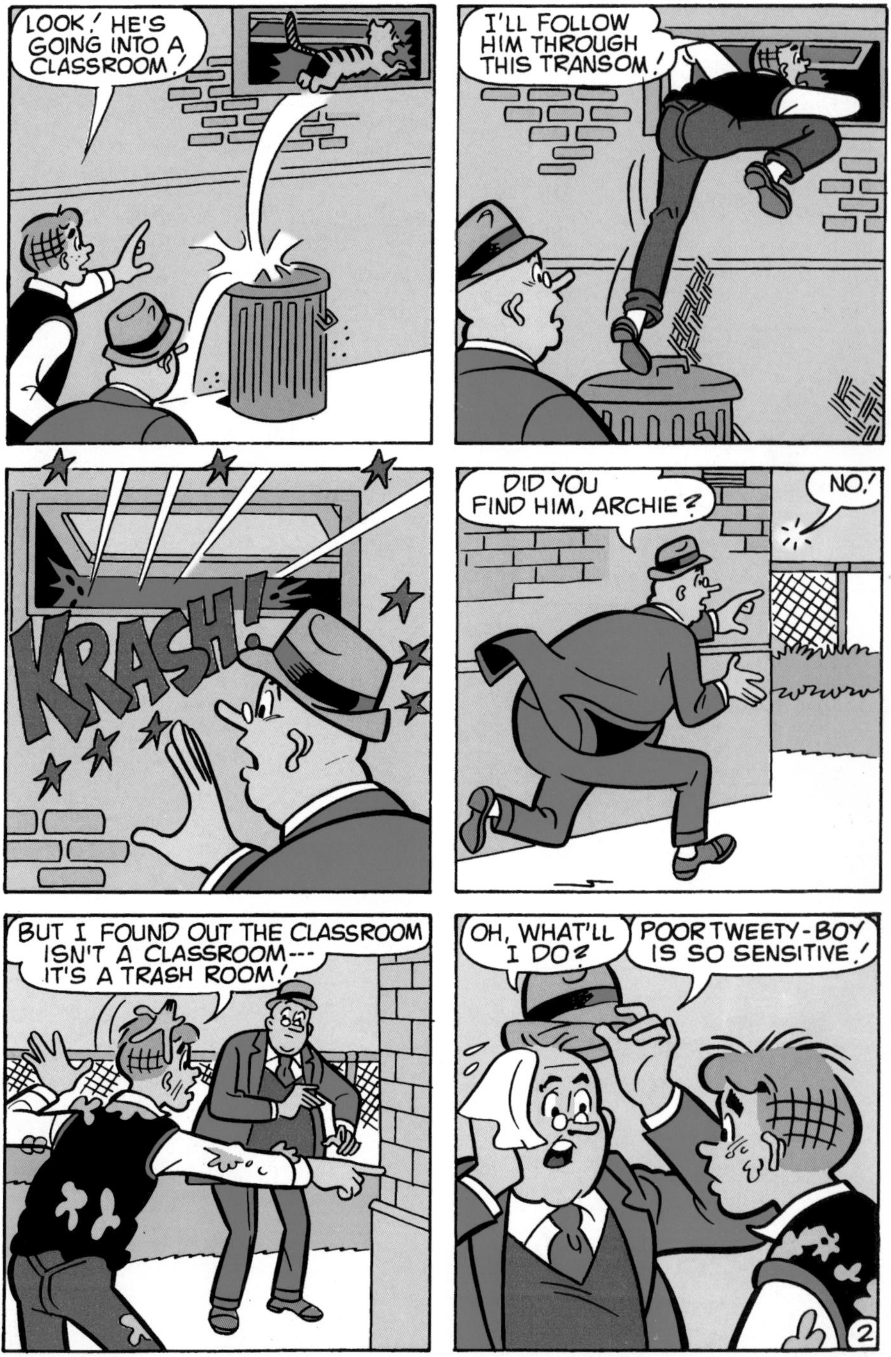
LOOK! HE'S GOING INTO A CLASSROOM!
I'LL FOLLOW HIM THROUGH THIS TRANSOM!
KRASH!
DID YOU FIND HIM, ARCHIE?
NO!
BUT I FOUND OUT THE CLASSROOM ISN'T A CLASSROOM--- IT'S A TRASH ROOM!
OH, WHAT'LL I DO?
POOR TWEETY-BOY IS SO SENSITIVE!
2

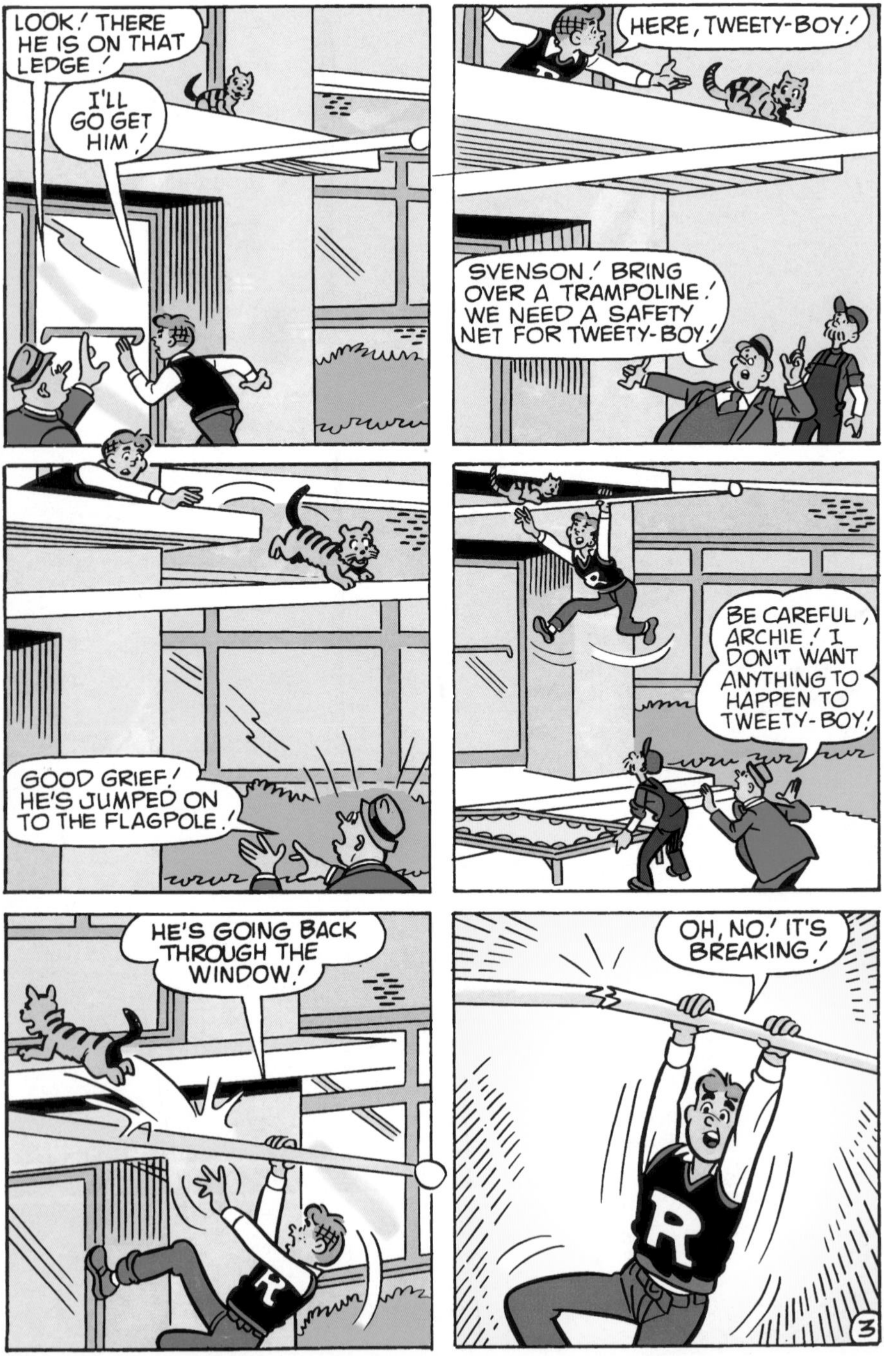
LOOK! THERE HE IS ON THAT LEDGE!
I'LL GO GET HIM!
HERE, TWEETY-BOY!
SVENSON! BRING OVER A TRAMPOLINE! WE NEED A SAFETY NET FOR TWEETY-BOY!
GOOD GRIEF! HE'S JUMPED ON TO THE FLAGPOLE!
BE CAREFUL, ARCHIE! I DON'T WANT ANYTHING TO HAPPEN TO TWEETY-BOY!
HE'S GOING BACK THROUGH THE WINDOW!
OH, NO! IT'S BREAKING!
3

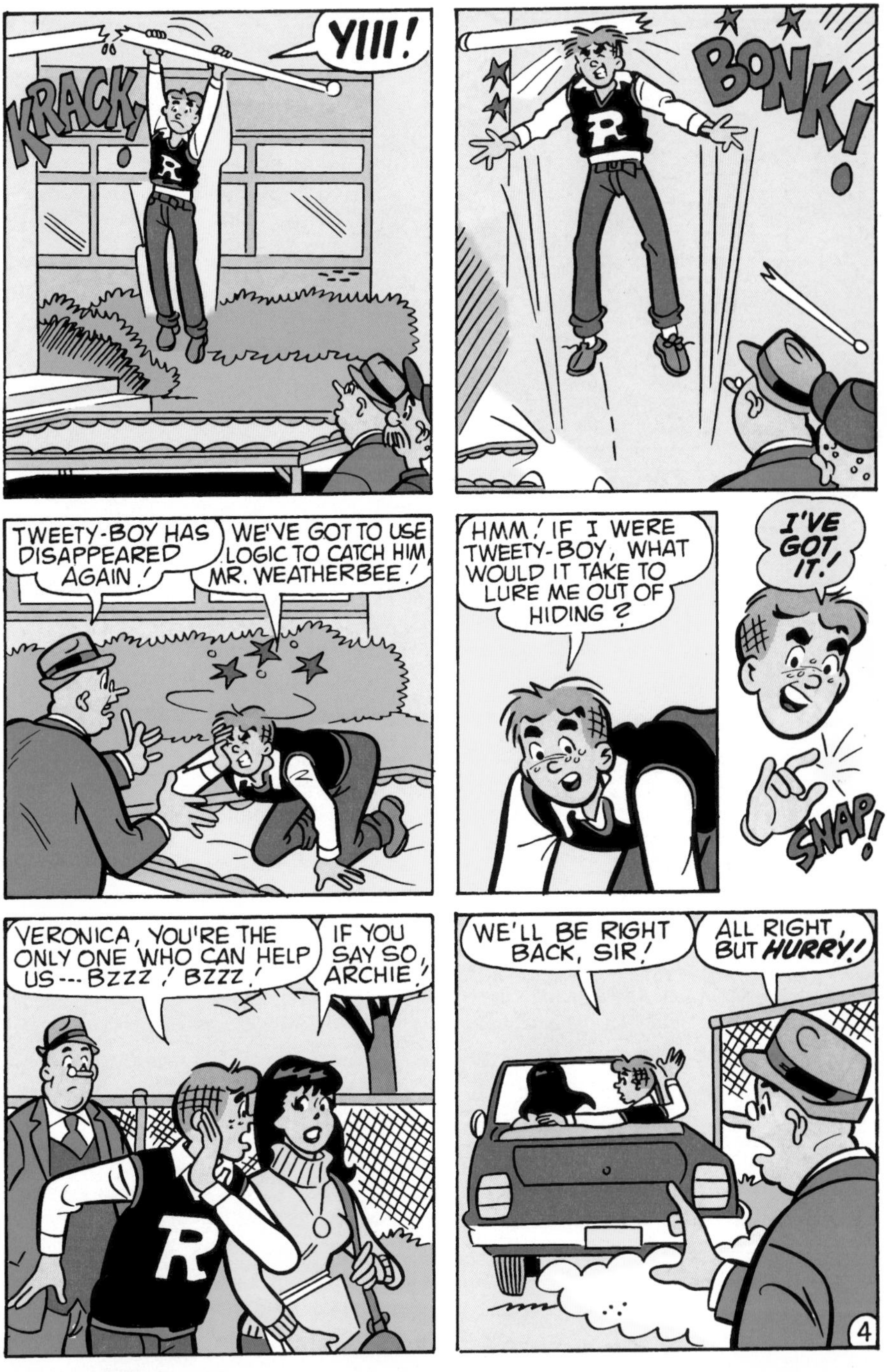
KRACK!
YIII!
BONK!
TWEETY-BOY HAS DISAPPEARED AGAIN!
WE'VE GOT TO USE LOGIC TO CATCH HIM, MR. WEATHERBEE!
HMM! IF I WERE TWEETY-BOY, WHAT WOULD IT TAKE TO LURE ME OUT OF HIDING?
I'VE GOT IT!
SNAP!
VERONICA, YOU'RE THE ONLY ONE WHO CAN HELP US --- BZZZ! BZZZ!
IF YOU SAY SO, ARCHIE!
WE'LL BE RIGHT BACK, SIR!
ALL RIGHT, BUT HURRY!
4

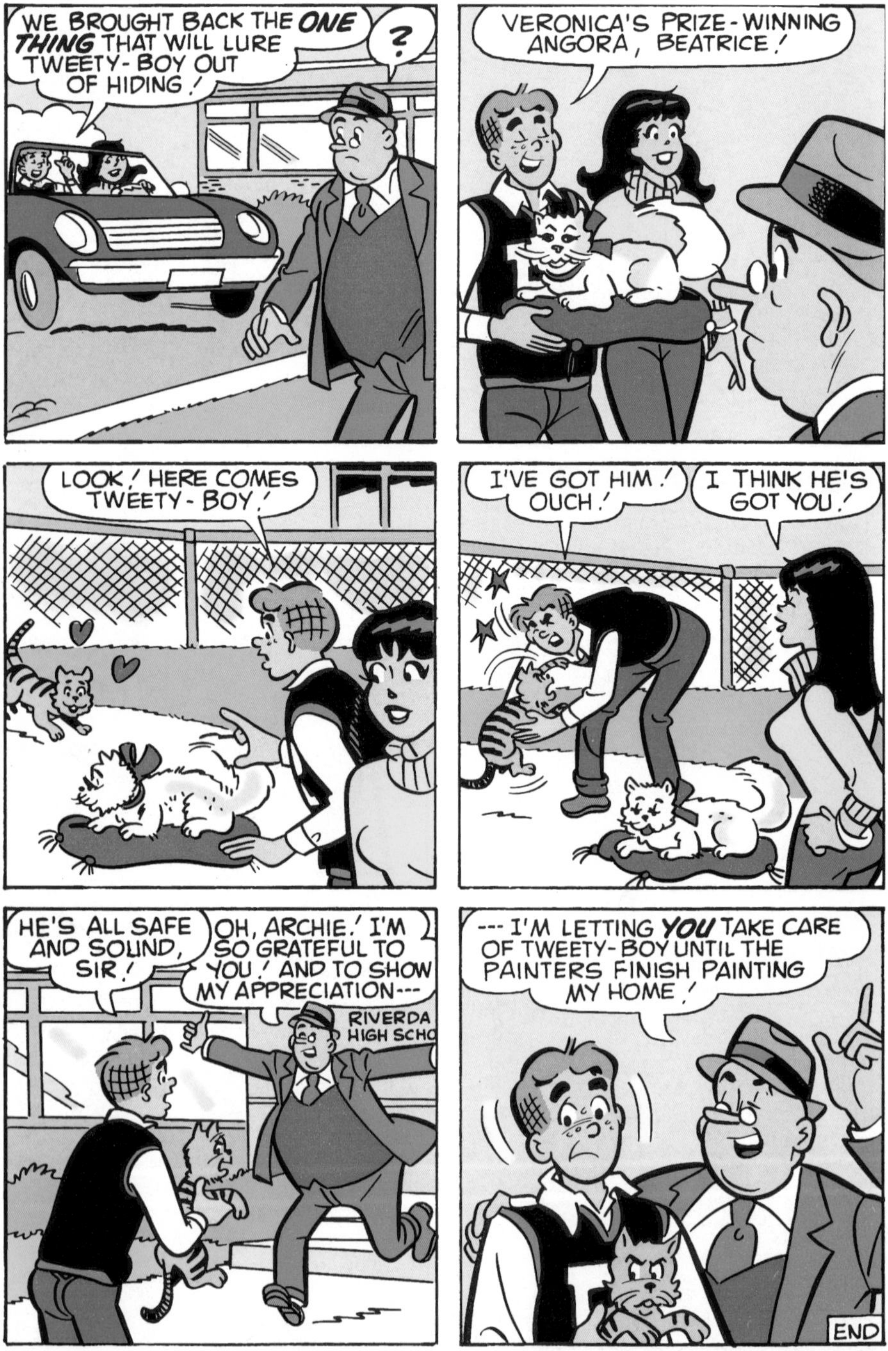
WE BROUGHT BACK THE ONE THING THAT WILL LURE TWEETY-BOY OUT OF HIDING!
?
VERONICA'S PRIZE-WINNING ANGORA, BEATRICE!
LOOK! HERE COMES TWEETY-BOY!
I'VE GOT HIM! OUCH!
I THINK HE'S GOT YOU!
HE'S ALL SAFE AND SOUND, SIR!
OH, ARCHIE! I'M SO GRATEFUL TO YOU! AND TO SHOW MY APPRECIATION---
RIVERDA
HIGH SCHO
--- I'M LETTING YOU TAKE CARE OF TWEETY-BOY UNTIL THE PAINTERS FINISH PAINTING MY HOME!
END

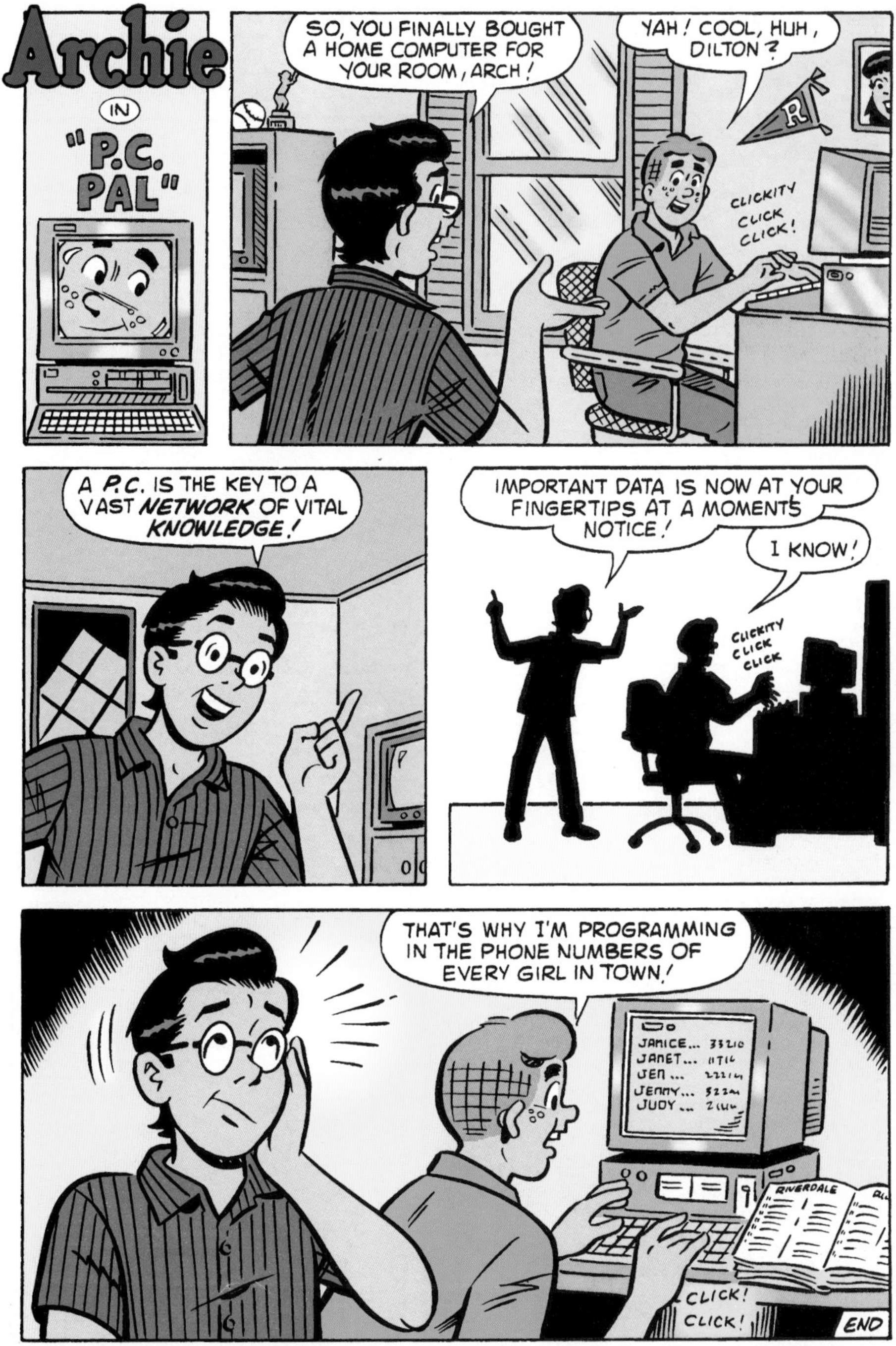
Archie
IN
"P.C. PAL"
SO, YOU FINALLY BOUGHT A HOME COMPUTER FOR YOUR ROOM, ARCH!
YAH! COOL, HUH, DILTON?
CLICKITY CLICK CLICK!
A P.C. IS THE KEY TO A VAST NETWORK OF VITAL KNOWLEDGE!
IMPORTANT DATA IS NOW AT YOUR FINGERTIPS AT A MOMENT'S NOTICE!
I KNOW!
CLICKITY CLICK CLICK
THAT'S WHY I'M PROGRAMMING IN THE PHONE NUMBERS OF EVERY GIRL IN TOWN!
JANICE...
JANET...
JEN...
JENNY...
JUDY...
RIVERDALE
CLICK!
CLICK!
END

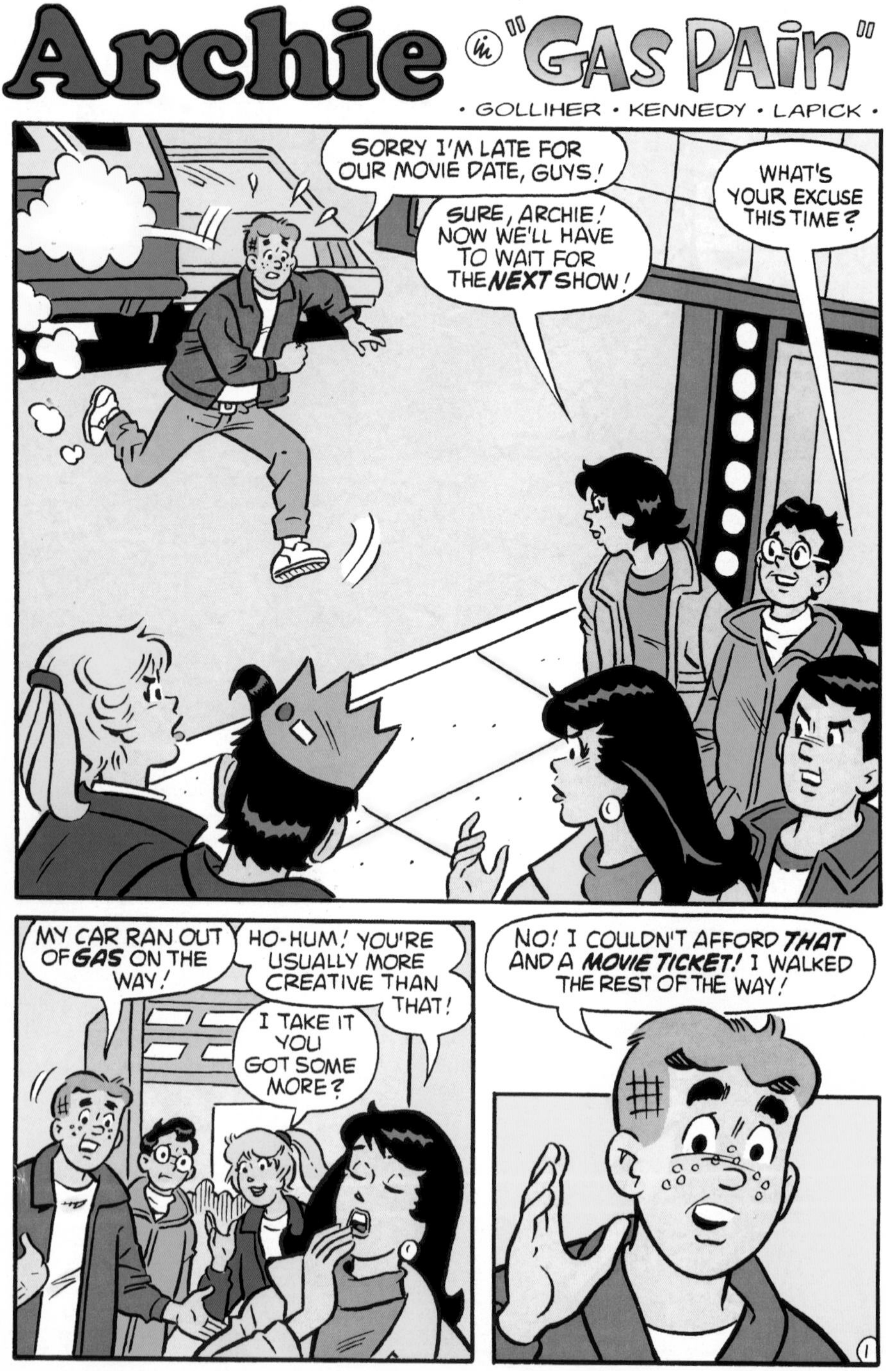
Archie in "GAS PAIN"
• GOLLIHER • KENNEDY • LAPICK •
SORRY I'M LATE FOR OUR MOVIE DATE, GUYS!
SURE, ARCHIE! NOW WE'LL HAVE TO WAIT FOR THE NEXT SHOW!
WHAT'S YOUR EXCUSE THIS TIME?
MY CAR RAN OUT OF GAS ON THE WAY!
HO-HUM! YOU'RE USUALLY MORE CREATIVE THAN THAT!
I TAKE IT YOU GOT SOME MORE?
NO! I COULDN'T AFFORD THAT AND A MOVIE TICKET! I WALKED THE REST OF THE WAY!
1

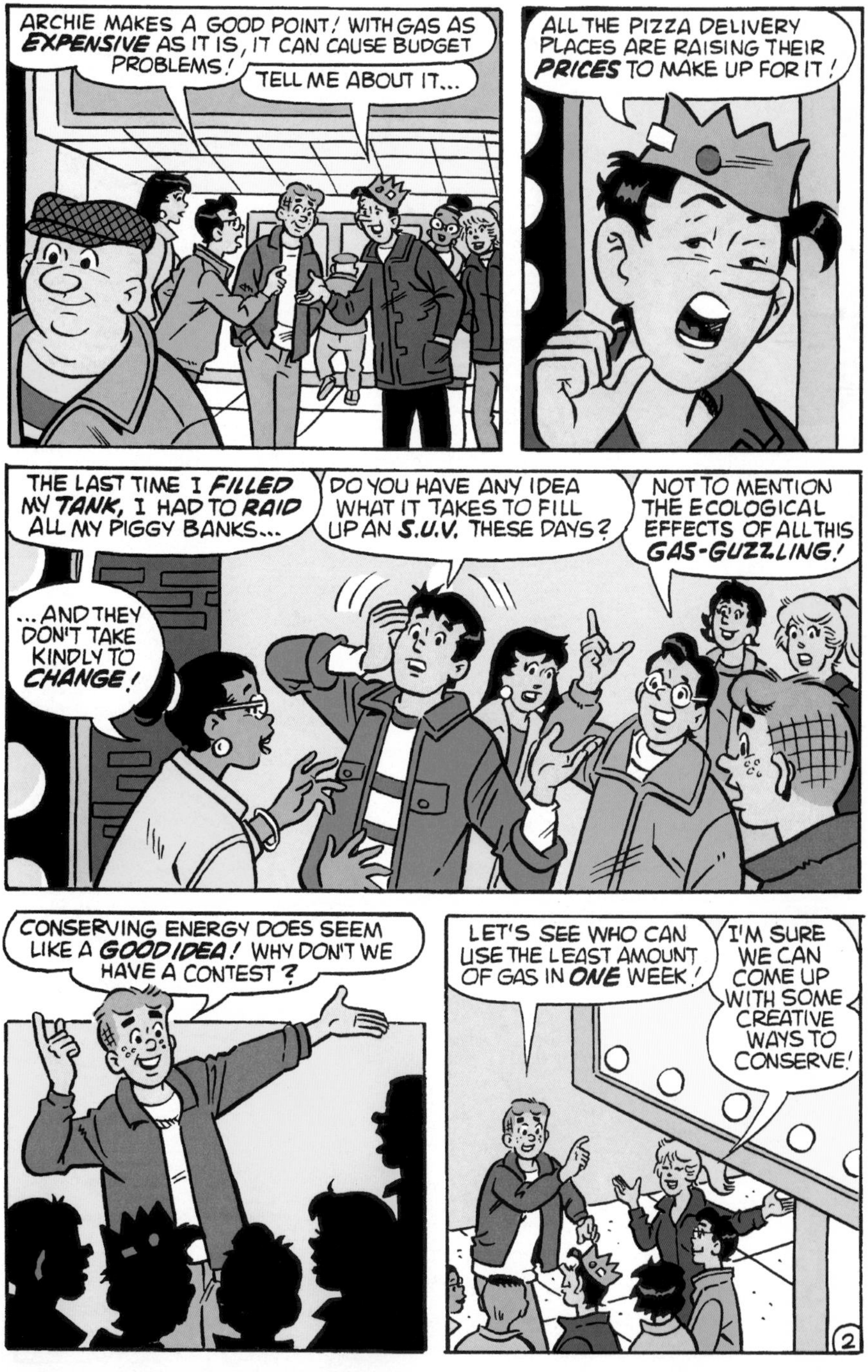
ARCHIE MAKES A GOOD POINT! WITH GAS AS EXPENSIVE AS IT IS, IT CAN CAUSE BUDGET PROBLEMS!
TELL ME ABOUT IT...
ALL THE PIZZA DELIVERY PLACES ARE RAISING THEIR PRICES TO MAKE UP FOR IT!
THE LAST TIME I FILLED MY TANK, I HAD TO RAID ALL MY PIGGY BANKS...
...AND THEY DON'T TAKE KINDLY TO CHANGE!
DO YOU HAVE ANY IDEA WHAT IT TAKES TO FILL UP AN S.U.V. THESE DAYS?
NOT TO MENTION THE ECOLOGICAL EFFECTS OF ALL THIS GAS-GUZZLING!
CONSERVING ENERGY DOES SEEM LIKE A GOOD IDEA! WHY DON'T WE HAVE A CONTEST?
LET'S SEE WHO CAN USE THE LEAST AMOUNT OF GAS IN ONE WEEK!
I'M SURE WE CAN COME UP WITH SOME CREATIVE WAYS TO CONSERVE!
2

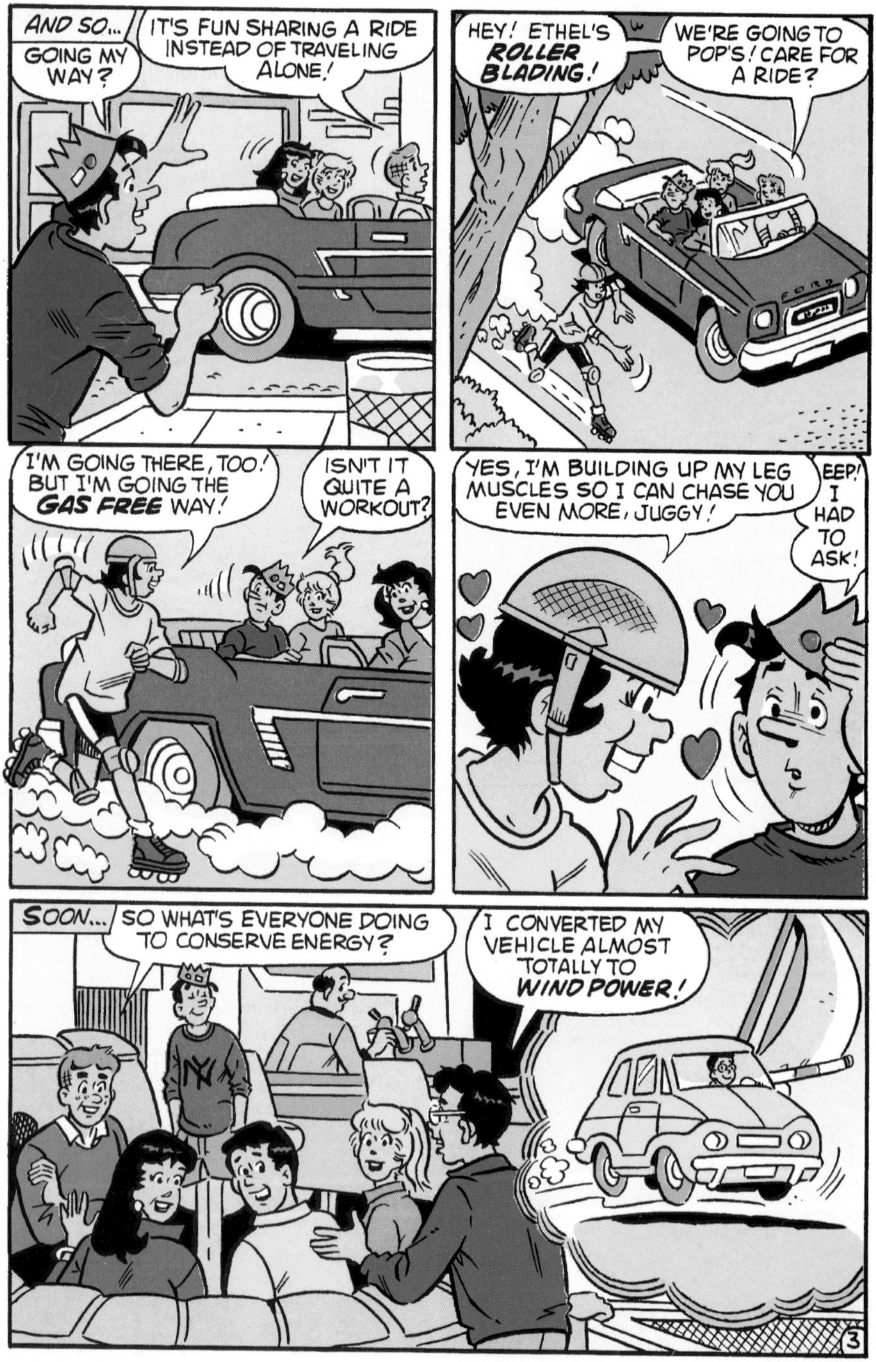
AND SO...
GOING MY WAY?
IT'S FUN SHARING A RIDE INSTEAD OF TRAVELING ALONE!
HEY! ETHEL'S ROLLER BLADING!
WE'RE GOING TO POP'S! CARE FOR A RIDE?
I'M GOING THERE, TOO! BUT I'M GOING THE GAS FREE WAY!
ISN'T IT QUITE A WORKOUT?
YES, I'M BUILDING UP MY LEG MUSCLES SO I CAN CHASE YOU EVEN MORE, JUGGY!
EEP! I HAD TO ASK!
SOON...
SO WHAT'S EVERYONE DOING TO CONSERVE ENERGY?
I CONVERTED MY VEHICLE ALMOST TOTALLY TO WIND POWER!
3

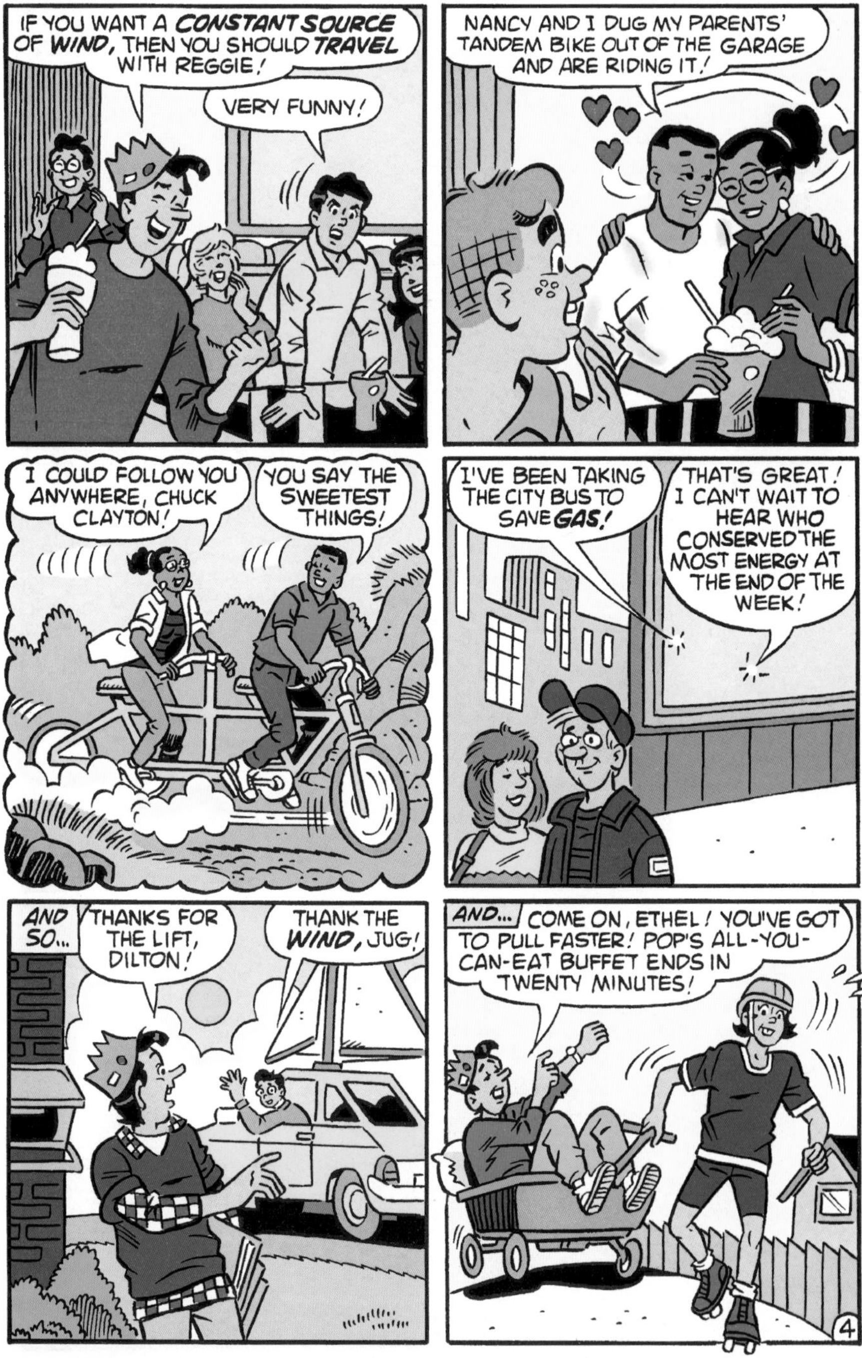
IF YOU WANT A CONSTANT SOURCE OF WIND, THEN YOU SHOULD TRAVEL WITH REGGIE!
VERY FUNNY!
NANCY AND I DUG MY PARENTS' TANDEM BIKE OUT OF THE GARAGE AND ARE RIDING IT!
I COULD FOLLOW YOU ANYWHERE, CHUCK CLAYTON!
YOU SAY THE SWEETEST THINGS!
I'VE BEEN TAKING THE CITY BUS TO SAVE GAS!
THAT'S GREAT! I CAN'T WAIT TO HEAR WHO CONSERVED THE MOST ENERGY AT THE END OF THE WEEK!
AND SO...
THANKS FOR THE LIFT, DILTON!
THANK THE WIND, JUG!
AND...
COME ON, ETHEL! YOU'VE GOT TO PULL FASTER! POP'S ALL-YOU-CAN-EAT BUFFET ENDS IN TWENTY MINUTES!
4

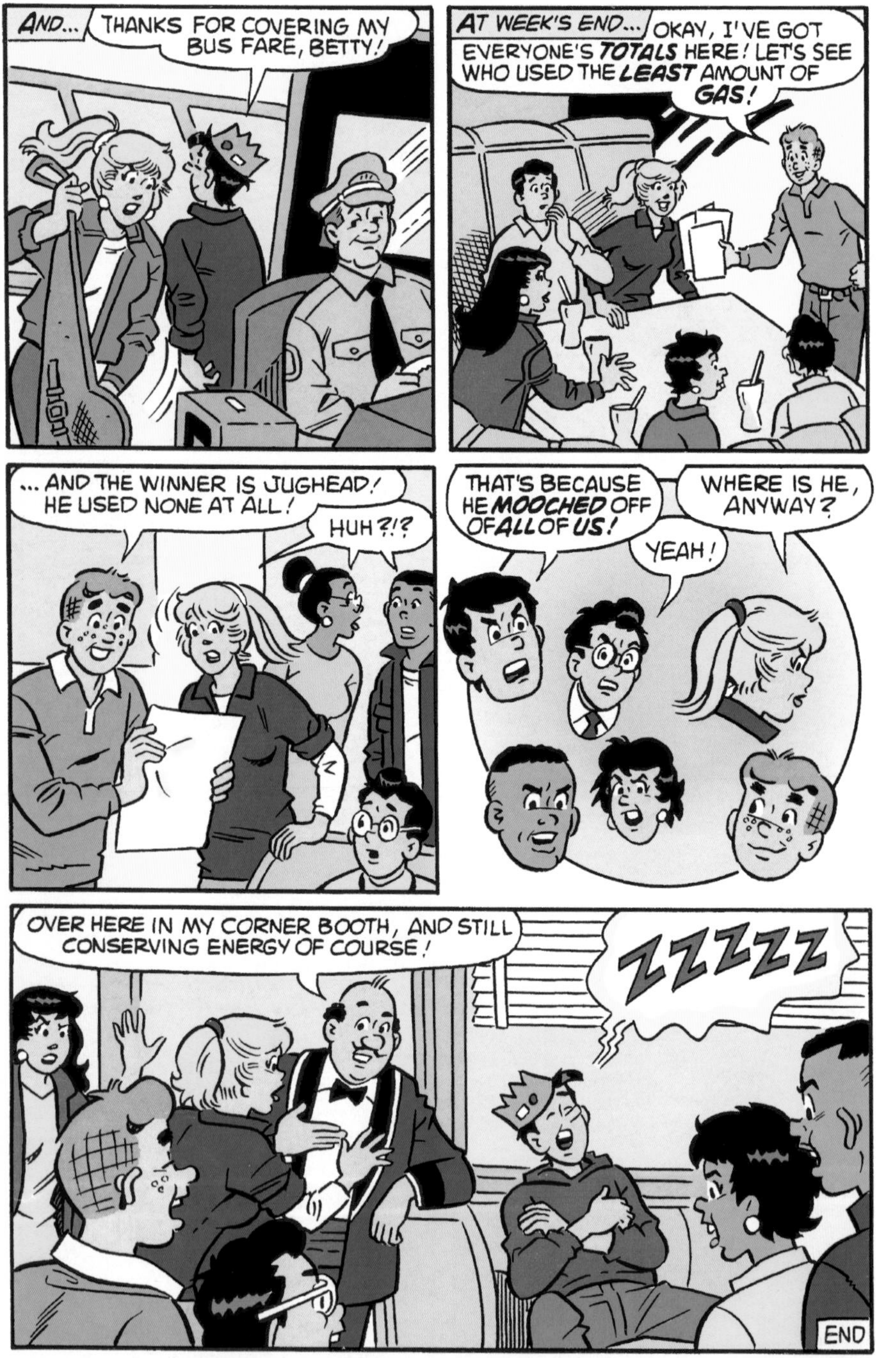
AND...
THANKS FOR COVERING MY BUS FARE, BETTY!
AT WEEK'S END...
OKAY, I'VE GOT EVERYONE'S TOTALS HERE! LET'S SEE WHO USED THE LEAST AMOUNT OF GAS!
... AND THE WINNER IS JUGHEAD! HE USED NONE AT ALL!
HUH ?!?
THAT'S BECAUSE HE MOOCHED OFF OF ALL OF US!
YEAH!
WHERE IS HE, ANYWAY?
OVER HERE IN MY CORNER BOOTH, AND STILL CONSERVING ENERGY OF COURSE!
ZZZZZ
END